CARDINAL EFFORT

a Generation X
Love Story

CARDINAL EFFORT

a **Generation X**

Love Story

DOUGLAS F. INGRAM

WITH SPECIAL THANKS to my wife, Terry. Your encouragement and enthusiasm kept me going, and I would never have been able to finish this without your help. You had this whole damned thing read aloud to you, one paragraph at a time, usually while you were sitting quietly beside me, reading real books by real authors. I can't imagine how much patience that took. I love you.

✧   ✧   ✧

AND DEDICATED to the memory of my friend Daniel who, without hyperbole, changed my life. I miss you, man. Rest in peace.

✧   ✧   ✧

I AM GRATEFUL for the efforts of my editor, Lisa Messinger. Her passion, dedication, and skill were exactly what this story needed, and I feel so fortunate that she took an interest in it.

MAY, 1990

CHAPTER 1

LEAH

Royce Murphy sat on his bare twin mattress and surveyed the humble bedroom, fiddling with his ponytail band. With the conclusion of the spring semester, he was only 18 credit hours short of the coursework required for his Bachelor's degree in English from Lancaster College in Dublin, GA. But May of 1990 was nearly half-over, and he still had much to do. Before Memorial Day weekend, he planned to move from the apartment he shared with Leah Carlisle and settle into the spare bedroom at his friend David's place, and to find a part-time job for the rest of the summer. The coffee shop where he had worked as a waiter and occasional cook since the previous August had closed for the season. With the vast majority of the 2,000 students returning to their hometowns for the break, there was little reason to keep the place open.

Moving from the apartment was not a major undertaking, logistically speaking. He had left the majority of his books, photo albums, and keepsakes at his mother's house in a southern suburb of Atlanta, and what he did have with him could easily be transported in the bed of a pickup truck. Parting company with Leah, however, would be far more taxing. They had lived together for a full year, ever since her original roommate abruptly quit school the previous summer and left Leah on the hook for full rent and utilities. He had seen her desperate "Roommate Wanted" post on the student center bulletin board and called her the same day.

She was barely five feet tall, with curly reddish-brown hair that was parted in the middle and reached a few inches past her shoulders. Her expressive blue eyes made it impossible for her to keep her emotions from revealing themselves. Her natural speaking voice was several decibels louder than most people's, and she tended to snort when she laughed. He knew immediately they would become good friends, even after the more prickly side of her personality emerged several weeks later. When they first met, she told him that every ounce of the "freshman fifteen" she had gained in her first year in Dublin had settled in her tits and ass, so she had decided to keep them.

In spite of their initial and mutual attraction, both decided to keep their relationship strictly platonic. Neither was interested in the complications that accompanied a long-term romance, and they knew their living arrangement was temporary. She was due to finish her nursing degree by mid-July, the end of the summer session of '90, and she already had two job offers and an ex-boyfriend who still carried a torch for her in her native Augusta.

There were two slip-ups, however.

The first came a couple of months after Royce moved in, when a couple of their neighbors invited them to a poker party. Fueled by wine and music and laughter, the card game was swiftly abandoned in favor of a bawdy game of Truth or Dare. By the time they'd returned home and closed their door, Royce and Leah were shedding their clothes.

The following dawn brought with it the realization that mistakes had been made, and they vowed not to let it happen again. Leah had assumed that bedding an English major would be an earth-moving romantic encounter, and Royce had expected her passion for music to translate into wild abandon in the bedroom. Instead, they shared a clumsy and awkward drunken romp that ended quickly and left them hugging their pillows in separate bedrooms, waiting desperately for sleep to arrive. They drank coffee together on their shady balcony the next morning, as usual, but barely looked each other in the eye.

The second encounter was far more memorable.

Just after New Year's Day, 1990, Leah was invited to perform in a country music showcase at a bar in Macon, but fretted over her two best friends' reluctance to join her and provide moral support. She knew Royce had a weak spot for Reba McIntyre, so she made her play. "I'll sing 'Whoever's in New England' if you'll come with me." He didn't argue. The black nylons and high-heeled boots she promised to wear for the performance were overkill, but she knew they were effective.

First place in the showcase was ten percent of the total cover charges for the night, but Leah was thrilled to finish second to the bar owner's niece and take one percent, which amounted to just over twenty dollars. They kept their coats on for the drive back to Dublin, because the heating system in his 1971 powder blue VW Squareback left much to be desired. On the radio, Elvis Costello sang that you could call her anything you'd like, but her name was Veronica.

"David told me the girls who are renting his spare bedroom are definitely moving out after spring semester," Royce said. He had been sitting on this fact for three days, hoping to find a good time to present it. "I'm gonna move there after they leave."

Leah looked wounded, but whispered, "Okay."

She wanted nothing more than to shower when they got home, around two a.m., while he opened a bottle of cheap grocery store merlot. He was proud of her performance and her composure, and of himself for getting through some truly dreadful country covers performed by overdressed and under-talented locals. He left his shoes and jeans in his bedroom and settled onto her overstuffed denim sofa.

She emerged from the bathroom, trailed by a cloud of steam and wrapped in her favorite turquoise towel. She lifted her waiting glass of wine from the coffee table and took a long sip. Settling onto his lap and straddling his thighs, she smiled broadly, taking his nearly empty glass from him and placing it on the side table. She kissed him deeply, but slowly.

"What do you want?" he whispered. "I need to know, first."

"I want to thank you. It means a lot that you came with me tonight."

"You know what I mean, Leah. What do you want, from this?"

She sat back up, adjusting the towel that was now hanging more loosely and revealing the top half of her milky-white breasts and several dozen accompanying freckles. Batting her lashes and cocking her head to the side, she answered. "Remember you once told me how much you enjoyed giving oral sex?"

"I do."

She kissed him again, harder this time. "I'll let you," she said through a giggle.

She rose and took his hand, making a token effort to tug him from his seat, and led him into her dark bedroom. Letting her towel fall to the floor, she pulled back the comforter, turned to face him, and sat on the edge of the bed. He paused just long enough to take a deep, settling breath, and dropped to his knees.

Her skin was warm and soft from the shower, and smelled distinctively of lavender. She rested on her elbows, propped up enough to watch what he was doing. He teased her a bit, with grazes of his tongue along her inner thighs, but soon snaked his hands beneath the small of her back and leaned in closer to the spot that was most in need of attention.

"Oh! That's very…um…Oh, that's…" Additional words eluded her.

He continued to experiment with alternating pressure and pace, manipulating her clit with his tongue until her climax was inevitable. "Royce?" she cooed, "Please don't stop doing that, right there." Her thighs spasmed and locked tightly against his ears, until the waves finally subsided.

Gathering her breath, she back-peddled and twisted to her right until her head found her pillows. "Come here."

He stood. "I need to go get a condom."

"Well, hurry. I might fall asleep first."

"You won't," he said confidently, retreating toward his own bedroom and pulling open the top drawer of his dresser. The thin layer of dust on the box of Trojans prompted a quick peek at the expiration date.

Still good.

Returning to Leah's bedroom, he unbuttoned and removed his flannel shirt and dropped his boxer-briefs to the floor. She watched him intently, with an appreciative grin. Unwrapping the condom and rolling it down onto his upturned erection, he remembered a comedy bit from MTV. "Any man can look heroic putting one of these on. Just don't watch too closely when it comes off later."

He climbed onto the bed and positioned himself between her thighs. Sliding into her slowly and carefully, he did his best to shake off the memories of their previous encounter.

They moved together in concert, slowly, with fingers exploring and teeth nibbling. He found an angle and depth that froze her, and intensified his motion. Her breath quickened and shuddered, and she urged his hips with her ankles crossed against his lower back. "Yes," she breathed, in a raspy moan. "Just like that. Please."

Her vaginal muscles tensed and pulsed around his shaft, a dozen times or more, and she threw her head backward. He did not relent, ushering her through spirals of bliss and reveling in her uncharacteristic vulnerability.

After a motionless pause to catch their breath, Royce tried in vain to replicate the magic he had just conjured. But in the process, his own desire betrayed him, and he suddenly slipped past his point of no return. She held him tightly as he came, her fingernails leaving indentations on his back. The removal of the condom was as awkward as he had predicted, but she missed it. She scampered nude to the kitchen to pour two more glasses, draining the last of the merlot.

Royce rested on his back, and she curled up against him on her side, with her right leg thrown over his.

"When you move out, who'll kill the bathroom spiders, you selfish bastard?" Her tone wasn't even half-serious, and he laughed. She rolled onto her right side, with her back to him. He rested his hand on her hip and gently caressed it until she fell asleep, then gathered his clothes and made his way to his own bed.

They spent the final five months of their time in the

apartment like a long-married couple, tied to routine. They shopped for kitchen and bathroom supplies together on the weekends, but their disparate schedules did not allow for much reflective interaction. She often worked nights at the local hospital, leaving for and arriving home from work just as he was going to bed or heading to campus, respectively. On the rare occasions when they watched a movie or a show together, she would stretch out on the sofa with her feet in his lap, as he absently massaged them over a book he was reading for class.

But they never again shared a bed.

✦ ✦ ✦

On May 13th, Royce rose from his bare mattress and made a pot of coffee in the tiny kitchen, expecting Leah to wake at any moment for her morning shift in the children's ward. He left her an empty cup on the counter, with a spoon propped inside for her to add her two scoops of sugar, and settled onto one of the two uncomfortable metal chairs at the bistro table.

He picked at the broken pieces of plastic covering the edge of the table and sipped from his cup until she finally appeared in the doorway. She was barefoot, wearing the black Nine Inch Nails T-shirt he'd given her after attending the *Pretty Hate Machine* tour, and a pink cotton panty. Her arms were crossed tightly to her chest.

"Thank you for making coffee. When is Luke getting here?"

He checked his watch. "About an hour."

She shifted her weight to her other leg and pulled at the hem of her T-shirt. She'd worn it to bed almost every night for the past several months. "Will you be wanting this back?"

"It's yours, Leah." Royce smiled. "It wouldn't fit me, anyway."

"Are you paying him to help you move?"

Royce nodded at his coffee cup. "Case of beer and a top-off of his gas tank, that's all he asked for. Fortunately, I can get both of them at the same place."

"Always so *practical*, aren't you? I should go shower, before he gets here." She turned toward the bathroom and tugged her shirt over her head before leaving his sight-line, twitching her shapely hips with each purposeful step.

✧   ✧   ✧

ROYCE STUFFED HIS contact lens case and soaking solution into an outer pocket of his fraying suitcase, along with his toothbrush and toothpaste, the last of the morning items he wasn't able to pack in advance. His bedroom window was open, so he heard the distinct sound of Luke's Chevy pickup from half a mile away. He walked to unlock the front door and watched through the blinds as Luke climbed the wooden steps to the balcony.

Luke Miller stood six-foot-four and had shoulders as broad as a garage door. Country strong, with a drawl to match, but smart as hell. He was studying chemistry, with the ultimate goal of becoming a pharmacist. Working in his father's thriving construction business kept him busy, however, and sometimes he would take only one class a semester. He was a Dublin local, and lived in the basement apartment in his parents' house. He was only two inches taller than Royce, but seemed far bigger.

"Dude! You ready?"

"Totally. Thanks again for the help."

"Lemme take a look at what we're loading, so I can get a plan in my head. She still here?"

"Yeah, in the shower. Everything's packed."

Luke scratched his chin at the doorway to Royce's bedroom and evaluated the load. Twin mattress and box spring, with a disassembled metal headboard and frame, and a three-drawer wooden dresser. A few boxes of books, a duffel bag and laundry basket filled with clothes and bath towels, a dual-cassette stereo and receiver with two detached speakers, a hand-me-down set of golf clubs and a Wilson tennis racquet, a metal tool box and an acoustic guitar in a weathered black case. And three stolen milk crates that usually served as a stacked bookcase, but for today stored a clock radio, a cordless phone/answering machine, a 35mm Canon camera, and a few dozen cassette tapes.

Luke picked up the racquet and performed an awkward slow-motion forehand and backhand. "You ever play with Carlito?"

"Yeah, whenever I'm feeling too good about myself and I need to get my brains beaten in."

"Let's get the mattress and box spring first. They can stand up along one side and the other stuff will stack up against 'em."

Returning to the apartment after their fourth trip to the truck, Leah emerged from the bathroom in dark blue scrubs and a tight sensible ponytail. "Always good to see you, Luke!"

"Uh-huh." Luke's expression suggested that his memories of rebuffing her advances were vivid.

Thirty minutes later, all items in place, Royce and Luke climbed into the cab and set off on the three-mile trip to Royce's new home in Kingston Hall. "When's Dave due back from Europe?"

"Not until after Memorial Day. They fly in that Monday, but he may hang with his parents for a couple days."

"Well, I'm sure he'll have stories. He always does."

✧   ✧   ✧

KINGSTON HALL WAS technically considered faculty housing and unavailable to the student body. David's father was an associate professor in Economics at Lancaster's satellite campus in Macon, however, and he was offered the use of the two-bedroom apartment for the rare occasions when he'd have to drive to Dublin for a semester's night class schedule. The rent was ridiculously cheap, so Dr. Carson extended his lease after David graduated high school in his native Virginia Beach and enrolled at Lancaster.

The building was unremarkable and institutional, with a brick facade on its three stories that faced Mayfield Drive, and was situated three blocks from the campus proper. Street level was on a parallel to the second story, with stairs leading down a hill to the first-floor entrance. David's place was on the top floor, accessible via a broad central stairwell, where every sound echoed within the cinder-block walls.

Royce and Luke spent another half-hour or so unloading the bed of the pickup and finishing the task before the oppressive middle Georgia heat settled in. "I can help you put stuff together. I got time," Luke offered. Royce shook him off.

"Thanks, man. I just need to get my car and drive it over. Let's swing by the Circle K on the way to Leah's, and I'll fill up the truck and grab your beers. You've done more than enough. We'll give you a call when Dave's back."

"A'ight."

☼   ☼   ☼

After squaring up with Luke and collecting the VW, Royce stopped by the Calhoun Student Center. He had about ten minutes to dash through the lunch line before it closed, and hoped the bulletin board downstairs might have some new job postings for summer work. Calhoun's dining plan was exactly the kind of affordable arrangement that students needed, and there were no restrictions limiting access to people who lived in the dorms. Royce, David, and Luke had all bought a lunch and dinner package, even during the summer semester. The only drawback was the dinner hours — Calhoun was open for service from 4:45 to 6:15 p.m., which forced students to eat at the same time as senior citizens showing up at local restaurants for the early-bird specials. It was no wonder most students kept a stash of ramen noodles, microwave popcorn, and assorted canned foods handy for a night-time snack.

Royce wrapped up a sandwich and walked downstairs to check the employment board. It was mostly bare, since the vast majority of available labor had gone home for the summer, but a newly placed index card caught his attention.

Data entry / light clerical. Hours flexible. $5 / hour.

He grabbed a pen from his pocket and scribbled the phone number down on a napkin. *I can type,* he thought.

CHAPTER 2

YAWNOC

Kingston Hall was arranged in two wings, with five units each. Two two-bedroom apartments sat opposite one another on the top two floors, on either side of the stairwell, with a superintendent's suite on the bottom floor across from an activity room. The lower level suite, during the building's more popular times, was usually occupied by a graduate student who accepted free housing in exchange for being the go-to contact for any problems that might arise for the residents. The activity room had coin-operated washers and dryers and dated vinyl seating. Royce needed to do some laundry, and stopped by to check out the facilities on his way back from Calhoun. The pool table that had once been the focal point of the room was gone, but the indentions in the linoleum allowed him to picture what the room must have been like when Kingston was fully occupied. As of now, however, the apartment he and David would share was the only unit in use on their side of the building.

Royce took his time settling in, but made it a priority to set up his stereo in the living room beside David's TV. He snaked the wire antenna beside the window frame and taped the tip as high as it would reach. The campus radio station's transmitter only broadcasted at ten watts, but when he twisted the knob, the signal came through loud and clear. Harriet Wheeler of The Sundays was telling him about the time she kicked a boy. The days he spent as a volunteer DJ at the station during his freshman and sophomore years seemed like a very long time ago.

David had a matching sofa and easy chair in the living room, along with a chipped wooden coffee table. There was no overhead light, but there were two floor lamps on opposite corners of the room. A dining area was separated from the living room by an arched doorway, but it was stacked with boxes of keepsakes and possessions that David had brought from Virginia but had never unpacked. The tiny kitchen was to the left of the dining area. David's bedroom, the larger of the two, faced the street, and Royce's was in the back, with the bathroom in the hallway between them. His room had a window that overlooked a wooded area, where the school's archery range had been, before it was moved out to East Campus beside Coyote Lake.

☼   ☼   ☼

THE NEXT DAY, Royce called the number on the napkin and set up an interview with Sal Russo of something called Yawnoc Productions. (He heard it at first as "Y'all knock," until he asked for the spelling.) Sal seemed happy to take his call, and gave the impression that they needed someone quickly. Royce scratched down the driving directions and changed into slacks and a navy polo shirt.

He took the Dublin bypass southbound, and turned onto Statesboro Highway about five miles from town. He kept his eyes peeled for Sammy's Bar, which, according to Sal's instructions, was no more than a mile from the destination. The street number matched with a large ranch-style house, situated on a corner lot, with a circular driveway that ran behind the house and connected the highway to a side street. A Cadillac Seville and a beat-up Ford Ranger were parked beside one another, in front of a renovated room that had clearly once been a two-car garage.

He grabbed a couple of copies of his resume from the passenger seat and entered the office. Sal stood to greet him from behind his small desk at the back right corner of the room. He was short and slender, and wore tight jeans, boots, and a western style shirt. His eyes bulged behind Coke-bottle lenses and the hairline that receded from his temples made his widow's peak even more prominent. His hair was gray and slicked back. "Royce?" he asked.

"Yes, sir. Mr. Russo?"

"Sal," he insisted amicably. "Come have a seat and I'll tell you how it works."

Sal explained that the Dublin office's primary venture was the Southeastern Showtime Circus, a one-ring show that toured small towns in Georgia and northern Florida twice a year, for about four months at a time. The circus was used as a fundraiser for local charities, called sponsors, with each campaign managed by a sales representative who would conduct ticket sales by phone a few weeks ahead of the performance dates. The sales rep would take 50% of the ticket sales revenue, with the charity receiving 25% and holding the remaining 25% until the circus came to town. On the date of the show, the ringmaster, Joey Vegas, was paid his portion in cash from the total sales.

Most of the reps were husband and wife teams who ran the campaigns in the same cities year after year. They would set up a phone room, employing locals as needed to make the telemarking calls. The tickets were sold as two-ticket bundles for $10, but a donation of $25 would buy you up to seven. Ticket buyers were encouraged to send back any tickets they didn't expect to use, along with their check, and were assured that unused tickets would be donated to local charities to allow less-fortunate children to see the show. The reps rented P.O. boxes for their incoming mail, and placed a forwarding order to the office address when they concluded the campaign.

Royce's primary responsibility would be entering into a database the ticket sales information for every town the circus visited. Sal handed him a stack of yellow sheets that had been pulled from a pad of carbonless paper, with each sheet containing the name, address, and phone number of the buyer. Sal called these sheets "taps," and explained that they were as valuable as gold, as people who donated one year were more than likely to donate again. The office was equipped with a Compaq DeskPro computer and a dot-matrix printer. A local computer whiz had written a simple database program to keep track of the taps.

"So," Sal concluded, "We need someone as soon as possible, and we're fine with working around class schedules for students. If you can commit to twenty hours a week, you could keep up with the work load."

"Oh, I'm sure I can get it done. And twenty hours a week would be easy to arrange, even after classes start next month. I'm enrolled for two, and they meet Monday through Thursday from ten in the morning until 12:30. I could be here by 1:00, at the latest. I can do full-time for four days next week, but I'm driving back to Atlanta on Friday for the Memorial Day weekend."

"Sounds good! See you Monday, then? Around ten?"

"I'll be here," Royce replied with a smile, standing and shaking Sal's hand.

"Oh, and next time you're on campus, would you take down the job posting?"

"Will do. And thank you," Royce said as he left the office.

He had a feeling that the whole operation was sketchy, but $100+ a week without taxes being taken out was a dream scenario for him. He could cover basic expenses, without adding too much to his student loan debt, and it was more than he was used to taking home from the coffee shop. The owner of the business, Bobby Lee Conway (Yawnoc backward, Royce later deduced), would be there for his first day on the job, and he looked forward to meeting the man behind the madness.

✿   ✿   ✿

THE INTERVENING WEEKEND passed slowly for Royce, alone in his new apartment, and he was grateful for Leah's invitation to join her for lunch after her church let out on Sunday. She listened intently as he described the job he'd accepted. "Welp, I've never heard of anything like that before!" she snorted. "He didn't give you any shit about your earring, did he?"

"This little thing?" Royce rubbed the thin gold hoop. "No. And didn't say anything about my hair, either." It was thick and straight, the darkest of brown, parted on the left side and reached his shoulders when he didn't wear it pulled back.

"I can always split if it gets too weird. I'll let you know how it goes," he assured her. He gave her a hug in the sandwich shop parking lot and drove back to Kingston. There were lists of necessities to be made, and he expected some birthday money to come his way during the Memorial Day festivities, since he would turn 23 on May 30.

When Royce arrived the following Monday for his first day at the circus company, Sal was on the phone and in the midst of what seemed to be a tense phone conversation. He took long drags on his cigarette and offered rushed apologies to the person on the other end of the line. He motioned for Royce to climb the three steps into the main house, which he did, tentatively opening the door. He walked into the galley-style kitchen, where a long semi-circular countertop/bar was framed by lighted glass shelving that housed twenty or so ceramic Emmett Kelly figurines. A wiry man in his forties sat behind the counter, holding a coffee mug in both hands. The air was thick with the smell of cigarette smoke. Looking up to acknowledge Royce's entry, he waved his hand to the four bar stools that surrounded the circular bar. "Cawwwww-see," he said in a thick drawl.

Royce hesitated, frowning with confusion. Bobby Lee Conway repeated himself. "*Cawwwww-see.* French for *sit down.* Ain't you cultured? You're about to be a graduate!"

"Sorry," Royce replied, taking the bar stool closest to him. "I chose Spanish as my language requirement."

"Sal said he'd hired a guy to do the taps. I'm glad. Split-tails don't have no sense of humor."

Bobby had deep-set piercing blue eyes that Royce imagined would look sad even when he was happy. His years as a rodeo cowboy had left his body wracked with constant pain in his joints, and nearly every movement caused him to grimace. The custom bar he'd had built in his kitchen was his own personal throne, however, and Royce got the feeling that a certain reverence was expected.

"Pleasure to meet you, Mr. Conway," Royce offered upon standing. "I should get to work."

As Royce turned to walk back downstairs to the office, Bobby called after him, "Let me know if the wop doesn't treat you right."

◊   ◊   ◊

SAL WAS STILL on the phone when Royce returned to the office and closed the door behind him, so he took a moment to evaluate his surroundings. Seeing the bar in the kitchen explained a lot about the office's dominant feature: a ridiculously ornate curved desk that was about the same size as the bar upstairs. The outward facing part of the desk was decorated with two-inch wide vertical mirrors, glued about a half-inch apart, and covering the entire face of it.

Sal's simple desk was to the right of the fancy one, and was cluttered with maps, accounting ledgers, and stacks of small envelopes. He was more relaxed now, leaning back in his chair with his boots propped up on the desktop, his ongoing conversation far friendlier than it had been moments earlier. The desk with the computer and printer sat beside the steps to the kitchen, with two bulletin boards mounted to the wall above it. On one was pinned a driving map of Georgia and northern Florida, and the other had a hand-written list of dates and city names, with highlighter and Sharpie pen marks beside them. Royce surmised that this was how he would keep up with his task list.

In the space between Sal's desk and the front wall of the office were a couple of filing cabinets and four metal shelving units sitting side by side. These were packed full with shoeboxes, each labeled with the name of a city and arranged roughly in alphabetical order. Royce pulled down the box labeled Ellijay, his friend Nico's home town, and found a stack of taps and a printout of the database inside.

Sal ended his conversation and came out from behind his desk with his hand outstretched. "Sorry for that. The ringmaster gets really antsy when we're trying to lay out the next route. Happens every time."

Royce shook his hand. "So, have you been with the company from the start?" he asked.

"No. Bobby's ex-wife handled the office during the first couple of years. I came in after they divorced. I used to run a segment of the rodeo tour in Oklahoma, so I've known Bobby for nigh on twenty-five years." His capped teeth made his smile that much bigger.

Royce nodded and turned to boot up the computer. "I like your set-up here," he said, motioning to the bulletin boards. "Seems easy enough to keep up with what I'm supposed to be doing."

"Yeah. Missy, who worked here a few years ago, came up with that. No one's figured out a better way to do it since then. But you're welcome to change things up if you want. As long as shit gets done, I don't much care how it happens."

✧   ✧   ✧

DURING HIS FIRST four days on the job, Royce fumbled through the database program, training himself and keeping quiet. His ears were always open, though, and he learned a lot about the inner workings of the company. Sal was busy with the deposits for the late-arriving ticket sales, which came from post offices in every city that hosted sales campaigns, bearing the yellow forwarding stickers. Sal put together the payments and sent them to the shows' sponsors, keeping meticulous notes concerning the 75% of the proceeds the sponsor was expected to send back to Yawnoc, since the checks were made out to them. Sal paid the reps their 50% in cash.

Royce also met Mae, Bobby's housekeeper. She was a heavyset and gregarious woman, with a graying mullet and several missing teeth. She did her best to keep Bobby in check, but since his cocktail hour began at noon every day, there was only so much she could do. He kept an eye on the clock, and announced to her daily as the living room clock chimed twelve, "It's time to build me a drink." She filled a highball glass with two shots of Smirnoff vodka and topped it with cranberry juice. This would be repeated roughly on the hour until her daily shift ended, so it's no wonder she strolled out to her pickup two or three times a week to make runs to the liquor store for vodka and cartons of Pall Mall cigarettes. Sal scribbled into his ledger book every transfer from petty cash for Bobby's vices.

Bobby owned his house outright, and didn't keep a checking account, so Sal kept up with the bills and had Mae purchase money orders from the post office to pay the water, power, cable, and other assorted monthly expenses. The salaries of the circus staff were apparently paid from the Lake City, Florida office, which was run by Bobby's cousin, and Bobby and Joey Vegas had some sort of nebulous agreement to split the show's proceeds throughout the course of a tour. This part of the arrangement seemed a mystery, even to Sal.

Royce shut down the computer at 4:00 on Thursday afternoon, as Sal reached for his receipt book. He flipped six fresh $20 bills onto his desk for the 24 hours Royce had logged, and handed him a pen to sign for it. "See you Tuesday, Sal. Have a good weekend."

"You, too," Sal replied. "Drive safe tomorrow."

Two weeks alone in his new surroundings had Royce particularly thankful for the holiday weekend. Luke was on call with the Dublin volunteer fire department every day, so they weren't able to get together socially. Nico and Carlos had each returned to their parents' homes for the summer and wouldn't be moving back to Dublin until August. And David was still in Europe with his family for a few more days. Royce woke up early after a restless sleep, packed the Squareback, and aimed for home. The subtle background noise from the cassette player told him that his second copy of U2's *The Joshua Tree* would need to be replaced by a CD before long.

He arrived at his mother's early enough to page his high school classmate, Eric, who returned Royce's call within minutes.

"Royce! You home for the weekend?"

"Yeah, man! I was hoping you might be available this afternoon."

"You're in luck. Whatcha needin'?"

"A half-ounce, if you have one. Eighty work for you?"

"Absolutely. Can you be at Kroger in thirty?"

"I'll be there," Royce answered.

Eric's product was high quality and fairly priced, and Royce was far happier dealing with someone he knew well. He found the emptiest section of the grocery store parking lot and waited. The '68 GTO Eric had been working to restore since his 17th birthday soon rounded the corner and pulled up alongside him. Royce settled into the passenger seat and shook Eric's hand. "How's business?" he asked.

"Good, man! You about done with school?"

"Yeah, I'll finish in December."

Eric reached into his T-shirt's breast pocket and pulled out a joint. "A little preview of what you're getting." He flipped the top of his Zippo lighter and took a long drag. "I'm buying direct from a grower in Kentucky now."

Royce took the joint and inhaled deeply. "Good to know. My new roommate has a healthy appetite, so I'm sure I'll be in touch soon." He handed the joint back to Eric, who carefully stubbed out the cherry.

"Here. Keep it. I've got a few more people to see."

"Thanks, man. I appreciate it. I gotta get home, myself." He reached into his pocket and pulled four of the twenties Sal had given him the day before.

Eric quickly glanced over each shoulder and passed a plastic bag across the GTO's console. "Tell your sister to call me if she needs anything." Eric smiled a salesman's smile.

"Will do. Thanks again." Royce watched the Pontiac speed off as he tucked the plastic bag into his glove box and set off for home. Jennifer would be home from school by the time he arrived, so he kept his sunglasses on to conceal his bloodshot eyes. It didn't work.

✦　✦　✦

"Been in touch with Eric, I see," Jennifer teased, hugging her brother. She had been the one to report Eric's new status as a dealer, and passed along his number.

"Yeah, I did. Here," he replied, handing her the stubbed-out joint. "He said to call him anytime."

Her high school graduation was scheduled for June 5th, the day after summer semester would begin, and Royce was heartbroken that he would miss it. They walked to the back porch together and shared a couple of puffs, formulating a plan to make the most of his weekend at home.

His mother, Kate, got home from work around 6:30

and the three cooked dinner together, like they had in the days before Royce had left for Lancaster. Kate had some chores for him, and he appreciated the opportunity to feel useful.

On Saturday, Royce and Jennifer packed an overnight bag and drove down to their father's weekend place at Jackson Lake. He knew Royce Senior would be interested in Yawnoc, and would have a lot of questions. "Well, I'll be dipped in doo-doo! We sent you off to get a degree, and you ended up joining the circus, anyway?" he teased.

Royce loved the quiet of the lake house and he didn't mind sleeping on the sofa so Jennifer could have the second of the two bedrooms. The three of them talked, drank beer, and played poker on the screened porch until well after midnight.

Royce was eager to get an early start on Sunday. He'd taken thorough notes on what he wanted to haul back to Dublin from his mother's favorite warehouse club, and he knew she would have some insights and suggestions, as well. Royce's father gave him a birthday card with a fifty dollar bill inside. "Thanks, Dad. I love you. I'll be in touch."

Jennifer had finals to study for, so Royce and his mother made the shopping trip alone. She examined his list and his budget, and nodded or frowned to evaluate his choices. It was a trip he'd made many times during his college years, but he always appreciated having an accounting professional with him. He loaded up on snacks and drinks, as Kate added a few more items to their cart — a couple of floor pillows, an oscillating fan, another set of towels and bedsheets — and made up the shortfall at the register. "I'm proud of you. Happy birthday." Royce wrapped her in a warm embrace.

CHAPTER 3

DAVID

The Squareback was packed full on Memorial Day Monday, and Royce was eager to get back to Kingston and stock his barren shelves. He would only be alone for a few more days, and he knew David would be grateful for a pantry full of options. And he wanted to put in as many hours at Yawnoc as he could before classes started.

He arrived for work at 10:00 a.m. on Tuesday to find a strange woman seated behind the large mirrored desk and, more alarmingly, Sal was nowhere in sight. There was a late-model Mercedes 560 parked in his usual spot in front of the office door.

The tiny woman stood and walked around the desk to greet him. "You must be Royce!" she exclaimed, her voice dripping with manufactured enthusiasm. "Just as tall and handsome as Bobby Lee said you were!" Royce figured the odds of Bobby referring to him as tall and handsome were somewhere between slim and none. Her bleached blonde hair could best be described as a dome-cut, blow-dried straight back and sprayed to immobility. She wore a tight pale-blue polyester business suit, shiny tan stockings, and tall white heels. "I'm Darla Boone, and I just moved in here with Bobby Lee over the weekend." From her drawl, Royce guessed that she'd been raised in Texas.

"Royce Murphy," he said, shaking Darla's extended hand. "Where's Sal?"

"Oh, he's just runnin' late today. I'm down here trying to make some plans. I'll be joinin' the sales team for the next tour!"

"Well, then. Congratulations. I'm sure you have a lot to plan for," he said, flipping on the power switch of the Compaq. "I'm new here, myself, but I'd be glad to help, if you have any questions."

"I might just take you up on it," she purred flirtatiously. "I could listen to that deep voice of yours all day!"

Royce rolled his eyes as Darla returned to her desk and fired up a cigarette from her Virginia Slims Gold box.

Sal arrived a half-hour later, looking ill and frazzled. He and Darla did not acknowledge one another, but he exchanged greetings with Royce.

What the fuck did I miss over the last three days? Royce wondered to himself.

The next couple of workdays passed quietly, but not without a few more valuable learning experiences for Royce. Sal spent a good deal of time on the phone with Joey Vegas, planning appointments during the fall tour, where Sal would drive to whatever city the circus was in to collect cash from the circus' cut of the sales proceeds. Joey had been robbed at gunpoint a couple of times, and was loathe to repeat the experience, but because of a couple of domestic violence incidents in his past, he was not able to apply for a carry permit to protect himself.

Royce helped Sal with some filing tasks, and found two loaded .38 revolvers in the file cabinets. *Let's hope these always stay right where they are*, he silently pleaded. He also learned that Sal's frequent trips to the bathroom were not because of an overactive bladder. Bobby had a hole jack-hammered into the concrete slab beneath the floor, and had installed a cylindrical safe, which was hidden by a small rug. By Sal's estimation, there was between $50,000 and 100,000 cash in the safe, at any given time, and it was his job to keep flawless records. This also explained the guns. Sal suspected Bobby had made withdrawals on Darla's behalf, and counted the contents daily. Bobby and Darla rarely appeared in the office during that week, but Royce could hear them giggling and doing God knows what in the kitchen.

☼ ☼ ☼

Royce told no one at Yawnoc that Thursday the 30th was his birthday, and made up an excuse for why he needed to leave an hour early. David was due back around dinnertime, and Royce wanted to be at the apartment to greet him. He kept the windows open, even though it was hot outside, and read "Paradise Lost" on the sofa while he waited. Before long, he heard a car driving up out front and looked out the window to see David's burgundy 1983 Civic Hatchback pulling into an angled spot next to his VW. He raced down the stairs and up to the street to bear-hug his best friend.

"Dude!" David yelled, "It's good to be back! You settled in okay?"

✧   ✧   ✧

DAVID AMBROSE CARSON was, simply put, the most unique and fascinating person Royce had ever met. He was a bit under six feet tall, toned and well-proportioned, athletically built from years of practicing *taekwondo*, but not overly muscular, and carried himself with a confidence that was seldom seen in a young man of his age. His signature attire was jeans, black Chuck Taylor high-tops, and a white T-shirt from his own hand-made collection. He used fabric markers to create designs based on his cinematic interests, typically horror and science fiction, or the occasional rock band tribute. In colder weather, he'd add an olive green cardigan sweater and/or a heavy Army surplus jacket, and sometimes fingerless wool gloves. His mousy brown hair was wiry, long, and unruly, but usually corralled under an ivy cap worn backward. His aesthetic was completed by square Buddy Holly glasses and a thick and bushy reddish-brown Van Dyke. Like his father, he was a member of MENSA, with a genius-level IQ.

They unloaded David's car and carried his duffel bag and a couple of small boxes upstairs. Royce sat cross-legged on David's bed while David unpacked his bag, and looked around at the *Fangoria* magazine fold-outs that adorned the bedroom walls. Some weren't too gruesome, like the iconic image of the young girl from the original *Night of the Living Dead*, but David had also hung the famous head explosion scene from *Scanners* and a particularly disturbing zombie kill from *Dawn of the Dead*. David had a nice comfortable queen-sized bed, but Royce hadn't once considered sleeping in David's room while he was away.

"Here, I got you something in Amsterdam. Happy birthday!"

"Oh, thanks, man! You didn't have to do that." Royce opened the small box and found a sleek and shiny black ceramic bong.

"It's called a tray grip style," David explained. "The indentations on the neck are finger grips, and the carburetor hole at the top goes under your index finger." The bong had a sturdy square base. "When it's filled with water, it's really bottom-heavy and stable. So, hopefully, no more bong-water spills."

"I wondered what happened to the rug that used to be underneath your coffee table," Royce smirked. The mouthpiece of the bong was oval and wide, and it reminded Royce of the day he and David had first met.

✧ ✧ ✧

IN THE SPRING semester of 1989, they were both enrolled in Theatre 101, a humanities elective. After spending half of the first day of class going over the syllabus, Dr. Weathers asked everyone to think about a dramatic event that had happened to them in their youth. "Who would like to share first?"

David raised his hand, "I got one."

Dr. Weathers nodded, and David continued. "I was nearly expelled from school on the second day of the second grade."

Dr. Weathers stood. "Okay, folks, pay attention. *This* is how you start a story."

"My dad's a professor, so we moved around some. I was in a new school for second grade. On the first day of class, we were told to stand up and recite the Pledge of Allegiance. When we came back the next day, we were told to do it again, and I refused."

Desks creaked as everyone leaned in closer. David's T-shirt was decorated with an album cover for British new wave band Sigue Sigue Sputnik.

"The teacher asked me why I wouldn't say the Pledge again, and I told her I'd said it the day before, and I'd meant it."

Royce could still hear the laughter that followed, including his own.

"Well, she didn't know what to say about that, and sent me to the office. The principal called my mother, and she came to take me home. She explained to me rituals were important, and usually there wasn't any harm in them, so I didn't make any trouble after that."

There were whispers of "wow" and "Jesus," and it took a long time for another student to be brave enough to follow with their own tale.

Royce hustled to catch up with David after class, finally overtaking him on the sidewalk outside of the building. "That was a fucking awesome story!"

They made small talk until it became obvious they were both headed to Calhoun for lunch. They went through the line and found a table together.

"I wish I'd had the balls to tell the first story I thought of," David said with a smile.

"Okay, this I gotta hear."

"I went to a performing arts magnet school in Virginia Beach, and a lot of my friends were really into *Rocky Horror*. So three of us went to the midnight showing one Saturday. We got there early and passed a bong around in the car. We were so high, it didn't occur to us that one guy was wearing black greasepaint for some reason, so we staggered up to the box office to buy our tickets and saw our reflection in the glass. The dude with the face paint had a flesh-colored circle around his mouth, and the other two of us had black circles around ours. We collapsed on the sidewalk laughing, and didn't get our shit together until the movie had already started. So we went home."

Royce cackled, and recognized immediately that he had a duty to introduce David to Nico, Carlos, Luke, Jennifer, and pretty much everyone else he knew. David's apartment at Kingston quickly became the principle hangout spot for Royce's friends, much to the chagrin of the Jills.

Neither member of the lesbian couple who had rented

David's spare room was really named Jill, but since they were inseparable, David gave them a collective name. They kept to themselves when David had the gang over, when weed was smoked and NES games were played, loudly and at all hours. When the time came for Royce to move in, David made sure the Jills had left their area clean before they moved out, and he had the locks changed before he left for Europe.

ROYCE FILLED THE ceramic bong with water from the bathroom sink and went to his bedroom to grab the baggie and a screen. They had missed the dinner hours at Calhoun, so David went to the kitchen to find something to eat. "Damn, dude! This is as full as I've ever seen this pantry. Thanks!"

"Don't mention it," Royce replied. "I'm just lookin' to get the most I can out of my last seven months down here."

David brought a boiler back from the kitchen and ate his macaroni and cheese straight from the pot with a big serving spoon. "Put in *A Fish Called Wanda*," he said, with his mouth full.

"Will do," Royce replied. He pushed the video into the VCR, and took his first pull from the pretty Dutch bong.

THE FOLLOWING MONDAY marked the beginning of summer semester. Royce was enrolled in a John Milton class on Monday and Wednesday, taught by Dr. Roberts, the chair of the English department. He was a mannered and gentlemanly fellow; charming, well-dressed, and soft-spoken. Royce's Tuesday and Thursday class was History of the English Language, taught by Dr. Gurski, an irreverent junior professor who was new to Lancaster but had jumped in with both feet, demonstrating particular enthusiasm for the theatre program.

As he'd promised when he had accepted the job, Royce dutifully arrived at Yawnoc at 1:00 p.m. daily once summer classes started, and until 5:00 tackled the taps and whatever other side tasks Sal needed done. The first week was particularly stressful, because the semiannual sales meeting was scheduled for Saturday the 9th, and Bobby and Darla were pressuring Sal to make changes to the sales rep handbook before the event.

"Darla, who has never done a sales campaign, is riding your ass about changes to the manual?" Royce asked with surprise, genuinely sympathetic to Sal's stress.

Sal nodded. He seemed even smaller than usual, huddled over the papers on his desk. His wife had a word processor at home, and was helping him with the edits, but it was small consolation. He could handle Bobby fine, but Darla was a variable he hadn't anticipated.

"I'm sorry, Sal. I know this must be tough. Let me know if I can help."

"Thanks. If I can get through the meeting and get all the reps back on the road, I'll be fine."

Royce was happy to have two summer classes that

didn't require a term paper, so he could avoid both the library and the computer lab in the basement of the English building. But David was working as many hours as possible at the Video Barn, since he wasn't taking any classes until fall semester, so they didn't get many chances to hang out until late in the evenings. On the plus side, this meant their weed supply was being organically rationed.

David continued to bring home obscure movies, most of which he ordered for the store, along with the latest Nintendo video game releases, which allowed them to devour the entire *Blackadder* series and overlooked gems like *Withnail and I* and *The Ninth Configuration*. It had taken some convincing from the other employees, but the Video Barn's owner had set aside a small rack in the back of the store and labeled it *Carson's Corner*, to feature David's selections. If David had something particularly disturbing or gory in the queue, Royce headed off to his room.

Royce's final exams were on Monday and Tuesday of the third week of July, and grades were posted Friday morning, so he went to the English building to check his. The two A's he had earned raised his GPA to 3.75, with *cum laude* virtually assured and *magna* within his grasp, as long as he could ace his final two classes in the fall.

He stopped by the apartment on his way to work, and found David sprawled out on his back on the sofa, his face even more pale than usual and his right hand extended out into the air. Drops of blood were spattered on the floor beneath his hand. "David! What happened, man?"

"Cut my finger on the lid of a tin can. I barely made it to the couch before I passed out." Royce examined the small cut, and hustled to the bathroom for a wet towel and a bandage.

He chuckled as he cleaned his friend's wound and wrapped it. "All that blood and gore you love, and this is what wrecks you."

"Those are special effects, Murph. Fake blood. This is *real* blood. *My* blood."

Just as Royce had finished cleaning David's real-life blood drops off the floor, the phone rang. A loud squeal made him wince and hold the receiver away from his ear. "I take it you passed your summer classes, Leah?"

"I did it! I'm finished! Woohoo!" she yelled again. "I called Memorial and told them I could start on August 1. Did you get A-pluses, professor?"

"Just regular A's, smart-ass."

She giggled. "So, if you were serious about helping me move out, my dad's bringing a U-Haul down next Saturday."

"I'm a man of my word. Call me when he gets there and I'll be right over."

"You're the best! Kisses!" she exclaimed, and hung up.

✧   ✧   ✧

Royce had two more weeks of full-time hours at Yawnoc before fall classes began, and they were eventful. Sales rep teams were in and out, collecting their printed taps and the tickets Sal had ordered from a local print shop in town, and working with him on their upcoming routes and schedules. The spring had returned to Sal's step, and Bobby was full of pride and optimism (and vodka) about the fall tour. The circus would come to Dublin on September 12 for its first two shows of the fall, before heading north, and Royce looked forward to meeting the performers and seeing the animals he had heard so much about.

The sales reps were about what he had expected, based on Sal's descriptions of them, though two teams stood out. Chuck and Bess Marshall were gruff and all business, displaying an air of entitlement as Yawnoc's longest-tenured contractors. They had been the loudest to object when it was announced at the summer meeting that Darla would be handling the Dublin campaign. Bobby was hurt, but not surprised. Darla was not the first girlfriend he'd given choice assignments to over the years, and the Marshalls always griped the loudest.

Ken and Sally Ross also made an impression on Royce. Younger than the other reps and smartly dressed, Ken and Sally were bright and friendly, and established a quick familiarity. They also appeared to be the only team who didn't smoke. Sally stood flirtatiously close to Royce, praising him for the good work he'd done with their taps, and touching his arm as she talked. Spotting a perceived interloper to the kingdom she had infiltrated, Darla rushed over and snaked her manicured hand into the bend of his other elbow. "Isn't he handsome? I'm-a definitely get him to work phones for me for Dublin's shows. That silky deep voice'll sell a ton of tickets!" Royce declined, as politely as possible, citing the insane amount of reading and research that would be required for his fall courses. Darla pouted, but batted her lashes at him, displaying the confidence of a woman who knew she had a couple more weeks to persuade him. He didn't understand why these women would spend an ounce of energy flattering the person who had the least amount of power or influence, but he figured he still had a lot to learn about the dynamics of the organization.

CHAPTER 4

CARLOS AND NICO

R oyce kept his promise to Leah, wrapping his hair in a bandana and skipping his morning shower to drive over and help with her move back home. She hugged him tightly and introduced him to her father, who shook his hand but looked at him warily. It was the *You have fucked my daughter, haven't you?* kind of accusatory look he had seen from other fathers. He wondered, if he ever had a daughter, if he'd have the same suspicions about the boys he would meet.

The day was hot and humid, typical of late July, and the bulky furniture became more of a struggle as the morning became afternoon. But they managed to get all of the heaviest items loaded before being chased inside by a rogue thunderstorm. Royce took a last look at the empty bedroom he had inhabited and then went to the living room to say goodbye to Leah's father. She walked him downstairs to his car and gave him another warm hug. "Are you coming back down to walk for graduation in the spring?" he asked.

"I'm planning to. Mom and Dad would be mad if I didn't. Thank you so much for helping me, Royce," she smiled.

"Of course," he said, climbing into his Squareback.

Leah glanced upstairs and then leaned into the open driver-side window, grabbing him by the back of his neck and planting a deep kiss. Her tongue felt blazing hot in his mouth.

"I still think about you when I touch myself," she purred.

He smiled and blushed. "Please keep in touch with me, Leah."

"I promise," she said, crossing her heart.

✿   ✿   ✿

ON SATURDAY, AUGUST 11, Royce and David tried to distract themselves with *Super Mario Bros. 3*, but they both kept glancing at the phone, willing it to ring. Nico and Carlos were due to arrive at the apartment they would share for the upcoming school year, and would need help getting settled. Finally, around 2:00 in the afternoon, they got the call. Royce tucked a thin joint into the breast pocket of his T-shirt.

Nico Conti had loaded his things early that morning in a small U-Haul truck at his parents place in Ellijay, and then stopped at the Lopez residence in Stone Mountain to collect Carlos and his stuff. They had spent the majority of the drive to Dublin squabbling like brothers, and were still bickering when they greeted Royce and David at the door of their new place.

"I still don't understand why you don't believe me," Carlos protested. He stood about five foot five, with dark curly hair, absurdly muscular legs, and a thin mustache.

"What's this about?" David asked.

"Tell 'em, Carlito," Nico sighed. He was around five-ten, with a husky build and a dark brown mullet he refused to update, despite the gentle ribbing he endured.

"Nico doesn't believe that I fucked a girl in the ass over the summer," he explained.

"No, no," Nico said, waving his finger at Carlos. "No, no. That's not it at all." Royce was eager to finish unloading the van, but sat down to witness the latest drama.

Nico continued. "I believe the butt sex. What I refuse to believe is that you were fucking this girl doggie style and she turned around and said, 'Why don't you move up a floor?'" David and Royce collapsed in laughter and it took almost a full minute to compose themselves.

"She did, though," Carlos muttered, and the laughter began again.

Royce tried not to think too much about the fact that Carlos, Nico, and David would all be completing their degrees the following spring and graduating alongside him. In a relatively short period of time, he had come to rely on their camaraderie. He had passed seamlessly between his high school's cliques, sharing good times with jocks, drama and chorus kids, and college-prep nerds, developing a few close friendships but a much larger network of comfortable acquaintances. But college had been a different animal altogether, and his first couple of years at Lancaster had been, to put it mildly, a lonely time for him.

It was not always idyllic, of course, and the *move up a*

floor argument was only the latest in a long line of petty disagreements. David was a master of smoothing hurt feelings, however, and what better way to side-step a potential landmine than by employing a cheesy love song? Royce remembered the first time David and Nico found themselves cross over a joke taken too seriously, and the silence that had hung in the air afterward. David offered a modified Aaron Neville/Linda Ronstadt lyric as an apology: "You know, Nico, I don't know much."

Nico smiled. "But you know you love me?"

David continued, "And that just might be all I need to know."

Not long after, Luke took a little verbal jab from David a little too personally, prompting David to quote Patrick Swayze. "Luke, man, you know you're like the wind."

"Through your tree?" Luke asked, completely disarmed.

"Through my tree," David confirmed.

✧　✧　✧

Nico and Carlos drove the rented van back north on Sunday and retrieved their cars. Nico's 1988 Buick Electra was the go-to vehicle when they were traveling together, so it was essential that it made it back to Dublin. Royce called Luke later in the afternoon, to make sure his lunch and dinner schedules would coordinate with all of theirs most days. There was a lot of catching up to do, and Royce was thrilled to have his friends back together for the home stretch. He double-checked his alarm clock and settled into bed with the bittersweet feeling that his final semester of college was about to begin.

Shakespeare's Tragedies was the last of the required courses for his B.A. in English, and he chose Contemporary American Literature as his final five-hour elective class. It was taught by Dr. Alan Russell, not one of Royce's favorites, but it was offered at 9:00 a.m., just before the Shakespeare course at 10:00, and efficiency was important to him.

Dr. Carol Dalton, Lancaster's resident Shakespeare scholar, ran every 5K, 10K, and half-marathon that was held anywhere within driving distance of Dublin. She was very tall, about five-ten, and Royce would wager that her body fat percentage was in the single digits. She kept her dirty blonde hair in a short layered cut, and was fond of Laura Ashley dresses and sandals. The earpieces of her reading glasses were scarred with teeth marks. If it weren't for the recurring and unwelcome dream, which always began with Royce slowly peeling off her blue sundress with embroidered daisies, he would have enjoyed even more having her as a professor.

He was able to nail down John Irving as his essay subject for the American Lit class, approaching Dr. Russell on the first day of class to stake his claim. He had already read Irving's entire catalog, from *A Prayer for Owen Meany* backward, and had a plan for a term paper examining common themes across his works. He kept Anne Tyler in his back pocket, in case someone beat him to John Irving.

✧   ✧   ✧

Royce, David, Nico, and Luke met at Calhoun at 11:00 a.m. for lunch every day during the first week of classes, and Royce got to Yawnoc at noon for a four hour shift. Darla and a local woman she'd hired to help with the phone sales campaign called local businesses in the afternoons, but she didn't pressure Royce to stay into the evenings to help make the residential calls. Sal kept to himself, ordering tickets and making logistics calls to stay one step ahead of the demand. He always had a ledger book open on his desk.

At lunch on Friday of the first week of classes, Luke asked the question they all had considered but no one had asked aloud. "So, who y'all got your eyes on?"

"Oooooh, that's a good question!" Royce chimed in. "Did Sun come back this year?" He looked to David for an answer.

"She did," David confessed, looking down at his burrito. "I have two classes with her." David's focus was computer science, and he had made the mistake of mentioning his infatuation for his classmate during the previous spring semester. But if anything had come of it, he had kept it to himself.

"Well, we all expect her to be sitting here with us soon," Luke teased. "You aren't ashamed of us, are you, Dave?"

This was rich coming from Luke, considering he had

apparently been going out with the same local girl since his senior year of high school, but no one in the group had ever met her.

David did his best to deflect attention to Nico. "I've seen the little red-haired girl on campus this week, Nico. Are you gonna make a play this year or not?"

Nico opened his mouth to reply, but was interrupted by his little sister, Gina, a sophomore and a far more observant Catholic than her brother. "What day is it, Nico?" she asked as she walked by the table. Nico looked at the cheeseburger in his hand and slammed it down onto his plastic plate. "God *dammit!*" His friends had made a pact not to remind him of the Friday Fast, since Gina kept her eye on him.

Nico tried to turn the tables, and targeted Royce. "You haven't sworn yourself to celibacy for the next four months, have you? I know Leah's gone, but there must be someone else. It's gonna be lonely last semester if you're counting on just us for companionship. What was that other girl's name? Shelley?"

Royce recalled the first day of his Shakespeare class, a few days earlier. In addition to dodging Dr. Dalton's eyes, he watched Shelley show off the engagement ring she had been given over the summer break.

"Shelley's engaged," he said softly. "And y'all are way wrong about Leah. We were never a thing." He glanced at an empty chair at their six-top lunch table, and lamented the fact that Carlos had an 11:00 class. He would have loved to move the spotlight onto someone else.

"Well, y'all looked like a thing," Nico pressed. "Except for when she was flirting with Luke, that is."

Royce silently bristled. He knew Leah was hard to take, sometimes, when she was out of her element. She had invited herself over to David's a couple of times, after Royce had moved in with her, and hadn't made much of an effort to fit in. When the guys were together, they smoked weed, played Nintendo, and watched action movies or goofy comedies. Leah didn't smoke, didn't game, and grumbled about the movie choices. She wore out what small welcome she had within the first couple of hours of her first visit. Luke had shut her down in the most Luke way imaginable, on her first attempt to flirt with him. "Our names are Luke and Leah. Seriously. George Lucas has already shown us why this could never work."

✧   ✧   ✧

OVER THE NEXT couple of weeks, Darla concluded the Dublin sales campaign and gathered her taps, tickets, and supplies from the office for a two week stint on the road. She was to run sales for the Toccoa and Dahlonega shows, and then return to Dublin for the show's performances in mid-September. Bobby was disconsolate. Royce and Sal watched through the office windows as Darla and Bobby loaded her suitcases into her Mercedes and hugged each other goodbye.

"Why doesn't he just go with her? Or go to visit?" Royce asked Sal.

"He doesn't have a driver's license," Sal replied. "He's had three DUI convictions, and did some time in jail when one of his passengers was injured in a wreck on the last of 'em." Sal shook his head. "He sold both his cars when he got released, and hasn't been behind the wheel since."

Royce walked up the stairs to the kitchen and caught Mae looking out the kitchen window at the tearful good-bye. "Pathetic," she groaned.

"Not a fan of Darla?" Royce asked. He tried to steer clear of taking sides in the mini-dramas at the office, but always kept his ears open for gossip.

"You know why she wears all those tight clothes and stockings, don'tcha?" Mae asked with a slightly catty tone. Royce shook his head. "She used to be *real* fat. She lost about a hundred pounds, after getting that stomach-stapling thing. She's real sensitive about the loose skin she's carrying, so she always wears clothes as tight as they'll fit."

Royce's mouth dropped open and his eyes widened with horror.

"It's true!" Mae continued. "I accidentally walked up on her when she was getting out of the shower once. She looked like one of them Shar-Pei dogs! She's had some surgeries, but that shit still leaves scars."

Royce shook his head in disbelief and went back downstairs to the office before Bobby returned to his throne. He'd be asking for another drink, and the less Royce considered Darla's body, the better. He tried to think happy thoughts, like the fact that Dr. Dalton had not yet worn the blue sundress with the daisies on it.

On Friday, David and Royce walked back to their apartment alone after dinner, packed a fat bowl in the Dutch bong, and queued up a tape of *Raising Arizona* in the VCR. Royce planned to drive home the next morning for the weekend, so he took a pad and pen into the kitchen to make a list of what they needed. David had already given him some money for Eric's product, because there were some necessities that his mother's warehouse club wasn't allowed to sell.

CHAPTER 5

SHOWTIME

Royce's Labor Day weekend trip home was a virtual mirror of Memorial Day weekend. He hooked up with Eric for another transaction, and then he and Jennifer packed an overnight bag and went down to the lake house for a visit with their father.

Jennifer was excited to show her big brother the pictures she'd taken at her graduation, and to fill him in on her first few weeks of classes at Emory University. She was living at home and working with Kate in the accounting department at a busy Atlanta law firm, and she was eager to pursue a legal degree of her own. He was struck by how much he and his sister looked alike, both with strong cheekbones and noses, deep brown eyes, and thick dark hair. Their paternal grandfather's grandmother had been a full-blooded Cherokee, and they both exhibited her genetic features prominently.

On Labor Day, Royce made the trip with Kate, with less money to spend than the last time they shopped together but with fewer items on his wish list. They took two cars so he could leave straight from the warehouse for the four hour drive back to Dublin. His load was a bit unwieldy, with cardboard case packs of food and drinks, his laundry basket, and assorted other items, so it would take several trips to move it all into the apartment. David was on the sofa with a book in his hands and some British comedy in the VCR. Royce dropped his first load and went back downstairs for another.

He could almost empty the remainder of the Squareback with the second trip, but not quite. He made one more round trip, grabbed the last few boxes, and locked the car before climbing the stairs for a third time. Casting an accusatory eye at David, he said with all the sarcasm he could muster, "No, thanks. I don't need any help."

David looked up from his book. "Dude. *Ask.*"

Two words. Just two words, but they hit him hard. David was right, and he knew it. He walked into the bathroom, closed the door, and sat down on the lid of the toilet. David had no way of knowing how much Royce had brought back, and all he had to do was ask him for help and David would have put down his book and walked with him to the car without hesitation. Royce appreciated every influence he had inherited from Kate — her love for classic movies and literature, her focus and drive to tackle whatever big task might be in front of her, and above all, the dedication and selflessness that it took to raise two children as a single mother, from the time Royce was eight and Jennifer was four. But he knew he had internalized a number of her negative tendencies, as well, and it took a conscious effort to suppress them. He could be quick to sense a slight and long to hold a grudge and, like today, to use passive-aggressive language instead of speaking directly. He always tried to be measured and contemplative in conflict situations, but sometimes he slipped.

He pulled some toilet tissue and wiped the tears that were forming at the corners of his eyes. David was in the kitchen, carefully putting away the new supplies, when Royce gathered himself and came out of the bathroom to stand beside him.

"I'm sorry, David. I know better."

David placed a reassuring hand on his shoulder. "I should have gone downstairs with you when you first got here," he added with a grin, "You know how I appreciate a full pantry."

Royce packed a bowl and suggested they watch a couple of episodes of *Twin Peaks* that David had recorded in the spring. The second season was only a few weeks from its premiere. They didn't have very many appointment TV shows, but they both were huge David Lynch fans.

✧   ✧   ✧

THE FOLLOWING WEEK of classes was abbreviated because of the holiday, but it was a struggle for Royce. He had no love for the selections Dr. Russell had chosen for Contemporary Lit, and he found it difficult to muster any enthusiasm for the class, even with a midterm exam looming in a couple of weeks. He was spending his library and computer lab time wisely, though, and reasoned that the essays he was writing for his final grades would bear far more weight than the midterms. Making matters far worse, however, was Dr. Dalton's decision to wear the blue sundress with the embroidered daisies. Royce fought his mental images and kept his head buried in the textbook for the entirety of class, even when called upon to offer his thoughts on a passage from *King Lear*.

Dr. Roberts, the department chair and Royce's favorite teacher, stopped him in the hallway after class. "Royce! Have you had much contact with the headhunters?"

"I've been doing some work for them, yes. Trying to build a portfolio." Dr. Roberts had published a paper decrying the decline of Standard American English in the workplace, which had received the attention of a few large corporations. A couple of placement agencies in Atlanta reached out to him, and asked if he might steer some of his impending graduates to them for recruitment. Royce periodically received editorial assignments on floppy disk, or small technical writing jobs, and he did his best to complete and return them promptly. He knew how tight the labor market was for people with humanities degrees, and wanted to do whatever he could to get a leg up on entry-level post-graduate positions.

By Friday, the circus office was abuzz about the show coming to town, but the logistics had Sal on edge. Darla returned mid-week from her sales campaigns, so Bobby was all smiles again. Royce didn't know how much he and Sal could take of Bobby's presence in the office, either micro-managing Sal on things that were already set in motion, or complaining about how to host the caravan of trailers, performers, and animals headed their way. Darla's calming influence was immediate, so Royce and Sal finalized the last of the plans in peace. "You may want to stop by Sammy's on your way to work on Monday," Sal suggested. "A lot of the show is going to be parking there."

✧   ✧   ✧

MONDAY AFTERNOON WAS a blur. Royce found a place to park in between two hulking RVs, and walked into Sammy's Bar for the first time. Bobby Lee was holding court, as expected, with Darla watching him with admiration from her seat at the bar. He was already well into his liquor allowance for the day, and stalked a pool table like a predator. Sal was sitting alone at a two-top to the left side of the bar, so Royce pulled up a stool beside him to watch the action. Every strike of the cue ball was hit at least twice as hard as necessary, as though Bobby intended to punish the balls for some offense known only to him. Targets that could have been nudged into a pocket were instead slammed and left to the whims of gravity to fall into place.

"This is why Darla walks funny, sometimes, I bet," Sal quipped.

Royce chuckled, and watched as Bobby pounded the eight ball into a corner pocket to defeat another opponent. He took an awkward victory lap around the table, with exaggerated high steps that had a pronounced hitch in them due to his gimpy knees. He sang as he pranced, "Animal crackers in my soup!" Royce wondered if this was the first time in recorded history a Shirley Temple song had been used by a victor to taunt the vanquished.

Sal rose and motioned for Royce to follow him. "Come on, let's meet some people." They went out the back door of the bar, and Royce trailed behind as Sal knocked on the door of the largest and newest RV in the back parking area. A short, portly man in his fifties opened the door, dressed in a navy blue Adidas track suit, and sporting a wavy red toupee. "Royce," Sal said with an air of reverence, "May I present Mr. Joey Vegas." Royce shook the ringmaster's hand and imagined how differently he must have to present himself to serve as the master of ceremonies for the circus. "Pleasure to meet you, Royce," Joey Vegas said in a baritone Southern drawl. "Let me get Lord Connelly for you."

Joey disappeared into the trailer and returned with a miniature horse on a black leather leash. Lord Connelly was the circus's signature act, and was owned and trained by Joey. Royce knelt on the RV's metal steps and carefully stroked the horse's chestnut coat and ivory mane. "He's beautiful," he said.

"And what's more, he knows it!" Joey said with a hearty laugh. "He can be quite a diva. Though not as much as Ashanti, of course." He nodded to Sal, "Have you taken him to Gloria's van yet?"

Sal shook his head. "No, but it's our next stop."

Royce gave Lord Connelly a few more pats and followed Sal across the parking lot, waving goodbye to the horse. Along the way, they passed three of the show's clowns practicing their act. They stood in a triangle, about twenty feet apart, and bounced nine tennis balls on the asphalt to one another, in a coordinated juggling routine that taxed Royce's visual ability to keep up. In high school, he had mastered the three-ball cascade, but he was flummoxed by the intricacies of the clowns' movements. As much as he wanted to continue to study them, however, he was motioned onward by Sal to an RV in the far corner of the lot.

Lady Gloria answered Sal's knock, and with an infectious smile motioned for the two of them to enter her trailer. She was a small and slender woman, also in her fifties, and wore cut-off denim shorts and a heather gray tank top. Her hair was jet black and dead straight, except for an inch-wide streak of gray on each side of her face that ran from her temples to the tips of her bob.

"I think Mistress Ashanti must have been expecting you!" she exclaimed, in an accent Royce could only vaguely place as middle-Eastern. As he contemplated the accent of a Persian student he'd met the year before, a glorious black leopard bounded from her cage in the main seating area and pounced onto the bench next to him.

Her coat was the shiniest of black, and she placed her head on Royce's lap and curled up on him as though they were long-lost friends. He caressed her as he would a house cat, even though she was five times the size.

Her purr shook the seat as she nestled into a comfortable position.

"You've made a friend!" Gloria smiled, combing her hair with her fingers. "Ashanti is usually so stand-offish."

Royce tried to catch his breath as the majestic cat nibbled playfully at his fingers. "I have nothing to compare all this to," he said. "This is all very new to me." The three exchanged small talk for a little while about the show and Lady Gloria's act, until Sal rose to indicate it was time to go. Royce thanked her for her hospitality, and told her how much he looked forward to seeing her performance.

Sal and Royce were only a few steps away from Gloria's van when Sal dropped some gossip. "Joey and Gloria have been an on-again, off-again item for years. But even in their happiest times, they keep separate living quarters. I bet there are members of the crew that don't even know about them," he winked. Royce looked around for the clowns, but they had already ended their practice session. He had work to do, and was eager to get down to the office to finish a couple of projects.

✧ ✧ ✧

EVEN AFTER MEETING Joey and Gloria, Royce was unsure what to expect from the show, so he didn't invite David and his other friends to join him for Wednesday evening's performance. He drove to the YMCA just ahead of the posted showtime of 7:00 p.m., and walked through the red and white striped curtains that had been hung outside the gymnasium door. The smell of freshly popped popcorn was inviting, and classic big band circus marches were piped through standing speakers. Refreshment and merchandise vendors flanked the entranceway, calling to the audience as they arrived: "Popcorn! Peanuts! Candy! Get it while it's handy!"

Royce approached the circus ring, which was bordered by curved bleachers on three sides, with folding chair overflow seating that could be moved in, if necessary. He dodged a swirl of children who were running back and forth at ringside, waving battery operated light-up souvenirs and ignoring the parents who tried to corral them. Shiny gold streamers framed the back of the stage, hiding the wings and the performers' path to the ring. A banner with the show's name on it hung above the entrance portal. He caught sight of waving arms from the corner of his eye, and turned to find Sal, Bobby Lee, and Darla in VIP seats on the top row of the risers, at stage left. Knowing they wouldn't be heard over the murmurs of the packed house, they motioned for him to join them.

The stage lights dimmed and a pair of spotlights twirled in circles as a pre-recorded welcome blared through the speakers. "Ladies and gentlemen, children of all ages, please welcome your master of ceremonies, Mister Joey Vegas!" Joey entered the ring in a sharp-looking black tuxedo, which had reflective pinstripe threads that sparkled under the lights. His toupee, too, seemed to glow brighter than it had when Royce first met him. He took a deep bow and raised a cordless microphone. He thanked everyone for attending, and for their support of the YMCA, the show's local sponsor for the performance.

The opening act was a pair of twin sisters from China, dressed in pink sequined leotards. They couldn't have been more than 15 or 16 years old, Royce estimated. They were both acrobats and contortionists, and their well-rehearsed routine was mesmerizing. The crowd erupted when they completed their performance. Then came the trio of clowns, who worked outside the edges of the ring while stage hands removed the acrobat props and installed wooden stands and metal rings for the next act. The clowns selected several children as targets for their up-close gags: balloon animals, plastic flowers rigged with water-squirting mechanisms, buckets of water that magically became confetti, among other staples.

The clowns were followed by a Bangladeshi animal trainer and his three rhesus monkeys. Royce leaned over to Sal and asked why some of these acts hadn't been parked at Sammy's on Monday, like the others. "The monkey trainer, Nazir, and the Zhou twins and their guardian prefer to keep to themselves," Sal explained. "If there's an RV park in a tour city, those acts park together and help each other out. I'm not sure any of them speak more than ten words of English. Just personal preference."

Royce nodded and turned his attention to the back of the house. The two spotlight operators were perched on ten-foot scaffolding at opposite corners, and the sound and lighting techs manned make-shift booths at the base of the scaffold on the left. A cluster of electrical wiring snaked along the base of the walls to connect their locations. Royce checked his program and asked Sal if he would come with him to the technical areas. His theatrical experience made him curious about the set-up, but he wanted to get back to his seat in time to see Ashanti and Lady Gloria.

Sal climbed down the bleachers, as subtly as he could, and Royce followed. The sound and lighting techs both immediately recognized Sal, and pulled their head-phones aside as he introduced them to Royce. Royce nodded and smiled, and motioned with his hands to let them know he didn't mean to be a bother. He just wanted to watch. The clowns had returned to the ring, with subtle wardrobe changes, and were performing a comedy routine involving an old-timey hand-cranked movie camera and a series of pratfalls. There were a number of sound and lighting cues during the routine, which the techs handled masterfully, and their skill and precision delighted Royce immensely.

Royce settled back into his seat on the bleachers just as Joey Vegas introduced Lady Gloria and Ashanti. Joey gave Gloria a kiss on the cheek as she took to the ring, and Royce marveled at her stage presence. The tiny bare-foot woman in shorts and a tank top was now wearing black heels and a sparkly red dress with a slit that ran all the way to the top of her thigh. Every movement she made commanded the audience's attention. And the overgrown kitten that had curled into his lap two days earlier now followed her training and behaved like a dangerous jungle predator. African drum beats pounded through the speakers as Ashanti raised herself onto her hind legs and bared her long, sharp white teeth, to the delight of the crowd.

Joey walked to the center of the ring as Gloria and Ashanti retreated to the sound of well-deserved applause. The opening bars of Henry Mancini's "Baby Elephant Walk" ushered Lord Connelly to the spotlight, accompanied by a handler Royce had not yet met. The tiny horse pranced around the perimeter of the ring, led by Joey Vegas, jumping small equestrian bars along the way, to the squeals of the youngest in the audience. He twirled in circles on command, and ascended a low platform, then jumped to another and back again. With an elaborate flourish of his hands, and a bow to the audience, Joey gave his cue to the other performers to join him in the ring.

The music crescendoed, and the spotlights twirled as the performers returned to the ring in the order in which they had taken the stage. They smiled and waved, and reveled in the adoration of the ovation the crowd gave them. They turned and filed out, through the portal at center stage, as Bobby took Darla's hand and motioned for Sal and Royce to follow them through the stage-left curtain. Royce looked over his shoulder to see the audience forming queues at the merchandise tables, and understood for the first time why the circus only needed to take 25% of the proceeds of the ticket sales, with excess money left over.

Behind the gym at the YMCA was a large locker room, which the circus crew had partitioned into dressing areas using curtains hung from ropes. Royce and Darla stood back a few yards while Bobby and Sal glad-handed the performers and staff. "Wasn't it great?!" Darla squealed, snaking her hand through Royce's bent elbow. "I'm just so proud of all of them!"

"I really enjoyed it," Royce confessed with a smile. He hadn't been at all sure he would. He felt a hand touch the small of his back and turned to find Sally Ross, the sales rep, standing close behind him.

"Sally!" Royce said, a little too excitedly, "I didn't see you in the audience."

"Ken and I got here late, so we stayed in the back." Royce nodded to Ken, who was standing at the entrance of the locker room. Ken nodded back, though his expression strongly suggested that he was not happy with his wife's proximity and body language. Royce decided it was time to go.

"I have some reading to do before class tomorrow, so I should probably get going," he said to Darla and Sally. Both of them encouraged him to stay, but he repeated his apology and back-pedaled toward the door of the locker room. He almost bumped into the Zhou twins, who had returned to the ring after the cast recessional to sign autographs and pose for pictures with audience members. Royce bowed to them and clapped his hands to indicate his appreciation for their performance. The girls giggled and skittered off to their changing area.

Royce wiped off the condensation from the Squareback's windshield before starting the car and driving back to Kingston. David was watching some obscure horror movie when he got home, and hit 'Pause' on the remote. "How was it?" he asked with genuine curiosity.

"Weird, as usual. Show was good, though. Better than I expected." He left David to his movie and went to curl up on his bed to read *Macbeth* until he couldn't stay awake any longer.

CHAPTER 6

RUMBLE

Royce helped Nico, Luke, and Carlos plan a birthday celebration for David on September 30, and the guys arrived as scheduled at noon that Sunday.

If David wasn't surprised, he did a good job of faking it.

Their first stop was David's favorite Chinese place for lunch, and then Nico drove them to the mall for a 1:30 showing of *King of New York*, the new Christopher Walken movie. Royce cut his eyes at Luke several times during the film, wondering how many lines he would memorize and incorporate into spot-on imitations for later use.

Royce packed a bowl upon their return to Kingston while the others bickered over which Nintendo games Luke would dominate first. But they all knew it wouldn't matter. If someone beat Luke in an NES game, it was because he let them.

After several hours of Luke's relentless command of whatever games they chose to play, Royce grabbed the phone and ordered pizza. Nico, Carlos, and David were tired of Luke's unbeaten streak, and decided to watch videos and play Spades instead. Bon Jovi's "Wanted Dead or Alive" was first up. David scowled at the lyric

"I've seen a million faces and I've rocked them all." He threw a cushion at the TV and said in a raised voice, "Jon Bon Jovi, you haven't rocked a day in your god-damned life."

Luke passed out on the sofa around 8:00, and Nico and Carlos said their goodbyes half an hour later. In spite of Luke's snoring, David and Royce were able to watch the season two debut of *Twin Peaks* in relative peace. "Thanks for today, man," David said as the opening credits began. "I knew you were planning something, but I didn't know what."

✧　✧　✧

Aside from another appearance by Dr. Dalton's blue sundress, Royce's life was peaceful for the next several days. But all that changed on October 11th.

He was looking forward to a quiet day in the office. It was Bobby Lee's birthday, and Sal was hosting a party at his house. Darla and Mae would both be attending, so Royce would have the entire house and office to himself. He was ahead of schedule with the tap entries, but hoped to press hard, free from any distractions, to give himself more of a cushion. He was making gratifying progress until around 4:00, when the sound of a roaring engine broke his concentration.

Darla's Mercedes slid to a stop in the driveway, trailing blue smoke from its tires. Bobby climbed out of the driver's seat and slammed the door behind him. He marched purposefully and drunkenly, storming into the office and throwing his cowboy hat at the tacky mirrored desk. He paced the length of the room, over and over, distractedly running his fingers through his gray hair. After several silent seconds, Royce ventured to ask, "What's wrong, Bobby?"

"I fired Sal," he replied. "Fuckin' wop was stealin' from me."

"What?" Royce said with astonishment. "That doesn't make any sense. He keeps such detailed records. I've seen him."

Bobby stopped pacing and turned toward him. His blue eyes were bulging and his face was beet red. "Yeah? Well, you gotta keep good records if you're stealin', don'tcha?" He walked behind the mirrored desk and flopped down into the chair. He continued, far more softly. "And then... and then today, my god-damned *birthday*, I find out he was trying to fuck Darla."

Royce shook his head and tried to speak, but felt as if all of the air had been sucked out of his lungs. The whole thing was unreal. Finally, he managed to force out a couple of sentences. "I don't understand. Not a bit of this sounds like Sal, at all. At all."

Bobby stood and pointed a bony finger toward Sal's desk. "I'll pay you forty thousand a year to sit in that desk," he said.

Royce's tongue felt numb. "I... I don't know. I'm still in school until the first week of December. I'm too close and I've worked too hard, and I'm not going to quit now."

"I know, I know," Bobby nodded and started pacing again. "We can work somethin' out. Think about it tonight, but I gotta know tomorrow one way or th'other." Both men looked out the window as Mae's pickup rounded the driveway and parked beside the Mercedes. Darla exited the passenger side and sprinted into the office, somehow keeping her balance on high-heeled sandals. She grabbed Bobby and wrapped her arms around his waist.

"I'm so sorry, baby," she said, "Let's go upstairs. Please?"

The wind was out of Bobby's sails, and Royce feared he might collapse. Instead, he leaned on Darla and staggered up the steps into the kitchen as Mae walked into the office.

"Wow," she sighed. "Just when you think shit can't get any stranger."

"What the fuck happened?" Royce asked her.

"I have no idea, honestly. Chuck Marshall was in Bobby's ear from the time we got there, sayin' God knows what. Bobby kept gettin' more and more agitated, and then Darla disappeared for about half an hour."

Royce turned around and shut down the computer. "Does any of this sound like Sal to you? I mean, stealing from the company and trying to sleep with Darla? I just can't imagine."

"Not to me," Mae agreed. "But I just push a vacuum and buy groceries. I'll letcha know what I hear, though."

Royce smiled. "I will, too. Tell 'em I went home, okay? I have a lot to think about." Mae patted him on the shoulder as he picked up his backpack and left.

☼   ☼   ☼

DAVID HAD ALREADY left for work by the time Royce got home. Royce waited until just before the dinner hours at Calhoun ended before walking through the line, hoping to avoid anyone he knew. He had so much on his mind, and didn't feel capable of small talk. When he got back home, he found himself pacing like Bobby had, and checked his watch repeatedly, thinking about when his father might be home from work. Eventually, he decided to page him.

Royce Senior called back within half an hour, as Royce sat entrenched on the sofa with a notebook and pen, trying to collect his thoughts. His father listened carefully and thoughtfully, realizing midway through the conversation that his son had already decided to take the job. He finally offered his thoughts. "Well, I don't see any way in the world you'd make that kind of money in an entry-level position in Atlanta. If you think you can handle the job, you should probably do it. It's not forever, you know. You can come home anytime you want, and your mom and I will do what we can for you."

Royce brushed a tear from his eye. "Thanks, Dad. I appreciate it. I'll do my best."

"Save your money, son. I know you know how to be careful."

"I do. Thanks again. I gotta call Mom now."

Kate was less enthusiastic about Royce's decision,

and needed more information. He wrote down every question she had, regarding taxes and weekly payments and how to protect himself against liabilities. "I don't mean to be a wet blanket," she said, "but we were kinda hoping you'd be home soon."

"I was, too," he replied. "I miss y'all. Tell Jennifer I said hey. I'll let you know what I find out."

He went to bed early and was already asleep by the time David returned from the Video Barn.

✧   ✧   ✧

Royce blew off his Friday classes, a rarity, and arrived at the office around 9:00 a.m. He wanted to talk with Bobby before he started drinking, and they had a lot to cover. He absently thumbed the corner of his yellow legal pad, staring at Sal's desk and waiting to hear signs of life from the kitchen upstairs.

Mae opened the door to the office, smiled, and said, "I told him you were here. He'll be up in a few. You want some coffee?"

"I would, thanks," he replied gratefully. "I'll be right up."

Bobby and Darla made their way to Bobby's throne as Royce was finishing his coffee. "My new office manager is here!" Bobby said in a hoarse voice. "Let's get down to business."

"If I grab a takeout plate from the dining hall, I can get here half an hour earlier. Can I count on you to handle visitors until I come in? The taps are up to date, but I'll need to hire someone quickly to stay ahead," Royce began.

"Shit, I can handle the reps, no problem," Bobby replied. "Hire whoever you want. Same deal you got."

Bobby's intense blue eyes and unusually professional demeanor were intimidating, but Royce soldiered on. "Okay, then. The deal. How would my pay work?"

Bobby explained that Royce would be paid $500 a week, in cash, with the other $14,000 coming from two $7,000 lump payments at the end of each tour. The fall tour payment would be pro-rated, but Bobby was already working on the numbers, because Sal would be due his percentage.

"You need to verify with Strickland about the tickets," Bobby continued. "I don't know what he's printed so far, but y'all seem to be on top of that. Verify with the wop when he gets here."

"Sal's coming in?" Royce asked, bristling at the slur.

"He wants to collect his shit. And I need some things from him, too."

They were interrupted by the doorbell, and Darla welcomed in a tall, barrel-chested deputy sheriff. Royce rolled his eyes. "Is that really necessary?" he asked.

"Protect yourself at all times," Bobby replied. "Boxing rules apply to real life, son."

Well, let's get ready to rumble, I guess, Royce said to himself.

✧   ✧   ✧

HE WENT TO work on the taps, and Sal's Cadillac pulled into the driveway a little while later. Royce had never seen a man look so broken. Sal's signature slicked-back hairstyle was dry and disheveled, and his narrow shoulders were slumped. Bobby and the deputy walked through the kitchen door, with Darla nowhere in sight, as Sal entered the office. Royce greeted him with a warm handshake and a half-embrace with his left arm. Sal pulled him close and whispered, "None of this is true. I think you know that."

"I do," Royce whispered back. "I'm so sorry, Sal."

"You watch out for Chuck Marshall. And Darla, too," he warned.

Sal walked to his desk and collected a framed five by seven formal photo of himself and his wife from a Mexican cruise they'd taken, along with a few wallet-sized school photos of their grandchildren. He dropped a couple of boxes of business cards on the desk, and tried to give Royce the keys to his desk drawer that contained the petty cash box. "Don't bother," Bobby said gruffly. "The locksmith is on his way."

Sal reached into his breast pocket and pulled out a computer disk. "This has the sales rep handbook on it," he said, handing it to Royce. "I didn't want you to have to start from scratch." He managed a crooked grin. "Oh,

and this," he said, scribbling a series of numbers onto the desk calendar, "This is my home phone number. If you need anything, anytime…"

Mae opened the door from the kitchen and walked tentatively down the steps. She glared at Bobby as she moved toward Sal and hugged him tightly. "I'll miss you, Sal!" she said sadly, patting the much smaller man on his shoulders. "You take care of yourself, okay?" Sal reached under the frames of his glasses and dabbed at his eyes.

He gathered his personal things and turned toward the door. "You can do this, Royce. Don't ever doubt it. Please take care of the show for me," he said, and closing the door behind him, he was gone.

Royce waited respectfully until Sal's car had exited the driveway before he took a seat at the desk. He was as angry as he could ever remember being, with no clear outlet. He motioned to the deputy but directed his words to Bobby. "You and I are going to count every dollar in the safe and the petty cash box while he's here," he barked, "and we're establishing a baseline."

"Well, look how you look!" Bobby said, his blue eyes wide and wounded. They opened the safe and the cash box and started counting. Royce took Sal's ledger books and flipped to the most recent page. The totals matched Sal's numbers, exactly. Royce made Bobby initial and date the pages, knowing that any shortfalls moving forward would be his responsibility to investigate. *Protect yourself at all times*, Royce repeated to himself.

The locksmith arrived while Royce was on the phone with Strickland's about the current status of ticket orders. Strickland verified that they were up to date, and agreed to rush a box of business cards for Royce. The locksmith gave Royce and Bobby each a key to the desk drawer, along with the new combination to the safe. Royce scribbled a help wanted ad onto an index card, hoping he could find someone quickly to take over his data entry position.

Mentally and physically exhausted, he posted the ad to Calhoun's jobs board when he returned to campus, and built a takeout box from the dinner line rather than eating in the dining room. He looked at himself critically in the floor-length mirror in his apartment's hallway. Hair in a ponytail, thin gold earring, a Pixies tour T-shirt, olive green shorts, and Chuck Taylors. He shook his head. "Not much like an office manager," he said aloud. *And not someone who would command respect from sales reps twice his age*, he thought. He checked his wallet for the only-in-case-of-emergency credit card and began a mental checklist for another shopping trip.

✿ ✿ ✿

As USUAL, SHAMROCK Mall was deserted on Saturday afternoon. Lancaster was a suitcase college, and the majority of the student body left the campus in its rear-view mirror on Friday in order to spend the weekend at their parents' house. Royce entered the menswear department of Macy's full of uncertainty. He was fortunate to find a familiar face. "Royce?" said a voice from behind him.

He turned to see Angela, who had come to Lancaster as a freshman at the same time he had. She was petite and fair, with long, wavy blonde hair and green eyes. He explained his situation and asked if she could help. She leaned forward and said softly, "I get so fucking bored here on the weekends. If you'll trust me, I know I can put together a good look for you."

She pulled a cloth measure from behind the cashier station and recorded the numbers for his arms, shoulders and neck. "Y'all boys wear such baggy clothes," she sighed. "It's like y'all don't even know how hot it is when you wear something that fits."

He vetoed a couple of her flashier choices, but otherwise accepted her selections without question. He asked about dress shoes that could be worn with jeans, and she immediately returned from the shoe department with sharp-looking pairs of black and brown loafers. He bought matching belts to go with the shoes, along with eight long-sleeve shirts, eight short-sleeve shirts, and three new pairs of jeans. *This will be my uniform,* he decided.

As she packed four large bags at the register, he asked with a grin, "You get commission on this, right?"

"I do," she said with a hundred-watt smile. "But I'd have done it for minimum wage, too."

BOBBY AND DARLA had driven to meet Joey Vegas over the weekend, and there was a new bag of cash waiting on Royce's desk when he arrived on Monday. There were no messages on the answering machine, and he hoped he wouldn't have to wait too long for applicants to help him with the taps. He was still ahead of schedule with them, and could devote an hour or so during the day to entering more, but knew he should be going through Sal's records and finding out exactly what he didn't know about his new position. He carefully counted the cash, making doubly sure that it matched the total Joey and Bobby had written on the envelope, and put the money away in the safe.

He drove by Strickland's on his way to the office on Wednesday to pick up two sets of tickets and his business cards. The cards looked like something his father would have, and even had the same name on them. He was beginning to feel less and less like a child playing dress-up. The phone rang on his way out the door, but something told him to stop and answer it.

"I was wondering if your data entry job was still open," said a soft but confident voice on the other end. She said her brother had seen his ad, and that she was looking for part-time work.

"Can you come by tomorrow afternoon?" he asked. She agreed, and gave her name. He wrote *Chloe Webb* on his calendar for Thursday.

CHAPTER 7

CHLOE

The sun's reflection off the windshield of a Mazda RX-7 flashed briefly through the blinds, distracting Royce from his calendar. The car circled the driveway, parked behind his VW, and an absolute stunner stepped out of the driver's seat. She was slender and leggy, about five-foot-eight, and she wore a pink sweater, an acid-washed denim skirt, black nylons and leather ankle boots. Her dark brown hair was cut in a shoulder-length bob, straight on top but wavy at the bottom, with wispy bangs that reached the top of her round blue-mirrored sunglasses.

Please be Chloe, he whispered to himself, and rose to meet her at the office door.

She spoke first. "Hi, I'm looking for Royce?"

"And you found him!" he exclaimed, cringing internally at the over-eagerness of his reply. "I love your car. Is that an '83?" he asked, trying to recover.

"An '82," she corrected, removing her sunglasses and slipping them into her purse. "It was my oldest brother's."

He motioned toward his desk and sat down, suddenly aware of his increased heart rate and body temperature.

He surreptitiously wiped his palms on his jeans as she took the seat across from him. "I brought this," she said, handing him a resume printed on heavy gray paper.

He scanned it quickly. "You're from Savannah," he observed with a smile. She nodded. She had honey-brown eyes with thick, long lashes, and a delightful scattering of freckles across her cheeks and the bridge of her nose. She was quite tan.

"The Key Academy? I hear it's an excellent school."

"I *really* loved it," she gushed. "The *best* teachers in the state." He placed her resume on the desk and tried to relax his shoulders. An awkward silence fell as they stared into each other's eyes.

"Lemme level with you, Chloe," he began. "I've never interviewed anyone before, and I'm not quite sure where to go with this."

"Oh, good! We're being *honest*!" she said, smiling broadly with relief. "No offense, but I was expecting someone older."

"Well, if you'd come here a week ago, that's what you would've gotten." He explained that Sal had been dismissed abruptly and he had taken over, so now he needed someone to fill his old position. He told her a bit about the company and the show, described the job duties, and explained that the owner lived in the house attached to the office.

"A circus? How interesting! Is it the one that was in town a while ago? I didn't go, but I saw some posters."

"Yes, it was here last month. But today it's in..." he checked the calendar on his desk, "Cedartown. North Georgia leg of the tour."

She leaned forward and tucked a lock of hair behind her right ear. "May I ask about the pay and the hours?"

"Well, I'm still in classes until the first week of December, so I don't usually get here until 11:30. How does noon to five sound, for now? And it's five dollars an hour cash, every Friday."

She raised her left hand and tapped her index finger to her chin. "Can I talk to my brother and sister-in-law first? I moved here to help them after their baby was born, but they don't need me quite as much as they used to. That's why they encouraged me to find something, at least part-time. I'll start taking a class or two in January."

"Of course," he said, smiling pleasantly. "Honestly, no one else has called about the job yet. But I do need someone as soon as possible. Can you give me an answer tomorrow?" He handed her a business card, in case she'd misplaced the number.

"Sure," she replied, standing up and adjusting her skirt. He escorted her to the door and opened it for her. The air was cool and crisp, and it reminded him of why autumn was his favorite season.

"It was a pleasure to meet you, Chloe, and I hope we'll be working together."

She took a look at his card and slid it into the outside pocket of her purse. "I'll call you tomorrow afternoon,

Mr. Murphy," she said with another disarming smile. He appreciated her tongue-in-cheek formality.

He waited until her car was out of sight before he picked up her resume. The air around his desk still carried the tropical aroma of her perfume, and he inhaled deeply as he continued reading.

Bobby Lee swung open the door from the kitchen and leaned into the office. "She's a purty one, ain't she?" he slurred playfully. Royce had caught him looking through the window in the kitchen door a couple of times while she'd been interviewing, but ignored him.

"She is," Royce replied casually, refusing to make eye contact and pretending to write something on his calendar. "Very pretty."

"Y'all would make some handsome babies, says I," teased Bobby, then closed the door and returned to his semi-circular throne.

Royce was intrigued by a number of items on Chloe's resume, particularly that she had spent the past two years taking classes at a junior college, which seemed unusual for someone who had graduated from such a prestigious high school. She also listed the Madison Inn as her employer from her junior year of high school until just a few weeks ago. Like Royce, she had participated in both show choir and theatre during high school. And she had been a member of Key's state championship ladies golf team.

After work, he drove back to the apartment and

changed clothes before walking with David to Calhoun for dinner. It was his good fortune that his friends' chatter was lively, because he could sit quietly and temper his excitement about Chloe. A lull in the conversation might have encouraged him to blurt out the details of their meeting, and he didn't want to invite any more teasing, especially since he didn't even know if she would accept the job. He wondered if she was speaking with her family at that very moment.

✧ ✧ ✧

HE ROLLED UP to the office around 11:30 on Friday morning and sat down with the plastic bowl of chicken soup he had brought from Calhoun. There was one message on the answering machine.

"Royce? Hi, it's Chloe. I know you aren't at the office yet, but I wanted to let you know I have decided to take the job. I'm not doing anything this afternoon, if you have the time to give me a little training on the computer. Anyway, call me when you get in."

She repeated her phone number for the callback. Royce nearly knocked over his soup in his haste to grab the phone.

She arrived less than an hour later, and parked behind his car again. She was dressed more casually, but was just as gorgeous in dark blue jeans, white Keds, and a black V-neck sweater with the sleeves pushed up her forearms. "Welcome back," he beamed as she came in.

"Thank you!" Her eyes sparkled when she smiled. He was hopelessly smitten. If she had only been living in Dublin for a couple of months, he thought it possible that she wasn't yet seeing anyone. Whether she had a boyfriend in Savannah, however, was a different and far more likely scenario.

He invited her to sit down in the rolling chair in front of the computer desk, grabbed his own, and wheeled it over to sit beside her. *The same perfume,* he thought, inhaling as subtly as he could. The taps program was not at all complicated, and he walked her through the process. He watched her long fingers click across the keys to make a few tap entries, and she quickly mastered the simple procedure. She typed fast, and would need far less time than he did to finish a city.

The sound of ice cubes falling into a highball glass in the kitchen signaled to Royce that Bobby Lee had declared the bar to be open. Mae always made his first few drinks stronger than the ones she mixed later in the afternoon, so Royce thought it was best to take Chloe upstairs to introduce her sooner rather than later. He led her up the steps and entered the kitchen first. She stood beside him at the circular counter as he spoke.

"Bobby, Mae, this is Chloe Webb. She'll be taking over my old job." Mae smiled warmly and waved a soapy hand from the sink as she continued to wash dishes. Bobby rose and shook Chloe's hand. Sitting back down behind his throne, he said, *"Cawwwww-see,"* and motioned to the bar stools, but the pair remained standing. He pulled his reading glasses down his nose and peered over them, carefully studying Chloe.

"You got some Oriental in you, don'tcha?" he queried.

"Bobby, that's not – ," Royce began to protest, but Chloe stopped him with a gentle touch to his forearm.

"My maternal grandmother was born and raised in Hawaii, but her parents were from Osaka. You're very perceptive." Her wry smile suggested she would've preferred to use a different adjective. "My other grandparents are all boring old Anglo-Saxons."

"Well," Bobby said, but failed to follow it with any other words. After a few seconds of thick silence, Royce explained they had more training to do, and led her back down to the office.

After the door was closed behind them, he spoke quietly. "I'm so sorry about that. Bobby is, uh, blunt. And rude. And also a drunk. Fortunately, however, he very rarely comes down here."

"It's okay, honestly," she reassured him. "I grew up with two older brothers, so I developed a thick skin against little things like words."

Royce saw no need for any more computer training, and he leaned backward against the awful mirrored desk. She sat down in her desk chair and crossed her long legs in his direction. "That desk is… something," she laughed. "Did the other office manager sit there?"

"Oh, hell, no," Royce chuckled, "Sal hated this desk

even more than I do. I switched chairs with it, after he left, but I wouldn't be caught dead sitting behind it."

She swiveled back toward her own workspace and frowned. "Would you mind if I brought some pictures or plants or something to put here? It's kinda drab and depressing. Oh, and a small radio. I work better with music."

"Of course. Whatever you'd like."

She shifted gears, delightfully. "So, Royce. You said you were in school until December. How much longer until you graduate?" He was flattered she had remembered that detail from their conversation the day before, and almost convinced himself she was flirting with him using her tone of voice and body language. She rarely broke eye contact, and used her hands a lot when she spoke. Her habit of brushing her hair back behind her ears was fast becoming his favorite gesture.

"I am officially done in December. I'd planned to move back to Atlanta after I finished my coursework, but it looks like I live here now." He told her about David and about Kingston Hall, but he was cut short by a phone call from the printer about his latest ticket order.

He sat down at his desk and reviewed the notes on his calendar with the printer. Chloe pointed to the closed door beside his desk and silently mouthed the word "Bathroom?" He smiled and nodded, and she grabbed her purse and went inside. He was wrapping up his call when she re-emerged, and he felt more than a twinge of guilt for checking out her ass as she returned to her seat.

"You're really good on the phone," she said after he hung up. "It's probably why I thought you'd be older. That, and the deep voice, of course."

He felt himself blush. "Thank you. I'm in a bit over my head, so I'm trying to give the illusion of competence."

"My mother would be impressed. She has always been a stickler for good phone etiquette, and has had to let people go from the inn because they couldn't properly deal with calls from potential guests."

He pulled her resume out of a file folder on his desk and scanned it again. He didn't want her to know he'd read it enough times to memorize it. "The Madison? It's your family business?"

She explained that her father had been a logistics executive for a shipping firm at the Port of Savannah, but was laid off when the company was sold eight years ago. He combined his severance payment with their family savings and bought the inn, which had been a dream of her parents for many years. "They've always been such host-y people. Every big family gathering, for holidays or whatever, was always at our house, for as long as I can remember. They cooked these huge meals and made sure everyone was taken care of."

She told him that her father had developed a serious case of rheumatoid arthritis while she was in high school, and she had been helping her mother run the inn ever since. There were only six guest rooms, but between maintaining the place and cooking breakfast every day, there was no way any one person could do it with the small cleaning staff they employed. "My mother finally found an assistant she could fully rely on, over the summer, so she encouraged me to follow my own path for a change."

But apparently, around the same time, Chloe's sister-in-law had given birth and contracted a potentially deadly infection from the C-section. Her brother needed help with the newborn, so she moved into their two-bedroom apartment in Dublin in the middle of August. "I stayed in Savannah until after August 13th, because I wanted to celebrate my 21st birthday with my friends, but I packed my bags the day after."

"Wow," he replied, with genuine awe. "So you put college on hold to help your parents, then moved to a different city to help your brother?"

She shrugged and smiled. "I go where I'm needed."

He opened his mouth to speak, his mind quickly weighing two potential comments, but a voice in his head with more wisdom overruled him: *You just leave it right the fuck alone, Royce.*

"What did you do for your birthday?" he asked, beginning a much safer line of conversation.

"Oh! So much fun! My friends and I went on a Savannah River booze cruise. It was a disco theme night, so we got all dressed up in 70s fashion and danced and drank entirely too much." She said the boat usually hosted "beach music" parties, but she was thrilled the disco night fell on her birthday. "I was born and raised on the coast, so there's only so many times I can listen to Jimmy fucking Buffett and that stupid 'Brandy' song."

He countered playfully, "Well, she *was* a fine girl, as I understand it."

She rolled her eyes, smiling at his joke. "After three or four drinks, everybody's cocktail waitress looks like a supermodel."

"And you won a championship with your high school golf team?" he inquired. "How'd you get into the sport?"

"Well, my dad and my brothers played almost every weekend. I knew if I wanted to spend time with them, I'd better learn to play, too. We made a fun foursome, eventually. They were good teachers."

"Have you played any of the courses here yet? There's a nice municipal course not far from here that only charges five dollars to walk nine after noon, even on weekends."

"No, I haven't, but I'd like to! I haven't played since Memorial Day weekend. Some of my old teammates and I entered a charity tournament at Crosswinds."

"Well, I'm not awful, so if you'd like to play, I'd be happy to go with you." He hoped he had not overstepped, so her reply was a relief.

"Yes, I'd like that!" she said, her honey-brown eyes bright with enthusiasm.

He contemplated asking her if she'd like to continue their conversation over dinner, but thought better of it. He glanced at his watch, prompting her to check hers, as well. "Shit," she said, "I totally lost track of time. It's my night to cook dinner, and I need to run by the Pig for some groceries." She stood and extended her right hand. "See you Monday?" she said cheerily.

"See you Monday, Chloe." He watched her walk out to her car, then gathered his things and left the office about half an hour early. His brain was buzzing, and he knew any attempts to gather himself and get any more work done would likely be futile. He and David crossed paths in the stairwell at Kingston, as David was leaving for work. Royce had not noticed that he was taking the steps two at a time, but David did. He smiled. "Good day?"

"*Great* day!" Royce replied. "When will you be back?"

"Around eleven," he answered. "I'll be expecting an explanation for this mood you're obviously in." He adjusted his backward ivy cap and nodded goodbye.

Royce changed clothes and walked alone to dinner at Calhoun, where he made plans with Carlos to play tennis together the next day. Upon returning to the apartment, he fished his weightlifting gloves out of his dresser, to make sure they were still there. He suddenly felt an urgent need to work out. He replaced the screen in the bong and packed it tightly, leaving it on the coffee table for David's return. On his walk back from dinner, he'd had an idea about his John Irving term paper, so he spent the next couple of hours combing through *The Cider House Rules*, *The Water-Method Man*, and *The World According to Garp*, highlighting passages and writing notes on a yellow legal pad.

When David got home, he grabbed a Coke from the fridge and ate a late dinner directly from the Burger King bag he'd brought in. They made small talk about weekend plans while David ate, then passed the bong back and forth until it was cashed. "So, this mood you're in?"

Royce had intended to be coy and evasive, but the THC had other ideas. "I may be in love with the girl I hired to help me in the office. She came in today for a little training and starts on Monday." He didn't realize until right then that he had inadvertently left the weight-lifting gloves on the arm of the sofa.

"So you're playing tennis with Carlito and going to the gym this weekend because you don't know how long you have to tone up some, before she sees you naked for the first time," David concluded. "Solid strategy."

"That is correct. Unless I find out she's dating someone in Savannah. In which case, I'm going to be depressed. I'll still look better naked, but I'll be the only one who notices."

"So you have designs on fucking your secretary. I'll be sure to nominate you for Executive of the Year for 1958," David teased, snickering at his own wit. The words did sting Royce a bit, though. He had already considered the cliché, but was trying not to think about it. He and Chloe were peers, after all. It wasn't like it was Sal sleeping with her. Or maybe he was engaging in the kind of "juicy rationalization" that Jeff Goldblum talked about in *The Big Chill*. He reached for the baggie to pack another bowl, in hopes a deeper bake would keep him from musing any further on power dynamics in office romances.

"I got that," David said, reaching for the bong and unscrewing the bowl. "I picked up a new release," motioning with his head to the Video Barn bag on the floor. David bopped into the kitchen with the metal bowl and a small nail to scrape out the ashes. He banged the bowl against the inside of the trash can three times, and adopted a high falsetto voice with a Latina accent. "Hello? Who ees eet?" Three more bangs and then, "Who ees there, please?" Royce giggled, reaching into the bag and sliding *Best of the Best* into the VCR.

CHAPTER 8

DON'T FUCK UP

Royce and Carlos met at the campus tennis courts at 2:00 on Saturday afternoon, and by 3:15, Carlos had easily dispatched him in two sets, 6-1 and 6-0. Royce was soaked in sweat, even though it was a relatively cool 78 degree overcast afternoon, while Carlos still looked fresh. Carlos was the number three player for the Lancaster Cardinals men's team, so in any match with him, Royce was satisfied to take one game. He usually accomplished this with an array of sliced backhands at unpredictable depths, defensive lobs, oddly-timed rushes to the net, and by avoiding Carlos's forehand when serving to him. And he ran down every single shot he could, even if he could only manage to get the ball back over the net and in bounds, with no hope of creating a winner from his efforts. *Just make him hit one more shot* was his mantra. *Maybe he'll make an error.*

After the second or third time they'd gone to the courts, two years prior, Royce asked him if he got anything out of playing with him. Carlos always played hard, and up to the best of his ability, but Royce was afraid he was wasting his friend's time. "Yeah, I do." Carlos assured him. "In matches with the team, my opponents usually just want to sit on the baseline and pound the ball back and forth. Try to overpower me. Bang big serves, hoping for aces. You're sneaky." He smiled a million-dollar smile, the kind you see on Wheaties boxes. "You make me think about what might happen next and react to it. And I can always use practice on backhand service returns."

They shook hands and parted ways. Royce had considered stopping by the library to do more research for his Shakespeare paper, but decided he was too sweaty and gross to be in civilized company. He opted instead for a shower and a nap before going back to campus for dinner.

On Sunday morning, he was relieved to find that he wasn't too sore to jog to the athletic center to work out. The weight room was empty, so he took a moment as he put on his gloves to assess his appearance in one of the full-length mirrors. He had played basketball in high school, run cross-country, and played plenty of tennis with friends; all activities that had given size and strength to his leg muscles. But he was never able to duplicate that same kind of gratifying shape above the waist. The best he could accomplish was "slender, but with some definition" in his chest, back, and arms. He was six-foot-two, however, and enjoyed compliments about his hair and his voice, so he resigned himself to be as confident as he could with his current physique, and to work on what he could change. He wondered, as he set the weight on the machine and grabbed the lat bar, whether Chloe judged herself as harshly or as gently, in turn.

✧   ✧   ✧

SHE ARRIVED FOR work on Monday at noon, carrying a small box. "Hi! How was your weekend?" she asked as she strolled in.

"Good. Yours?" He ached all over from the weekend's activities, but tried not to grimace too much.

"Oh, same old thing," she sighed. "Helping with my nephew, Jacob, and not getting enough sleep. I don't get out much."

"Whatcha got in the box? Need any help?"

She unpacked a small radio, offered a suggestive smile with her eyebrows raised, and handed it to him. He snaked the cord down behind the back of the computer desk and plugged it in, then extended the metal antenna. The dial was set to his favorite radio station in Macon, and he was pleased the signal was strong. The station's format was called "rock hits," and they played a nice mixture of songs from the past ten or fifteen years, along with new releases from "alternative" labels. Not a lot of deep cuts, but a wide enough assortment so they wouldn't necessarily be listening to the same songs every day. Billy Idol was singing about rocking someone's cradle of love.

She'd also brought an eight inch tall flowering cactus in a terra cotta vase, and a five-by-seven, white wood framed photo of her standing on a beach between two tall young men, arm in arm, with a lighthouse in the background. She wore a pale green beach wrap and her signature blue-mirrored sunglasses. Royce tried to ignore the fact that her black bikini was clearly visible beneath the wrap. The ocean breeze had tossed her hair into an agreeable mess.

"North Beach at Tybee?" he asked.

"Yes! You know it?"

"I do. Lighthouses are a hobby, and I've been to that one many times."

"This was taken by my sister-in-law, in June, while Michael was home on leave." She pointed to the taller of the two men. "He's a hospital corpsman in the Navy. And that's Mark," she said, pointing to the other man. "I live with him and Kimberly."

"It's a great shot. Y'all look really happy."

She clutched the photo to her chest and smiled before placing it delicately beside the cactus.

✿　✿　✿

HE WAS PROUD of himself for not being too distracted by having her in the office during their first week of working together. He had a lot to do, and was still making sense out of Sal's accounting ledgers. He was attempting to re-work them in a way he could better understand, but they were a lot more involved than he had expected. He didn't realize that Bobby offered start-up loans to so many of the sales reps when a new tour's campaigns began, with no set payback schedule. The reps had their own page in a separate ledger, detailing payments and re-payments, but he had no idea how accurate they were. He was also combing through the files whenever he could, looking through the records of previous campaigns, to educate himself about which cities had been trending up or down.

The mail carrier came to the door every day, carrying larger and larger bundles of forwarded checks and cash payments for campaigns that had already closed. Royce worked out the deposits and sent them to the show's sponsors, and kept tight records on the funds that were to be returned to the show for its cut of the proceeds. He had Chloe check his math.

He kept his conversations with her as light and as casual as possible, talking about their families, music, concerts they had seen, favorite movies, places they would like to visit on vacations, and so on. He noted with growing interest that she never mentioned a boy-friend, and by Friday he had become emboldened. He had caught her humming along with the radio a couple of times during the week to Concrete Blonde's "Joey," and when it was played again on Friday afternoon he rolled out a joke he'd been secretly practicing.

"I'd like that song better if they sang Chloe instead of Joey, wouldn't you?" he asked, and then sang the mod-ified opening: *Chloe, baby, don't get crazy.* The line took several seconds to complete, since it was such a plodding ballad, and she made a slow and dramatic half-turn in her desk chair while he serenaded her.

"You know, I've always wanted a man to sing to me," she said with a smirk. Then she scrunched up her nose and added, "But not like that." She paused a beat before laughing, and it was the longest two seconds he had experienced in years. He was relieved to laugh along with her.

"In other news," she continued, "I could play golf with you on Sunday week, if you aren't busy. My mother insists on Mark and Kim bringing Jacob down to visit her at least once a month, and they're planning to go next weekend."

He was giddy but took pains to hide it. "Sure, yeah!" He was surprised his voice didn't crack. "You're not going along with them?" he asked, on another fishing expedition for information about a possible man in Savannah.

"No, not this time. Honestly, I kinda like having the place to myself for a couple of days."

"Not this time." Well, that could be taken more than one way, he thought. Perhaps the following week would bring some definite answers. Or maybe on the golf course?

✿   ✿   ✿

HE LIFTED WEIGHTS on Saturday and Sunday, but spent a fair amount of time in the campus library, as well. He had just over a month before his two term papers were due and, while he was confident about the John Irving research he had completed, Dr. Dalton was a stern grader for seniors, and the Shakespeare paper had given him a case of writer's block. With his new pressures at the office, he knew he couldn't afford to wait to the last minute to get the writing done.

He and Chloe faced a parade of sales reps coming through the office on Monday and Tuesday, but they were prepared. All taps that were needed had been entered into the database, with their print-outs placed in the appropriate city boxes along with the tickets, so most of the reps made their visits quick. They all seemed impressed with Chloe, who handled herself confidently in those first introductions to the staff. Royce received knowing glances and nods of approval from most of the men, though fortunately their comments to her remained professional. He was thankful so many of the reps were teams of couples. The men wouldn't think of saying something inappropriate to a much younger woman while their wives were in the room.

On Tuesday afternoon, Royce asked Chloe about her plans for Halloween the next day. "Oh, our apartment complex is hosting a party for the kids tomorrow night. Everyone brings their candy and treats and passes them out. It's a lot easier than having the kids go door to door, up and down the stairs. I'm really looking forward to seeing all the costumes! What about you?"

"No plans, really. I'm picturing a dinner at the dining hall, followed by some friends coming back to the apartment for bong hits and horror movies. If I had to guess, I'd predict that *Halloween* kicks off the evening."

His prediction was correct.

By Friday, he was having trouble containing his excitement about the golf outing. "Are we still on for Sunday?" he asked hopefully.

"Yeah! I was thinking, do you want me to come by and pick you up? If the course is near here, I'll be driving right past the campus."

He thought it was an excellent idea, and wrote out his address and phone number on the back of a business card. He said a silent prayer that it wouldn't be raining.

✧   ✧   ✧

DAVID WAS BECOMING annoyed by Royce's pacing around the living room on Sunday, waiting for the call from Chloe to say that she was leaving her place. He had checked his bag about a dozen times, re-verifying over and over that he had enough golf balls and tees, and had cleaned his golf spikes and clubs two or three times. Finally, just after 1:00, the phone rang.

"I'm on my way," she said.

"Great. I'll walk downstairs and meet you on the street." He looked at David. "Well, it's showtime."

As he closed the door behind him, David called out helpfully, "Don't fuck up!"

The day was unseasonably warm and cloudy, and smelled distinctly of autumn in the South. He leaned against the back of his car to wait and, minutes later, she rounded the corner and parked in the open spot next to him. Her windows were down, and Queen's "Stone Cold Crazy" blared from the speakers. She pointed with her thumb to the rear of the car and popped the hatch. He squeezed his ratty black golf bag beside her light blue Callaway one, and dropped his spikes on top of her folded golf bag pull cart. She turned down the radio as he opened the passenger side door to climb in, carefully dodging the cassette case on the floor.

"So, where am I going?" she asked.

"Down the bypass. Pass the road to the office and turn left on the next cross street."

"Roger," she said with a nod, shifting into reverse and backing out onto the road. She wore a black Callaway cap, with her hair in a ponytail pulled through the opening above the back-strap. Her forest green polo shirt was untucked, and her black shorts were ridiculously short. She drove fast, aggressively working the clutch and the gearshift. He reached down and grabbed the cassette case, eager to get a look inside. Several Queen cassettes, along with Depeche Mode, The Cure, Tears for Fears, The Cars, and Duran Duran. The last cassette on the second row, however, surprised him.

"No shit! Lone Justice?" She smiled a bright toothy smile and nodded, raising her eyebrows.

"Well you know so many," he sang, mostly on key. She joined him for the rest of the chorus, entirely on key. *"Ways to be wicked. Oh, but you don't know one little thing about love."* She even delivered a spot-on imitation of

Maria McKee's unique and sexy pronunciation of "love." He was falling, fast and hard. It was time to dial the flirting up a notch, he decided. If she was seeing someone, or simply wasn't interested, he couldn't go another day without knowing for sure.

When they arrived and parked, they walked to the pro shop. He noted that not only were her shorts ridiculously short, they were skin tight, as well. He motioned to them and asked, "Is there even any room for a tee in your back pocket? That's going to be distracting for me."

She playfully nudged her elbow into his side. "This is the first time I've seen you in shorts, too, keep in mind. You've got some legs on you."

Royce slid a ten dollar bill to the clerk, a teenager named Bill, according to his name tag, and told him they wanted to walk nine. Bill said there were several foursomes in carts nearing the turn, and advised them to play the front, to avoid having to let a bunch of groups play through. Royce smiled and nodded. The front side was his favorite, and he knew he had a prayer of putting up a good score. He would settle for anything short of an embarrassment, however.

CHAPTER 9

RED TEES

They changed into their golf shoes and made their way to the par five first hole, their metal spikes making a pleasing crunching sound on the sidewalk. He pulled his three wood and took several swings to stretch out. She checked the scorecard, which she had slid into a leather holder from her bag. "Not going with a driver?" she asked.

"I should take that thing out of my bag," he replied. "Can't control it, so I don't use it." He teed up and took aim down the left side of the fairway. He made solid contact, sending the ball high and long toward the left rough, but it faded about ten yards during its descent and rolled to a stop in the fairway, on the top of the hill.

"Nice fade," she said.

"Purely involuntary. Stick around for the unintentional draw that comes with my irons off the tee, debuting soon on hole number three." He paused, realizing what he'd just done. "Apparently I also accidentally rhyme, sometimes."

She chuckled, grabbing the handle of her pull cart and beginning the twenty yard walk to the red tee box. She pulled her driver and used it in a few stretching exercises before teeing up a yellow Titleist. Her backswing was slow and deliberate, but her follow-through was lightning fast. The ball took off low and straight, climbing the hill and coming to rest not far from his.

They both made putts for par on the first hole, and remained level on the scorecard, trading pars and bogies back and forth as they approached the par three sixth hole. He aimed to the right side of the green and his ball drifted left toward the center, but came up a few yards short. Chloe hit a beautiful, towering seven-iron that left her ball less than ten feet from the pin. Her birdie putt stayed online until two feet from the hole, where it veered left and missed by three inches. She groaned in frustration. He decided another Concrete Blonde line was in order, and sang, *"Oh, Chloe if you're hurtin,' so am I."*

She pursed her lips and shook her finger at him. "I *will* throw this putter at you."

As karmic retribution for teasing her, he assumed, he lost his tee shot wide to the right on the next hole and carded a double bogey to give her a one shot lead. He bogeyed again on the eighth, against her par, and found himself down two shots on the tee at the last hole. They both found the fairway with their first shot, but she made a mess of her approach to the elevated green and bogeyed as he rolled in a short par putt. *At least I finished on a high note,* he thought, though the entire day felt like a victory.

On the way to the car, she tossed him her keys. "I know you want to drive it," she said with a smile. "Oh, and I'm keeping this," she added, folding the scorecard and putting it into a pocket in her golf bag.

Royce did want to drive her RX-7, and thoroughly enjoyed the trip back to Kingston. The steering was responsive, and the transmission was as tight as if it was brand new. He felt confident enough to roll the dice one more time. "When are Mark and Kimberly due back? Do you need to cook something for them tonight?"

"Oh, no," she laughed. "They'll have to pry Jacob from my mom's fingers! I don't expect them until late."

"Okay. Then would you let me take you to dinner?"

She studied him with a quizzical expression. "Yes," she answered softly, after a pause that tied his guts in a knot.

He breathed deeply in relief. "Excellent! Would you mind if I stopped at the apartment first, to change shirts? I feel like I'm carrying a pretty good chunk of that last sand trap around my collar."

"Sure! I'd like to see your place." He offered to take her by her apartment, too, if she wanted to change. The sun was beginning to set, and he worried that her itty bitty shorts were going to leave her legs too cold. "No, I'll be fine. I would like to ditch this hat and brush my hair out, though. Could I borrow yours? And maybe a jacket?"

"Of course," he replied, pulling the Mazda into the empty space beside his car. Unexpectedly, Nico's Electra was parked on the other side of David's Civic. Royce took his shoes and golf bag out of the hatch, led her to the front door and opened it for her. As they reached the top floor, they heard muffled laughter and playful bickering from inside the apartment. The door was unlocked, as usual, when someone was at home. The room fell silent as they walked in.

"Guys, this is Chloe," Royce announced proudly. "Chloe, meet David, Carlos, and Nico." The guys stood and offered their hands. Chloe said each name aloud as she greeted them.

"So, who won?" David asked. Royce motioned to Chloe with upturned palms. She gave a faux curtsy.

"But you hit from the ladies' tees, right?" teased Nico.

"Forward. The forward tees," Chloe teased, harder. "They don't have, like, little *tits* on them." David nearly choked on his Coke.

Royce pointed Chloe toward the bathroom, retrieved his hair brush from his bedroom, and handed it to her. He was thankful the sink was relatively clean. She peeled off her cap and removed her ponytail holder, frowned at the mirror, and set about making the best of it. Royce put on a clean shirt and a bit of deodorant, and walked back into the living room. "*Dude,*" David whispered, motioning toward the bathroom with his head. Nico offered a silent thumbs up, which Carlos doubled.

Royce beamed and whispered back, "We're going to dinner. I'll be back in a bit."

Chloe emerged from the bathroom, still fiddling with her bangs, and handed Royce his brush. He pulled his own band out, brushed his hair backward, and tidied his ponytail. He removed a grey fleece hoodie from the coat rack and offered it to her. She waved to his friends and said, "Nice meeting you guys!" and they made their way back down the stairs. Royce realized he still had her keys in his pocket and tried to give them to her. "Nope, still you. You already have my mirrors and seat set to Giant Driver," she joked, with another playful elbow to his ribs.

They agreed on Italian, and Royce drove them to his favorite place in town. She used his hoodie as a blanket to cover her bare legs, both in the car and at the restaurant. The dining room was almost empty, and they took a quiet table in the back. She asked him if he had taken golf lessons before.

"No," he answered. "I realized when I was about sixteen that I probably wasn't ever going to be great at any one thing, so I decided to try to become at least pretty good at *everything*. Golf, tennis, bowling, juggling. Any kind of physical activity." She was intrigued, and asked how he managed to do that. He almost didn't hear the words, suddenly struck by the way the candlelight flickered in her beautiful brown eyes.

"Well, I'm kind of a mimic. I can watch people who are really good at something, and make my body do almost the same thing. From a distance, it looks like I know what I'm doing," he said, laughing to himself. "If you get close enough, of course, you'll see I haven't put in nearly as much practice as the experts, so my results aren't the same. Golf balls drifting all over the place, forehands flying well past the baseline…" his voice trailed off as he noticed how broad her smile was, and how intently she watched him speak.

The conversation was interrupted momentarily by the arrival of their dinners, dropped off by a stout, efficient waitress. They both tore into the meal. It had been a long afternoon. He spoke again. "What are you thinking about studying, when you're able to start at Lancaster?"

She tapped her chin with her index finger as she finished the bite of pasta in her mouth. "I'm going to major in finance. I've always been fascinated with money. How to manage it, grow it. I'm keen on owning my own business one day, and I want to be as prepared as possible to make it successful. Maybe the inn? A franchise? I don't know. But *something*." The chin tap was officially Royce's second favorite of her mannerisms. He hoped to be able to add a dozen more to the list.

"That's ambitious!" he said, genuinely impressed. "I'm sure being so close to your mom and dad's business has given you a lot of insight."

She nodded. "A little too much insight. I teeter back and forth between being happy for them and terrified for them, depending on the vacancies."

They made short work of their entrees, and he left the waitress a healthy tip. "I should tidy up a bit, before Mark and Kim get back," she said, preempting his thoughts of inviting her back to the apartment. On the drive back to Kingston, she popped the Lone Justice cassette into the car's stereo, and they sang loudly along to "Sweet, Sweet Baby."

"Keep the hoodie for the drive home, if you want," Royce said as he opened the driver's side door and stepped out.

She shook her head, and handed him the jacket. "I'm good. It's not far, and I'll turn the heat up." He was a little disappointed; he liked the idea of Chloe's legs wrapped in his hoodie.

They stood awkwardly beside the driver's side door, until she took a quick step forward and wrapped her arms around his shoulders. He snaked his around her waist. The embrace lasted longer than a goodbye hug between friends. She breathed into his ear. "I had fun today. Thank you for inviting me."

"I had fun, too." He felt physical pain in his chest when she stepped back and climbed into the car. He watched her move the seat forward and adjust the mirrors, and grinned sheepishly at her. "Good night," he said, more than a little sadly.

"See you tomorrow!" she replied with a twinkle in her eyes, as if to remind him. He watched her drive away until she made a left turn and disappeared from his sight.

Nico, David, and Carlos were still on the sofa in nearly the same positions they'd been in when he'd left for dinner. "I didn't expect y'all to be here," Royce said to Nico and Carlos.

"David called and said we should come and check out this girl," Carlos said, enthusiastically.

David and Nico turned to him with their mouths open. "And I also said we wouldn't tell him that, right?" David scolded.

"Oh, right," Carlos replied, looking sheepish.

"So, you want to give me shit about trying to fuck my secretary until you meet her?" Royce reminded David.

"Well, to be fair," David defended himself, "You didn't tell me she was a sassy knockout."

Royce tried to stifle his grin. "She *is* a sassy knockout," he agreed proudly. He excused himself and walked to the bathroom to shower. Since the show was over, Nico and Carlos were gone by the time he finished.

✧ ✧ ✧

THE NEXT DAY marked one month until the end of fall semester, and Royce assumed that David was up early so he could get some extra time in the computer lab. As he was pulling on his backpack, however, David emerged from his bedroom with his CD player in his hands. He extended it toward Royce and said, "Okay, you've inspired me. I want you to take this and hide it from me until I ask Sun out. I'm going to keep being a pussy about it until I'm deprived of something important to me. So take it."

Royce accepted with a smile, carefully re-wrapping the cords so they wouldn't drag the ground. "Okay," he replied. "Good luck."

They were living in a transitional time. Nearly everyone they knew had seen the future and purchased a CD player for new music releases. But many of them had spent their teen years lovingly compiling a collection of cassettes, and a large percentage of the cars they drove had cassette players in them, so holding onto the old technology was important, as well. Few had the money for a wholesale replacement of the titles in their cassette collections with shiny new CDs. This is why the Columbia House music club offer of eight for a penny was so appealing. Royce and David were both longstanding members. They also both owned mismatched stereo systems, with a radio tuner, turntable, dual cassette player, and a much newer CD player made by a different manufacturer from the other components. Their cassette collections consisted of nearly as many carefully assembled mix tapes as studio releases. Royce had a CD alarm clock, which he bought specifically to employ as his wake-up music "Let the Day Begin" by The Call. He wasn't one to hit his Snooze button over and over, but having a song with lyrics that said, essentially, "Get up, man. You've got shit to do and you need to get on it," was all the inspiration he needed to crawl out of bed.

When Chloe got to the office, Royce greeted her with a playful, "How was your weekend?"

"Oh, it was so good!" she said, and whispered mischievously, "I had a *date*!"

"Is that so?" His spirit soared, hearing her use the word. "What did y'all do?"

"Well, we played golf, and then he took me out to dinner."

"Sounds like a good guy! Are you gonna see him again?"

"I don't know," she said mournfully, turning around to face the computer. "He hasn't asked me yet."

Their second date would be delayed, however. Chloe's high school friend Cassie was celebrating her 21st birthday in Savannah over the coming weekend, and Chloe planned to make the drive down right after work on Friday. Royce had Plan B already lined up.

"So, a week from Thursday, one of my favorite local acts is going to be playing at the Hound. The whole gang is going, and I'd love for you to join us, if you can."

"Well, for future reference," she answered with an inviting smile, "if your date plan involves live music, or a play, you can be pretty certain I'll drop everything to be there. Who's playing?"

"Vic Norton, a Lancaster alum. He used to play here six or seven times a year, but he's gotten a lot more popular now. He still tries to make it back a few times a year if he can manage, usually right before finals week."

"Cool! What kind of music does he play?"

Royce gave the question some thought, and considered tapping his chin. "Think *MTV Unplugged*, I guess. He strips down rock hits and reimagines them. He has his own original folky stuff, too, but he's better known for the creative covers. His version of 'She's a Beauty' by The Tubes is some genius level stuff."

She seemed truly excited about the show, and wondered aloud what she should wear.

David called Royce at the office on Wednesday, and asked him to bring home the CD player if he'd hidden it there. Sun had accepted his invitation for a date, and they had made plans for Saturday evening. The enthusiasm and relief in David's voice gave Royce a laugh, but he suppressed it until he hung up the phone.

On Friday, Royce prepared Chloe's weekly pay an hour early, so she could get on the road. She signed his receipt and he walked her to the door. "Drive safely, and have a great time." She looked over her shoulder to make sure they weren't being watched through the kitchen windows, and wrapped him in a warm hug.

"Thank you! I'll tell you all about it on Monday." She released him, but popped up onto her toes to kiss his cheek before waving goodbye.

Royce spent the better part of Saturday in the library and computer lab, over-analyzing his term papers, and didn't get back to the apartment in time to give David grief before he left for his date. "You're not going to wear that, are you?" was a popular piece of mental sabotage used by all five friends before a significant event. He stayed up late, in hopes of hearing David's report on the evening, but ended up going to bed just after midnight. David was still out.

David finally woke and came shuffling into the living room while Royce was having coffee and watching a news report about a church that had been hit by a tornado earlier in the morning while services were being held. David read the headline and said, "Oh, yeah, I believe in God." He could be coolly sarcastic when he didn't get enough sleep.

"You were out late last night, young man," Royce said suggestively, as David flopped into the easy chair. "How'd it go?"

David thought for a moment, combing his hair with his fingers. "It was good! It was good. Sun's a city girl, so she's about as miserable out here in the middle of nowhere as I am. I'd love to be able to date her in a big city. She and her roommate have a cool duplex, though, with a fire pit on the back patio. We sat out beside the fire after dinner and talked. Listened to music."

"Nice," Royce replied. "You wanna see if she can come to Vic's show on Thursday? Chloe's coming, so she wouldn't be the only outsider."

"A capital idea," he agreed. "I'll ask her."

✧ ✧ ✧

THURSDAY FINALLY ARRIVED, and with it another chance to see Chloe outside of the office. She teased that she'd borrowed something to wear from one of her Savannah friends the previous weekend, and she hoped he would like it. He told her Vic was scheduled to play at 9:00, but it would probably be closer to 9:30. "We're going over early, to get a couple of tables together. Nico's been having secret talks with a little red-haired girl he's had his eye on, so there may be as many as eight of us."

"Okay, good! I'll get there early, too, if I can. I've never been there, but I know where it is."

CHAPTER 10

THE HOUND

Two bars served as the primary competition for the patronage of Lancaster's students. They were within easy walking distance of campus, in the area the students colloquially referred to as "downtown" and, in fact, sat catty-corner from each other at the same intersection. The Embassy boasted modern décor and a large dance floor surrounded by neon lights. Their DJs played mostly Top 40 and dance hits. It was known as the unofficial gathering spot for the Greek community on campus.

Beckett's Hound, on the other hand, called to mind the style of an Irish pub. A little shabby and run-down, but warm and welcoming just the same. In the cramped entranceway, a hostess and a bouncer collected the cover charge on nights with live music, checked IDs, and applied wristbands to those of legal drinking age. Through a pair of maroon curtains, the Hound opened to a large room with well-stocked bars on either side and small tables and chairs between them. At the far end of the room, a wide arched doorway led to an even larger space with a dance floor and stage. The doorway was flanked on both sides by sturdy wooden stairs that led to the balcony.

Royce and David walked through the archway and

made an immediate left turn toward their favorite table. Both sides of the room had elevated seating areas running the full length from back to front, but the back table on the left side had several long nails sticking out of the nearby wood paneling where they could hang their coats. Royce reserved a nail for Chloe by hanging his umbrella on it. It hadn't rained on their walk to the Hound, but the sky was heavy with low gray clouds. They pulled the back two four-top tables together and arranged eight chairs around them. "Smithwick's?" Royce asked, and David offered a thumbs up. The DJ was in an R.E.M. kind of mood, apparently, as they had heard both "Driver 8" and "The One I Love" in the short time since they'd arrived.

As Royce waited at the bar for the drafts, two strong hands slapped down onto his shoulders. He spun around just in time to brace for Luke's hug. "Man! I feel like I've hardly had a chance to talk to you since your big promotion! How's it going so far?"

"Good, good! A lot to learn, but I'm getting there." Royce missed his lunchtime bullshitting sessions with the guys, but the half-hour he gained by taking out lunch from Calhoun had proven valuable. And Luke's schedule with the fire department prevented him from making it to dinner at least a couple of times a week.

"Dave said y'all both have dates comin' tonight. You're sure you trust 'em to be in the same room with Vic Norton and his *magical musical penis*?" Luke adopted a clichéd emcee voice for the last part of the question.

Royce smiled. "Well, it's a big room. And I'm sure it will be a target-rich environment."

Luke's older brother had played drums for Vic several years earlier, so Luke had heard more stories than any of his friends about Vic's legendary appetites. The phrase *Gets more ass than a cross-town bus* was frequently used. It would be a big surprise if Vic didn't leave the Hound after the show with two or three girls from the audience.

Royce was just about to ask Luke if he could get him a beer when Carlos and Nico walked in. He flagged them down and handed them the drafts he'd bought for himself and David. "Do me a solid and take these up to Dave. I'll get a pitcher and some more glasses."

His friends disappeared around the corner, and Royce stopped in the restroom. Chloe had never seen him with his hair down, so he checked again to make sure it looked right. He was wearing a gray Sonic Youth T-shirt, and had even put on his leather necklace with the steel ankh pendant that he was sure he hadn't worn in over a year. When he walked back into the bar area, Chloe was standing near the entrance, looking around.

He waved to get her attention, and her face lit up. She jogged over to him and delivered a leaping hug that forced him to spin them both around in a circle to keep his balance. He put her back down and she squealed, combing his hair back with her long fingers. "I fucking *love* it! Wow!"

"Thank you very much!" He blushed, and temporarily forgot where he was or what he was supposed to be doing. His scalp tingled. *The beer. Right.* They sat down on stools while the bartender pulled a pitcher of Smithwick's and put four glasses on a tray. He left a $2.00 tip in the hope he would get noticed just as quickly when the bar was crowded, and led Chloe through the arched doorway and up the steps to their tables.

He introduced her to Luke, the only one she hadn't met, and as they exchanged greetings, David distributed the glasses and poured a round for the four newest arrivals. Chloe pulled off her tweed knee-length coat to reveal a long-sleeved black fishnet shirt with a black tank top underneath it. These paired perfectly with her tight black jeans and the ankle boots she'd worn for her interview. Royce also noticed she was wearing a smoky gray eye shadow, which he had never seen on her before. She finished off her look with thick leather wrist-bands and large gold hoop earrings. He felt his knees weaken as he hung her coat on the nail with his umbrella.

He pulled his chair close to hers and whispered, "My turn to say *Wow*. You look incredible!"

"Thanks!" she replied, with a weapons-grade smile. "It's the top I borrowed from my friend," she whispered flirtatiously

"No," he countered. "It's all of it. All of you."

"You haven't seen *all of me* yet, silly," she teased. *Yet.* He pondered the word as he tried to maintain his cool.

He felt a bite of sadness for David and Nico, who were still waiting for the objects of their affections to arrive, both watching the archway diligently. The room was rapidly filling, as Vic's tech brought two guitars and a bass to the stage, propping them on their stands beside the microphones in front of a modest drum set. David's patience was rewarded. He stood and pressed his fingers to his mouth, whistling loudly to get Sun Choi's attention.

Royce had only seen her at a distance on campus, and rose to greet her. She was lovely, with fair and flawless skin and long, straight, jet black hair. She came across as shy, and a little overwhelmed at having to meet so many people at one time in such a social environment, but the trio of unfastened buttons at the top of her cream-colored sweater suggested she could also be self-confident and flirty. Royce took her coat from David and hung it on a nail, and she settled next to David and nuzzled her head against his shoulder. Royce excused himself, estimating he had time for one more pitcher run before the show started.

When he returned, everyone pushed their glasses to the center of the table and he topped off all of them. He was interrupted by a cacophony of squeals from the entranceway, where a dozen or so drunk girls rushed to the dance floor and staked their claim to the area in front of the stage. Nico's jaw dropped when he realized that the little red-haired girl, whose name was Susan, was among them.

It was no secret that Nico was a man of simple tastes, and he was drawn to Susan's conservative appearance and demeanor. The version of the little red-haired girl who arrived at the Hound was the polar opposite. Her hair was teased out, and her make-up could only charitably be described as garish. She and her friends were wobbly on their feet as they danced together to "Rio" by Duran Duran. Nico did his best to spin the situation. "She's pretty, made up," he offered.

David slapped the table. "She's *pretty made up!*" Everyone who had a glass to their mouth performed a synchronized spit-take, showering themselves and each other in Smithwick's foam and laughter. Nico stood so abruptly that his chair flipped over backward. He made wide circling motions with his index fingers, signifying everyone. "Y'all can kiss my *entire* ass!" he exclaimed, and stormed off.

Sun cast a concerned eye toward David, who reassured her. "He'll be back."

Chloe caught Royce staring at the empty stage. "What is it?"

"I was just thinking I'd like to spend a weekend with Vic's guitar," a shiny black Fender Newporter.

"You play?"

He nodded.

"Oh, this is one of those 'pretty good at everything' deals, right?"

"Well, I play a little. And it's my only instrument."

The house lights dimmed and the stage lights brightened. The bar area emptied as the patrons who had been waiting there streamed through the doorway. The DJ queued his mic and announced, "Please put your hands together for Dublin's own Vic Norton!"

Royce turned his chair ninety degrees to the right, facing the stage. Chloe did the same, but pushed hers backward so she was sitting beside him along the back wall. He put his right hand on her thigh and squeezed, as she interlaced her fingers with his.

He recognized Vic's second guitarist and drummer from previous shows, but the bassist was new. Vic pulled the strap of his Fender over his shoulder and said, simply, "Thank y'all for coming," and began the opening chords of "A Girl Like You," by The Smithereens. He was tall and wiry, with a mess of wavy light brown hair down to his shoulders, a colorful sleeve tattoo on his right arm, and a thin goatee.

Luke threw his head back in laughter, loud enough to get everyone's attention at the table. He mouthed to Royce, "Watch his eyes." The lyrics of the song were pleading and repetitive — *"I'll do anything I have to do, just to win the love of a girl like you"* — and Vic sang them directly to more than a dozen girls close to the stage. The seed was planted. His second song was an opportunity for the audience members to show that this wasn't their first Vic Norton performance. The end of the chorus of "Let's Go" by The Cars invited rhythmic hand claps and a collective shout of *"Let's go!"*

Nico had not yet returned to the table as Vic wrapped up his eight song first set with Fleetwood Mac's "You

Make Loving Fun," which left everyone perplexed. Carlos noted that Susan had also left her group of friends as some point. Royce took the empty pitcher from the table, along with the ten dollar bill David clandestinely slid to him, and went back out to the crowded bar area for a refill. Nico and Susan were sitting opposite one another in a booth at the back of the room, but Royce pretended not to see them.

"They're out there talking," Royce reported when he returned. Chloe grabbed Royce's hand and yelped when the DJ played Depeche Mode's "Enjoy the Silence."

"Dance with me, I love this song."

"But I don't really —" he began.

"Dance with me, I love this song," she commanded.

There were two dozen or more people on the dance floor with them, but Royce noticed only her. Her solo moves were fluid and sexy, but she returned repeatedly during the song to press herself against him so they could move as one. He had never encountered a woman with such a playful confidence in herself and her sexuality, but in contrast to previous infatuations with strong personalities, he was not at all intimidated by her. Their close-quarters maneuvers provided for a few light grazes of their lips against one another, and promise piled upon promise. She pulled him close when the song ended. "Meet you at the table. I need to find the restroom."

Royce floated back to the table on waves of beer and lust to find far more people there than when they had left it. Vic had come to say hello to Luke, and a wake of admirers had followed him. An older woman Royce didn't recognize was in Chloe's seat, so he stood against the back wall and listened to the conversation. Vic's tech brought a cello and its stand to the stage.

"You have a cellist?" Sun asked, excitedly.

"Only for the next song," Vic replied. "It's a new addition to the set list, but a good one. Do you play?"

Sun shook her head. "Violin. But I know a lot of cellists." She was blushing. David shifted in his seat.

Chloe returned and Royce introduced her to Vic. "You have a lovely voice!" she said.

"And you have lovely eyes," he replied. Royce rolled his.

Royce motioned for Chloe to take his seat, but she shook her head. "I already have a seat." He took her hint, sat down, and she curled up in his lap.

"Well, I should go. It's almost that time," Vic said, and the entourage followed him down the steps.

Nico returned to the table, poured himself a glass from the pitcher, and flopped down into his chair. "BBH'd again," he sighed.

The guys nodded in sympathy, but Chloe and Sun looked at each other with upturned palms and shook their heads.

"Boyfriend Back Home," David explained. "A suitcase college girl's way of letting a campus love interest down easy."

The house lights dimmed again as Vic and his band

took the stage. "Please welcome Maria Flores," Vic announced. He waited until the applause subsided before beginning a wonderfully soulful acoustic version of "Nothing Compares 2 U," expertly accompanied by Maria's cello. Predictably, the first few rows of girls in front of the stage erupted in cheers with the line *"I can put my arms around every girl I see."* Susan had returned to her friends, and she was in full voice.

Carlos stood to applaud at the song's conclusion, keeping a steady eye on Maria Flores and watching her until she sat down at a table on the left side of the stage. He quickly drained the last of his beer, ran his fingers through his hair, and set off to chat with the cellist. "Go get 'er, Carlito," Luke urged.

Vic played a couple of Royce's favorites in his final set, including Men at Work's "Overkill" and "Running on Empty" by Jackson Browne, along with two of his original songs, before concluding with "She's a Beauty." He thanked the crowd again and basked in a lengthy ovation.

Chloe leaned close, her cheek against Royce's. "I'd love to stay longer, but my little nephew gets up *awfully* early."

"Understood. I'll walk you to your car." Chloe said her goodbyes to David, Luke, and Nico, and pulled one of Royce's business cards out of her purse to write her phone number on the back of it for Sun. Sun reciprocated on a cocktail napkin. David and Royce smiled at one another, as this could only be a good sign.

"Can I get one of those, too?" Luke asked. "Just the

card, not your number." Chloe handed it over. Luke, for whatever reason, enjoyed collecting the business cards of his friends who went onto start their careers after leaving Lancaster.

Royce was relieved he'd brought his umbrella, as a cold steady rain was falling when they reached the Hound's front door. "Where are you parked?" he asked. She pointed north.

"Over there, in front of that old drug store."

They walked arm in arm, huddled beneath the umbrella and trying to avoid puddles and missteps on downtown's crumbling sidewalks.

"How many of my business cards are you carrying around with you?" he joked.

"Just a few. I took some out of your desk when you went to the bathroom the other day. I like having them."

They reached her car, and she turned to face him, standing close. "Thank you, again, for thinking of me. I had a great time."

"I think about you quite a lot," he said suggestively. Keeping a firm grip on the umbrella with his right hand, he leaned forward and cradled her face with his left. The touch of their lips was electric.

He had been told by more than a few women that he was a good kisser, and he attributed this to two factors. Many years before, he had read in one of his mother's magazines that a woman should demonstrate to a man how she wanted to be kissed. With his gift for mimicry, he could identify his partner's preferred style within just a few seconds, adapt, and imitate. Chloe liked her kisses slow and soft, with playful teases from the tip of her tongue, but otherwise gentle and patient.

The pace of the rain intensified and they both found themselves shivering. "Can you get away Saturday night?" he asked.

"Probably. But I'll let you know tomorrow."

"Drive safely. See you tomorrow."

She smiled and took a deep breath, her hand to her chest. He watched her drive away before turning back toward the bar. He got as far as the front door before deciding to walk home instead. He wanted to be alone with his thoughts.

He had hoped to get a report on anything he'd missed after leaving the Hound, but Carlos and Nico were no-shows for lunch in the dining hall the next day, so he and David counted on Luke to share any news. Nico, apparently, had resigned himself to the BBH situation, but it didn't help that he'd seen the little red-haired girl on campus for her Friday morning classes, looking rode hard and put up wet. Carlos, on the other hand, had managed to charm Maria, the cellist, until the house lights came up around 3:00 a.m. Carlos had mysteriously announced that he would be gone for the weekend.

Royce and Chloe took every opportunity to steal subtle touches and a few quick kisses at work on Friday, and she confirmed that she'd be available on Saturday after dinner.

CHAPTER 11

TATANKA

Royce and David packed a fat bowl in the bong after dinner. "I've invited Sun over tomorrow night, and I was thinking about making a subliminal tape."

"A subliminal tape?" Royce asked, giggling.

"Yeah. Like, recording my name into songs, hoping she'll be affected but won't know why. For 'Sharp-Dressed Man,' they could say *'Cause every girl crazy 'bout…DAVE!'*"

Royce fell over sideways, laughing. Gathering himself, he understood what was being asked of him. "I can make myself scarce tomorrow, no problem. That new Costner movie is, what, three hours long, right?"

"A sweeping Western epic, they say," David replied.

"Gotcha. You have a paper?"

"No, but I'll get one at Calhoun tomorrow at lunch. Thanks."

Royce called Chloe and asked, "Are you up for *Dances with Wolves* at 8:30?"

"Yes! Should I meet you there?"

"Nope. Your place is on the way for me. I'll come get you about 8:00."

"I like it!"

Royce took great pleasure in watching the unflappable

David running up and down the stairs to the laundry room, washing his sheets and towels, cleaning the bathroom, and tidying up the apartment.

"You gonna be okay?" he asked him.

"Got it all under control." His body language suggested otherwise.

After David left to take Sun to dinner, Royce rolled a small joint and tucked it into his pea coat, and shoved a Zippo into the front pocket of his jeans. He was eager to meet Chloe's family, but a bit nervous, as well.

Mark was a commercial interior designer, and traveled frequently to supervise projects he had a hand in creating. Chloe invited Royce in, where Mark's influence was obvious. The space was perfectly organized, tidy, and well-appointed, with no signs of the chaos that a newborn would normally bring. Both Mark and Kimberly greeted Royce warmly, though Mark ribbed him gently about losing to his little sister at golf. Jacob was asleep in his crib in the living room, but Royce made it a point to rub his back and whisper, "Hello, young man. It's a pleasure to meet you."

Chloe hustled down the stairs and climbed into the Squareback's passenger seat. "So, what's David up to tonight?"

Royce pulled the Zippo from his pocket and lit the little joint on his way out of the apartment complex. He took a drag and handed it to Chloe. She cracked her window and pulled a long drag of her own.

"It's gonna be their first time, I think," he replied. "Or at least David thinks so."

"So soon?"

"Pretty sure it's pronounced like *sun*."

She slapped his shoulder, hard. "Okay, fucker, don't do that. They've only gone out a couple of times, like we have, and I'm not quite ready for that yet. You understand?"

"Yes, I do. I'm sorry." Royce took another long drag. "But they've known each other for over a year, taking classes together and working on group projects and stuff. I think she's probably been into him for months, waiting for him to ask her out. It's different than meeting someone for the first time a month ago, like some people I can think of."

She smiled, reluctantly. "It is, you're right. I just don't want you to get bored or give up on me."

"Not gonna happen," he said, pulling the VW into a parking space outside the theater.

David was right. The movie was a sweeping Western epic, deadly serious and packed full of important messages and themes. But around the one hour mark, Chloe spiraled into a giggling fit she couldn't escape. John Dunbar, the main character played by Kevin Costner, was attempting to communicate with an assemblage of Sioux regarding buffalo. He put his hands to his head, with index fingers pointing upward to mimic horns when he learned the Sioux word was *tatanka*. She imitated the character's motions and whispered, "*Tatanka*! Buffalo!" before doubling over in suppressed laughter.

Royce rested his hand on the small of her back and whispered, "You know this is going to become a thing, right? Whenever there's a misunderstanding, we'll just say *Tatanka*! Buffalo!" She covered her face with her hands and fought to regain her composure.

When the movie ended, he took her hand and led her to the parking lot. "We should talk," he said. "Waffle House?"

She smiled. "Okay, yeah, let's do that."

They ordered coffee and a slice of pie, apple for him and chocolate cream for her. They sat in a booth in the far corner, as private as a public place could be. He looked over both shoulders before asking, quietly, "So, tell me what you like. What you don't like. These are things I need to know." He pulled her feet into his lap and slid his hands into the cuffs of her jeans, massaging her calves. She closed her eyes.

"Well, I like *that*," she smiled, tapping her toes together. "Let me think for a minute." She brushed her hair behind her ears. "I've only been with three guys before. I dated someone in high school for almost two years. The other two were… mistakes."

"I know about mistakes. I've had them, too."

"Oh? What's your number, then?"

He answered honestly. "More than three, but less than… ten?"

Her eyes widened. "I can't say I'm surprised."

"I guess the chorus and theatre girls at my high school were more generous with their affections than at the Key Academy," he offered with a shrug.

"Maybe. Todd and I were together for pretty much all of our junior and senior years, and I was faithful to him." Her expression suggested there was a lot more to the story, but he didn't press. He waited until the waitress had refilled their coffee cups before continuing.

"Okay, then, I'll start. Things I like," he said, "Atmosphere, mood-setting. Comfortable clichés, I guess. Candles, music."

"Yes! Good! I like those, too!" She tapped her chin with her fingers and giggled. "I like to be on top."

He laughed and nodded enthusiastically. "I do not object!"

"Okay," she continued, in a far more serious tone. "I don't care for oral sex. On me, I mean. I know it's not a popular stance."

"That's interesting." He was thankful she had told him, but disappointed to hear it. "What is it you don't like?"

"I can't relax." She fidgeted in her seat. "I mean, I know I'm supposed to enjoy it, but I have this weird mental block and I can't get outside of my own head. It ends up being awkward for both of us, so I'd just rather skip it."

He tried to offer non-verbal reassurance by wrapping his long fingers around her ankles and holding them tightly. "I feel the same way about sex talk. Like, during the act. I've been told, 'Talk to me!' but I can't ever find the right words. Everything comes out sounding like either bad porn or some bizarre clinical description of what particular body parts are doing. I cringe, and take myself completely out of the moment."

"Well, thank you," she said, smiling brightly, "I'll remember not to ask you to talk to me until afterward."

It was getting late, and he knew they both were tired. He excused himself and called David from the pay phone on the wall between the bathrooms. David said the coast was clear — he was minutes from leaving the apartment to take Sun back to her duplex. He drove Chloe home and kissed her goodnight at the door to her apartment. When he got home, David was all smiles and walking on air. His evening had gone better than he had hoped, though, as expected, he was tight-lipped about the details. He hadn't even needed the crazy subliminal tape.

✧   ✧   ✧

THE CIRCUS CLOSED its fall tour the following day, in Milledgeville, GA. On Monday, Joey Vegas was at the office when Royce arrived at 11:30, to drop off the final cash envelope on his way back to Florida for the holidays. Joey and Bobby sat at the kitchen throne, griping and bitching about the fact that a relatively populous stop like Milledgeville didn't have a local sponsor, and both of them blamed Sal. Royce sat quietly and listened. He knew there was a delicate balance, in terms of sponsorships.

Daughtry Village, a statewide charity that owned several properties near Georgia's best pediatric care facilities and offered free or deeply discounted housing options for the parents of children who were undergoing critical treatment, was the company's fall-back option when they were unable to secure a local charity to sponsor the circus. The raw sales numbers confirmed people were more likely to donate to a local sponsor — a Lion's Club, Chamber of Commerce, Fraternal Order of Police, YMCA — but these options were not always available.

On the other hand, Royce had overheard conversations between Sal and Daughtry Village representatives that clearly suggested they wanted to have more dates dedicated to their efforts, rather than simply being used as a last resort. It was a thin line for Sal to walk, as alienating Daughtry could result in them pulling their sponsorship altogether and putting tour dates in jeopardy. But too many Daughtry dates risked a sales rep rebellion. And now Royce had to walk the same line, without Sal's years of experience. Chloe's arrival at the office broke the tension.

Royce opened the door from the kitchen to the office and asked her to come upstairs. "Chloe Webb," he said, formally, "Meet our ringmaster, Joey Vegas."

Joey stood and puffed out his chest. "Young Chloe!" he said, in his booming stage voice, "I've heard so much about you!"

If he had, it had come from Bobby.

She blushed and extended her hand. "It's so good to

meet you, Mr. Vegas! I'm so sorry I haven't had a chance to see the show yet, but I hear great things."

Flattery was the way to Joey's heart, and she had scored a direct hit. She continued, "Is Lord Connelly with you? I'd love to meet him." Her eyes sparkled.

"I'm sorry, Miss," he said, shaking his head. "I've sent him back to Florida ahead of me, with Lady Gloria. I hope Ashanti hasn't eaten him by the time I arrive. Sometimes I stop here by Bobby's for a few hours and it's three days later before I find myself leaving."

"Well," she said, "Another time, then. I'm looking forward to it." She and Royce excused themselves and walked down to the office.

✧ ✧ ✧

Royce closed the office at 3:00 on Wednesday, giving him and Chloe a head start on their trips home for Thanksgiving. He was not at all happy about not seeing her for the next four days, but family was important to both of them, and he looked forward to seeing Jennifer and his parents. He knew she would have stories to share with him when she returned, too. David, Nico, and Carlos would all be leaving town for the holiday weekend, so there was no reason for him to cut his trip home short.

He split the weekend as best as he could, between his mother and father, and he was grateful to have Jennifer with him for both extended family gatherings. He talked with Kate and Royce Sr. about the new job and about his studies, but only told Jennifer about Chloe. "I know your next few weeks will be nuts, but I hope I can meet her soon. It's been a long time since I've met one of your girlfriends," she said, nudging him with her elbow.

He met with Eric and bought a full ounce of his best stuff, feeling like a grown-assed man with a real job.

✧   ✧   ✧

CHLOE CALLED HIM when she got back to Dublin on Sunday evening. "So, I have some bad news and some fucking awesome news."

"Okay," he replied, settling himself in the easy chair. "What's the bad news?"

"Well, next weekend looks like it's going to be… biologically undesirable, for what we both have been waiting for."

"I have a comment on that, but I'll hold it for the awesome news."

"Good! The awesome news is that Mark and Kim are taking Jacob back down to Savannah for the weekend on Friday the seventh, so I'll have the place to myself. My dad's sister and her family will be in town, and they've requested an audience with the baby. You'll be finished with school, so I'd like to invite you to come see me, for a celebration dinner. I borrowed some of my grandmother's recipes, and I thought we could try them out together."

"I accept!" he said with a chuckle. "We can talk about the particulars later."

"Yes," she giggled, "So what's up for this weekend?"

He told her about an accidental tradition that had been established at Kingston on the weekend before finals. He and David had the guys over for a sort of *If you don't know it by now, you won't* party, to blow off steam before taking exams and turning in term papers. The details didn't vary much from what a regular weekend gathering would look like, but it was the timing that mattered. This one would be different, however, because in addition to the five regulars, Sun and Chloe would be joining.

✿ ✿ ✿

ROYCE BREEZED THROUGH his final week of classes, wrapping up discussions on *Othello* and Flannery O'Connor's *Everything That Rises Must Converge*, and feeling confident that his term papers needed only minor revisions before they were submitted. At the office, however, Bobby was becoming more agitated and nervous about his first sales meeting in years without Sal, which was set for Saturday, December 15th. He called Royce upstairs to the kitchen repeatedly, asking for updates on the late deposits for the recently completed campaigns, and scribbling notes on his printed copy of the last sales rep handbook for Royce to revise.

For the most part, Royce agreed that Bobby's additions were necessary and important. They could no longer rely on Sal's encyclopedic knowledge of campaigns past, and so it was essential to have a record of sponsor names and contact numbers, phone room leads, and performance locations. Bobby had repeatedly asked for Sal to add these resources to the handbook, but Sal didn't type and seemed unwilling to burden his wife with the transcription of so many years' worth of information. But Royce had the computer savvy and access to technology that Sal had lacked, so he understood that it would fall on him to make things easier for everyone, moving forward.

The research was tedious and time-consuming, however, and required pulling files and looking at every one of the post-campaign review sheets that the reps filled out. He wrote the details long-hand on a yellow legal pad, and took the disk to the computer lab whenever he had free time. He organized the pages in the most logical fashion he could think of, and conferred with Strickland on how long he'd need to prepare enough printed copies in advance of the sales meeting.

He had long since made arrangements for a lunch meeting at The Fifth Quarter, the country-slash-sports bar a few miles north of town, but Bobby insisted upon verifying the details daily. "You've got lunch arranged?" he asked, and, "Make sure everyone gets three drink tokens." Royce nodded and re-verified, even though a three drink allowance sounded to him more like the standards of a comedy club than a business meeting. Then again, this would be his first official Yawnoc Productions event.

Chloe reached out her hand to squeeze Royce's every time he made a slump-shouldered return to the office from the kitchen. And when she thought she wouldn't be seen, she walked over to his desk and kissed his cheek. "You're doing fine," she said, rubbing his thigh underneath his desk. "You tell me if you need me to help." He gratefully accepted, asking her to check his addition with every new deposit. *Just get those term papers turned in*, he thought, *and you'll only have one big thing to focus on.*

✧   ✧   ✧

As AGREED, ROYCE and David woke up early on Saturday and set about cleaning the apartment. They always tidied before the guys came over, but Sun and Chloe would require much more effort. David retired to the bathroom mid-morning, and Royce assumed he was cleaning it. Instead, David emerged with a copy of *Fangoria* tucked under his arm and announced, "I'm not at all proud of what went on in there."

Royce shook his head, pausing his efforts to dust the coffee table. He handed David a scented candle and a lighter. "Dude," he scolded, "People will be here soon. You wanna take care of that?"

"Cool your jets. I'm on it."

Royce showered and made a run for more drinks and snacks, returning in time to assess their work and determine they'd done the best they could. He heard the familiar clatter of a Volkswagen four-stroke engine and rushed to the window, with the fear that someone was stealing his car. Instead, a fully-restored yellow '72 Super Beetle parked on the street, with Sun behind the wheel. He cast a critical eye toward David. "Why didn't you tell me she had a Bug?"

"You know I'm not a car guy," he replied with a shrug. "Sorry."

Royce hustled down Kingston's staircase and up the steps to the street as Sun was unloading a couple of grocery bags with an eye on the Squareback. "Oh, I've got it," she said. "I don't need any help."

He paused to catch his breath. "No, I know, I just came down to get a look at your car. It's gorgeous! May I?" She nodded, and he popped the hood and trunk and opened both. The bucket seats in front and the bench seat in back looked brand new — not even a crack in the black leather. Maple gear shift knob, leather-wrapped steering wheel, fresh carpet on the front luggage area, and chrome hubcaps so shiny that he bet Sun could do her makeup in their reflection. "Wow," he said, "This is impressive."

"Thank you so much! My dad's a huge Volkswagen enthusiast. He's got two buses, a half-dozen Beetles, and a couple of Things." She pointed toward the Squareback. "But he doesn't have one of those."

"You wanna take a look? I bought it from a fellow collector near my mom's place." Sun smiled and nodded.

"Your car wasn't here when I came by the other night. And David didn't tell me you had one."

"He's not a car guy, I guess," said Royce with a hint of sarcasm. He unlocked the hood and hatch. "It's nowhere near as carefully kept as yours, but it runs well.

I keep those thick floor mats in the back because the metal is rusted through." He laughed. "It would freak passengers out to look down and see the road flying by underneath their feet."

Chloe drove up and stopped in the street behind them. Rolling down her window, she called out, "Excuse me, is this the right address for the car show?"

"It is!" he exclaimed. "Free parking, anywhere you'd like."

Chloe greeted Royce with an enthusiastic hug and kiss, and hugged Sun, as well. "I'm glad you're here," she said.

"I'm glad you're here, too."

Royce had not considered until that moment how uncomfortable they both might be in this environment. He made a mental note to keep an eye on non-verbal cues. Luke pulled up and parked his truck alongside the row of cars.

"It was my understanding," he said, "that this was going to be an indoors thing. It's gonna get fuckin' cold out here when the sun goes down."

"And poor David's upstairs all alone," Sun sighed.

Royce reached for Sun's elbow. "Listen, next time you talk to your father, please let him know the Squareback is available. I've been thinking about buying something new."

Chloe raised her eyebrows. "Oh? This is the first I'm hearing about it."

Royce winked at her. "Yeah. My father's been talking

to some dealers he knows. It's a weird situation, since I don't have much of a credit history, and I can't produce any pay stubs or an employment contract. I'm counting on his connections."

CHAPTER 12

PROBABLY PORN

Royce took Chloe by the hand and they all went upstairs. Chloe followed him to his bedroom, where he kicked the door closed, pulling her against his chest. "Do you know how much I want you right now?" he asked.

She melted against him. "I do. About half as much as I want you." He kissed her deep and hard, but restrained himself emotionally as best as he could. *Just one more week.*

He pulled the ceramic bong and his weed supplies out of his top drawer. "Ooo, how pretty!" she said. "How does it work?" He gave her a quick demonstration, loaded a fresh screen, and packed the bowl full.

He had intended to add fresh water to the bong from the bathroom sink, but David and Sun had their own project going on in there. "Jesus, David," Sun scolded, "This is a mess!" She held a makeup mirror and a small pair of scissors, trimming David's unruly Van Dyke. Chloe stopped to watch, rubbing Royce's five o'clock shadow.

"I've been trying to talk him into growing some facial hair," she said to Sun.

Royce shook his head. "Believe me. It would never look like that."

David nodded in agreement. "I like being able to grow any formation of facial hair I want to, but I'm not crazy about having to shave from the bottom of my eyeballs down. I can look like Teen Wolf in about two weeks."

As usual, Nico and Carlos were the last to arrive. This brought the final count of the party to seven, an unwieldy prime number for even-numbered competitions like Nintendo or Spades. Fortunately, Chloe had brought Scrabble and Trivial Pursuit, a couple of games that were more fluid in the number of game-play participants.

Royce motioned for Chloe to take a seat in the recliner and sat on the floor in front of her. Sun and David took seats on the sofa with Luke. Carlos and Nico pulled the floor pillows to the coffee table and made themselves comfortable. Royce said a silent *Thank you* to Kate for adding the floor pillows to his Memorial Day shopping cart. Luke fished a Yawnoc business card out of his pocket and held it up dramatically.

"So, Royce," he said in a booming voice. "What else does this production company produce, besides the circus?"

Well, shit, Royce thought. Luke could have brought this up over lunch or dinner with the guys, at any time after Vic's show at the Hound, but he held onto it until the potential embarrassment level would be at its maximum.

Chloe leaned forward with her hands on Royce's shoulders. "Ooo, I'd like to hear this," she said. "I've been wondering the same thing."

David finished packing the bowl and handed the bong

to Royce, with a look that suggested he take another hit while formulating his answer. "Well, I only work with the circus, so I can only tell you what I've overheard. They own a large interest in a dirt racetrack in south Georgia, somewhere." He took a deep breath before continuing. "And there is apparently a successful video production outfit in north Florida, around Lake City."

"Video production?" Luke asked with raised eyebrows, sensing blood in the water. The smoke Chloe exhaled tickled Royce's right ear.

"Probably porn," Nico offered, without looking up from his Nintendo controller.

"*Obviamente porno,*" Carlos added with a nod.

Sun passed the bong to David, who blew a long trail of gray smoke into the air and paused thoughtfully. "I'm thinking it could be porn," he said.

Luke dealt the final blow. "Have you given any thought that it might be porn?"

Sun and Chloe offered the only sympathetic eyes Royce could find, but he gave his friends what they wanted. "Yes, fuck," he said. "I've thought it might be porn."

His four antagonists bellowed and high-fived one another. Sun kicked off her shoes and pulled her feet onto the sofa, sitting cross-legged, and spoke in a serious voice. "Okay, can I ask a question?" David rested his hand on her thigh. "You guys seem to enjoy giving each other grief, but is there a line you don't cross? I mean, David says you've been friends for a long time, but he also tells me stories about jokes you play on each other.

And I've seen it with my own eyes a couple of times. You haven't damaged any friendships along the line?"

The room grew quiet, as the guys looked at each other and wondered who would be the first to speak. Royce bit the bullet. "Well," he said, "Things have mellowed since the Trevor incident." He cast his eyes around at his friends as he reloaded the bowl, silently urging someone else to start the story. Chloe slipped off her flats, as well, draping her right leg over Royce's shoulder and stroking his thigh with the tips of her toes. She wore black textured stockings beneath her jeans. Royce smiled, recalling how distracted he had been on the first couple of days she had worn her navy blue sandals to work. She had taken note of it.

"Trevor," David began. "This was about a year ago. Trevor made Luke look small. He was six-foot-six easily, and probably 250 pounds. Offensive and defensive lineman for his high school football team. All he could talk about was Nikki, his sweetheart back home."

Luke and Nico nodded in unison, vividly remembering the event. Carlos held up his palms in innocence. He was out of town on a tennis tour during the unpleasantness. "Nikki was driving down to Lancaster over a long weekend, and so we decided to prank them," David continued. Sun covered her mouth with her hand, in anticipation of what was to come, and didn't remove it.

Royce took a heavy drag from the bong and handed it to Chloe, reluctantly taking his turn as narrator. "Nikki was tiny. Like five-foot-nothing tiny. We privately joked about how oddly mixed they were, in photos. So, David — sorry, dude, but it was your idea — thought it would be funny to make it look like Trevor was dangerously violent. And that we were all afraid of him."

Chloe nearly choked on her exhale. "Shit, guys. That is messed up."

Sun shook her head.

Luke continued, finally owning up to his participation. "The four of us were at Calhoun having dinner when Trevor and Nikki got there and sat at our table. Everything was just like normal, laughing and joking around. We tried to make Nikki feel welcome. We made sure David and Royce were seated closest to Trevor, since they're the best actors. They waited until Trevor made any kind of sudden move, like reaching for a salt shaker, and they'd both flinch, shielding their faces."

Royce giggled, in spite of himself. It was still funny, in a sick way, and the weed didn't allow him to display the appropriate amount of remorse. Chloe pinched his ears. Sun whispered through her fingers, "Oh, my god."

"After about the third time this happened," Luke continued, "Nikki was getting uncomfortable. Trevor saw what we were doing, and started to get agitated with us. And that didn't help matters, at all. What he didn't need to do right then, in front of Nikki, was raise his voice. But he did. So Nico and I shrunk down in our seats, like this was a regular thing for Trevor to do. Like we were expecting the worst."

Royce was relieved to see that David was also failing to restrain his laughter, and re-took the narrator role. "So Nikki got up and excused herself, with Trevor trying to explain we were joking. He looked back over his shoulder at us, while he was chasing her. I'd never seen a guy so angry. But I remember what David said. Do you?"

David nodded. "I guess that worked a little *too* well."

Luke took over again. "After dinner we walked back over here and dealt some Spades. Which we need to do soon, guys. Anyway, about an hour later, Trevor's banging on the door, mad as hell. Nikki had packed up and left, and he had an appointment the next morning and couldn't follow her back to Atlanta right away."

Sun looked at David. "Please tell me you did something to try to fix it."

"We did," he assured her. "We had Royce write an apology letter to her, and we all signed it and gave it to Trevor that night. He and Nikki had other problems going on that we didn't know about, so it wasn't all on us. I don't think she completely trusted him around the girls down here. He came back down a week later and moved his stuff out of the dorm. Last I heard, he enrolled at the same school she was going to, and they were working on things."

Luke nodded. "I'm the only one who keeps up with him, I think. I talked to him a couple of months ago, and they're doin' okay."

Royce rubbed Chloe's foot, hoping she wasn't too

angry with him. He pivoted the conversation to food to lighten the mood. "So, do y'all want snacks or should we order something more substantial?"

The delivery idea was overwhelmingly popular, though they were split 4-3 between pizza and Chinese. Everyone kicked in cash to the coffee table, and Sun dealt with the delivery drivers. She also set up the Scrabble board for herself, Chloe, and Royce, while the other four got loud over coin flips and Spades partners. "What's that about?" Chloe whispered.

Royce drew Sun and Chloe in close and explained, quietly. "So, Luke and Nico are notorious cheaters, and they can't be paired together. They have to flip a coin for partners." The girls look confused, so he continued. "They signal to their partner what suit they want thrown. Making a fist for clubs, or rubbing their ring finger for diamonds, or touching their chest for hearts. I'm embarrassed to admit how long it took us to catch them. David, Carlos, and I lost a fuck-ton of hands before we figured it out."

As the games began, Royce laughed to himself about the difference in seriousness at each end of the coffee table. David, Carlos, Nico, and Luke were loud and boisterous, cursing their failures and celebrating their victories. At the other end, Sun, Chloe, and Royce weren't even keeping score in the Scrabble game. It made him itch a little, not having a pad and pencil to establish a winner, but he never voiced it.

Sun and Chloe opted out of the next couple of rounds

of bong-passing, since they were driving, but Royce overheard them whispering about a possible shopping trip together on Sunday. They played Trivial Pursuit with Royce, and David asked to be dealt in, even though he was still engrossed in Spades with the other three. That didn't stop him from winning, however, even with his attention divided and not moving his own game piece to preferred categories.

Shortly after midnight, Chloe yawned. Royce whispered in her ear, "You're welcome to sleep here tonight, with me."

"I know, and I'd love to. But I need to be home in the morning for Jacob." She sighed. "Just one more week." She said her goodbyes a bit later, and Royce walked her down to her car. The other guests departed soon after.

✧   ✧   ✧

KNOWING THE COMPUTER lab would be busy on Sunday, Royce set his alarm clock so he could get there right when it opened. It took his best effort, but he resisted the urge to apply any major edits to his final two term papers. He read them over and cleaned up a couple of punctuation problems, but otherwise stayed only long enough to print out two copies of each. Finding none of his friends in the dining hall for the early lunch rush, he wrapped up a grilled cheese sandwich and tomato soup and walked back to Kingston with the realization that this convenience would only be available to him for a few more days.

He called Chloe later in the evening, and asked about her shopping trip with Sun. He could practically hear her eyes roll through the phone. "I bought *a* thing," she said, "but I had more in mind. It would have been a lot easier for me if I'd just asked you what you'd like to see me wearing."

He paused, searching for the right words to reply. "I'm flattered, truly. But you didn't have to do that. I didn't know that was why you'd gone shopping. I have no doubt you'll leave me breathless. You always do."

"We'll see."

✧ ✧ ✧

On Monday morning, Royce walked to campus and visited Dr. Russell's office to submit his paper. They engaged in a bit of small talk, regarding the circus office and Royce's thoughts on pursuing a graduate degree in English. "I could definitely see you as a professor, someday," Dr. Russell said. It was the first compliment Royce ever remembered hearing from him.

He stopped by Dr. Dalton's office next, wiping off the condensation of sweat his hands had left on the plastic sheet that covered his paper. He kept his distance and extended the folder to her. "I have learned a lot from you, Dr. Dalton, and I appreciate the thought you put into your classes," he said. He didn't realize until that moment he hadn't had the dream about her since the night before Vic Norton's show at the Hound.

"Well," she said, with the earpiece of her glasses in

her mouth, "I hope you won't be a stranger, since you'll still be living in town."

"I won't. My girlfriend is enrolled here now, and I have friends in the theatre department who I still want to see perform." They shook hands and he turned to leave, thinking *And I hope never to see you again while I'm asleep.*

His final errand was a trip to the registrar's office, where he had a friend who could give him early word on the final grades. He mustered as much charm as he could, and handed her his business card. "Wednesday, maybe?" he asked, hopefully.

"Maybe. But Thursday is more likely." She seemed sad to disappoint him. "I'll call you when I know."

✧　✧　✧

SATURDAY EVENING'S PLANS weighed heavily on Royce and Chloe's interactions at work, though the awkwardness faded a bit as the week progressed. He had been practicing a few songs on his guitar, though he dared not give any indication of what they were, as it would spoil the surprise. She began and abruptly aborted a few comments of her own, with a mischievous look in her eyes that suggested she, too, was keeping secrets.

Thursday afternoon, Royce got the call he'd been waiting for. His contact in the registrar's office said, "Russell and Dalton both submitted A's for you. The computer says you made *magna* by two-tenths of a point."

"Are you sure?"

"I double-checked the math. You're good."

"Thank you so much! Please let me know when you're heading to the Hound, and I'll send a pitcher your way."

He hung up the phone and sank back into his chair. Chloe had been listening silently to his side of the conversation, and raised her palms and eyebrows to request an update. He motioned to the area on the right side of the office entrance, where they knew they couldn't be seen through the window of the kitchen door. Darla and Bobby routinely snuck glances into the office from the kitchen, and they were not very subtle about it. Royce had a feeling it drove them crazy when no one was visible from that vantage point, and he found their interest in his interactions with Chloe to be unseemly for supposedly mature adults.

"A's in both classes," he whispered, with his hands on her hips. "*Magna* confirmed."

She wrapped her arms around his neck and rested her head against his chest. "I am so, so happy for you! I know how much you wanted this."

He reached down and squeezed her butt. "I won't let it go to my head, but it looks like I'm getting a number of things I've wanted this week."

✧　✧　✧

AFTER WORK ON Friday, they drove to his favorite butcher shop in town and selected a couple of beautiful New York strip steaks. He waited until Saturday to call his parents to deliver the news of his grades, knowing he'd be a nervous wreck if he just sat around the apartment waiting until it was time to leave for Chloe's.

Kate was ecstatic for him and gushed, and knew the pauses in conversation were because she was wiping away tears. She asked about his plans for coming home for Christmas, but he told a white lie that he was preoccupied by preparations for the sales meeting and hadn't given it much thought yet. Jennifer told him she'd done well on her first college finals, and that she was excited to catch up with him whenever he was able to get home.

His father beamed with pride, as well, thankful that his son's hard work had paid off with such a tangible achievement. It didn't take long, however, before their conversation turned to cars. There were two leftover red 1990 Miatas available, through his father's friend at the Mazda dealership, but they'd have to be sold and off the lot before December 31st. Royce reported that Sun's father had an interest in the Squareback, and they talked about what would be a fair sales price for it. His father asked for a phone number, and said he'd handle the negotiations with Mr. Choi.

CHAPTER 13

ALL NIGHT

R oyce filled his backpack with toiletries, condoms, and a change of clothes, stopped by the kitchen and added the cabernet from the fridge, picked up his guitar case, and headed out. David had been watching silently, but rose from the sofa as Royce turned the doorknob. "Hold up," he said.

Royce turned slowly, bracing for *You're not going to wear that, are you?* or worse.

David smirked. "You've got wine, your contact lens stuff, and some condoms in your backpack, I would guess. Your hair is down, and you're wearing a flannel shirt and carrying a guitar case. You are the Scruffy College Boy Seduction Starter Kit."

Royce chuckled, shaking his head. "Yeah, man, I suppose I am. I'll be home tomorrow, sometime."

As the door was closing, David called out, "Don't fuck up!"

    ✧   ✧   ✧

ROYCE PARKED IN the empty space beside the RX-7 and climbed the stairs to the second floor. Chloe opened her apartment door before he had a chance to ring the bell. She wore white ankle socks, gray lounge pants, and a bright red Lancaster Cardinals sweatshirt. She incorrectly sensed disappointment in his expression and said, "Yeah, I know. I was wearing less, earlier, but I got cold."

He shook his head. "You're beautiful. And something smells great."

She grabbed the front of his shirt and pulled him inside. "You should maybe say the *wrong* thing, from time to time, just to change it up." She had cranked the heat up alarmingly high.

On his way to the kitchen, he left his backpack and guitar beside the sofa. The steaks were in a shallow dish with the marinade, and she had put a cast iron skillet on the stove for him. He added some oil to the pan and turned up the eye. She busied herself with preparations for a spicy noodle side dish and a spinach salad while he opened the wine and poured two glasses.

"How would you like your steak?" he asked.

"Medium, please. About how long?"

"Ten or fifteen?" he guessed. "I haven't cooked with cast iron in a while."

"Good!" she said, peeling off her sweatshirt and tossing it aside. "We have time to make out a little before dinner."

She quickly pressed her chest to his, but not before he got a peek at the thin white tank top she was wearing. Her areolae were tiny, no larger than a nickel. Her kiss was hungrier than he'd ever felt it, deep and probing, rather than gentle and playful. He didn't want it to end, but he didn't want to burn their dinner, either. "I need to turn these," he forced himself to say.

"Okay. And I need to remember that we have all night."

The steaks were a bit more rare than he'd hoped, but the marinade was tasty. Some combination of soy, ginger, and garlic, plus a few ingredients he couldn't identify. Chloe had tossed the noodles in sesame and chili oils, and she had coated the spinach with a rice wine vinegar dressing. "Please tell your grandmother how much I enjoyed this," he said, continually attempting to avoid staring at her nipples through the tank top.

"I will," she replied. "She and Pop are still planning to come for Christmas. It's gonna be a zoo, with so many people in town to see Jacob's first one."

They washed and dried the dishes, and finished off the last of the wine around weighted pauses in their conversation. She stepped toward him, placed a gentle kiss on the side of his neck, and asked, "Would you excuse me for a few minutes?" She disappeared around the corner toward her bedroom. From her stereo speakers, he heard the spoken-word and bass line opening of "Three Days" by Jane's Addiction.

He pulled two condoms from his backpack and slipped them into the breast pocket of his shirt. He took off his shoes, socks, and jeans, and sat nervously on the edge of the sofa, taking deep breaths in a futile attempt to calm his heart rate. Three minutes passed, according to the clock on the VCR, before she came back around the corner and curled her index finger in the *Come here* motion. She had removed her socks and her lounge pants, revealing dark red polished toenails and a skimpy black silk bikini panty. He rose and followed her to her bedroom.

The room was dark, illuminated by a handful of strategically placed candles, as Perry Farrell appropriately sang *"'Til the shadows and the light were one."* She frowned and walked around to the far side of the twin bed, lowering the volume on her stereo and scolding, "You're just too darn loud."

He pulled off his flannel shirt, tossing it to the floor in front of the bedside table. She climbed onto the bed and knee-walked across it, wrapping her arms around his neck when she was in front of him. Taking her waist firmly in his hands, he pulled her closer.

"I thought you almost never painted your toes?" he said softly.

"I thought you said you liked it?" she breathed back, followed by another long, urgent, and hungry kiss.

She ran her right thumb back and forth, just inside the waistband of her panty. "This is the one thing I bought when Sun and I went shopping. I'm strictly a cotton girl, most of the time, but I liked the cut of these."

"So do I," he agreed, stretching his neck around her shoulder to get a better look. "Particularly in the back." A playful peek of tan lines confirmed that the back panel of the panty was smaller than the bikini bottom she wore to lay out in the sun. But not by much.

He was flattered that she'd created a mix tape for their evening, and focused on the lyrics to the opening song. Clearly she had chosen it for a reason. Both of them had purchased the CD when it had been released a few months prior, and "Three Days" was probably his favorite track on the album, even before this night. He grazed her spine, up and down, with the fingers of his left hand, and covered her left breast with his right. Her small nipple stiffened against his palm.

She tugged at the collar of this T-shirt, pulling his forehead to hers. With their eyes no more than two inches apart, she studied his gaze. Wordlessly, they sought and received verification. They were fully in the moment, together. He remembered her words: *We have all night.*

The intensity of their explorations increased along with the tempo and volume of the song. She held his face in her hands, then combed her fingers through his hair on both sides, gripping it into a tangle in the back. He moved his hands down to her ass, inside the silk fabric, spreading his fingers and squeezing roughly. His erection swelled in his boxer briefs, pointing hard left and reaching his hip bone, pressed tightly between their bodies. Dave Navarro's soaring guitar solo crescendoed, and Royce moved his right hand to the back of her head, securing a handful of her hair and pulling backward to expose her neck. Whimpered gasps escaped her lips as he licked and bit his way from her shoulder to her jawline, and then repeated the same trail on the other side of her neck.

The long opening song ended and another began, though he could not immediately identify it. She brought her hands to his chest and pushed back gently, prompting him to look up from her neck and level his eyes with hers. She grabbed the hem of his T-shirt with both hands and pulled it abruptly over his head, dropping it to the floor at his feet. Tilting her head slightly to one side, she purred, "Get in my bed."

He retrieved one of the condoms from the pocket of his shirt, and turned to watch as she undressed. The tan lines from the strings of her bikini had faded, but a pair of triangles in a lighter skin tone remained, with the nipples of her small breasts in their centers. Below her navel was another lighter triangle, pointed downward. Her pubic hair was trimmed into the same shape, about half an inch within its borders. When he looked back up to meet her eyes, she raised her eyebrows and cocked her hip impatiently.

He pulled his boxers down to his knees and let them fall to the floor. As he kicked them aside, his thick erection swung back and forth like a fleshy metronome. She stared down at it for what seemed like a long time, before tapping her finger to her chin and declaring, "Mmmm, that's going to be fun," and took the condom from his hand.

Stacking her pillows on top of one another, he climbed onto the bed and settled onto his back. She straddled his thighs, wrapping her fingers around the base of his shaft to hold it upright as she rolled the condom down.

She was slick with arousal, but took her time, lowering herself down onto him deliberately. "Give me a minute," she said, closing her eyes. "It's been a while."

"Oh, I'm not going anywhere."

Leaning forward, she snaked her arms underneath his and, palms up, clenched the pillows on either side of his head. Her movements were subtle, a slow rocking motion with her hips, drawing his full length inside her a bit at a time, accompanied by the familiar soft and teasing kisses. With his long arms, he could reach nearly every inch of her, and traced the lines of her body with lingering strokes of his fingertips.

It had been eleven months, nearly to the day, since Leah took him to her bed after the show in Macon, and he feared a hair-trigger reaction to an unaccustomed intimacy. Chloe's choice of pace and rhythm were a blessing. He concentrated on his breathing, mentally cataloging every second. He wanted to remember every sound, every sensation.

In a voice just above a whisper, she sang along with the Terence Trent D'Arby song on her tape: *"But the thought of you just caves me in / The symptoms are so deep, it is much too late to turn away..."*

As her voice trailed off, she drew her knees further up his body, clamping tightly against his waist. She pressed harder against him, on the downward strokes of her hips, using the base of his cock to stimulate her clit. He cradled the back of her head with one hand, and placed the other on the small of her back. She seemed surprised by how quickly her climax arrived, burying her face into his spread of hair and the pillow beneath it. She quivered and gasped, breathing *"fuck…fuck…fuck… fuck…"* into his ear as she rode out the blissful spiral. Even through the latex, he could feel a cascade of warm fluid, slowly making its way down and around him.

"Jesus Christ, Royce," she said, barely audibly, raising her torso and steadying herself with her elbows beneath her.

"You should do that again," he teased, with a deep kiss.

"Oh, I'm *gonna*," she assured him.

"I want to thank you for helping me solve my being-bad-at-sex-talk problem."

"Oh?" she asked, brushing her hair behind her ears, "Did I do that?"

"You did. Now I know I can just sing to you, instead. Of course, I don't know what's upcoming on your tape…"

She sat upright, reaching backward to steady herself with her hands on his knees, and began again the slow, steady rocking of her hips. Delighted by the new perspective, he raised his hands to her breasts and brushed his long fingers across her stiff nipples. She closed her eyes. The next song began – one very familiar to him.

He took her hand and pulled her back down onto his chest. With his mouth wide open, he kissed and bit her neck. She rode him urgently, grinding against him, her breath quick and shallow in his ear. Taking a fist-full of hair at the base of her neck, he whisper-sang along with Maria McKee, "*Your heart beats my blood, my breath fills your lungs.*"

She unraveled suddenly, her leg muscles quaking and squeezing his hips. "Oh! Fuck!" She raised her torso slightly and begged, "Pinch me. Please."

Cupping her swaying breasts, he clamped her nipples between his thumbs and the knuckles of his index fingers. Her orgasm seemed to crash and wane, and then crash again, rocking her entire body, far longer and deeper than the first. She bit his shoulder hard, groaning and gasping, the formation of words impossible. By the time the warm rush of fluid inside her reached the base of his shaft, he was undone. He moved his hands to her hips, digging into her skin with his fingertips and thrusting upward in long, rapid strokes. She froze, pressing her forehead against his. "Yes," she whispered. "Come for me."

He erupted, panting, holding her tight to his chest until the spasms of pleasure subsided. He kissed her long and soft, combing her hair with his trembling fingers. Rolling off of him and settling onto her left side, she stroked his face and said, "Be right back." His eyes closed, he listened as she ran water in the bathroom sink. He carefully removed the condom and tied it off, dropping it to the floor beside his boxers. She came back with a warm damp cloth, and gently wiped off his cock. Returning to his side, she rested her right leg across his and nuzzled her head against his shoulder. She grazed his bare chest lightly with her fingernails, sighed, and announced, "I like you."

"I like you, too," he replied with a chuckle. "I'd like to hear how you discovered that, uh, *technique*, for lack of a better word."

"What, none of the other 37 women you've bedded before liked to be on top?" she teased.

"It was nine – I counted after our conversation that night – and yes, some did. But always sitting upright and bouncing. Like in porn."

"I see. Well," she paused briefly to consider her words. "When I first learned how to… tickle myself, I would straddle a thick bolster pillow from our old sofa, and rub myself against it. It wasn't until much later I discovered I could do the same thing while sitting on a guy."

"I love it. 'Tickle myself.' That's perfect."

Her cassette player reached the end of the tape and loudly clicked off. She sat up and swung her feet to the floor, reached down to grab his flannel shirt, and put it on.

"Leaving already?" he asked.

"I have to pee. Then I'm going to eat ice cream in the living room while you play and sing for me." She blew him a kiss from the bedroom doorway.

He pulled on his T-shirt and boxers and affixed a messy ponytail with a hair tie from her dresser. He was studying the makeshift liquor cabinet in the living room when she emerged from the bathroom. She pressed her chest to his back and hugged him from behind while he considered his options. "Would Mark be pissed if I helped myself to some of his Crown Royal?"

"No," she replied, turning toward the kitchen, "But I'm sure he'd insist that you pour his little sister one, too." She filled two cocktail glasses with ice and searched the refrigerator for a mixer. He poured the whisky and she topped it off with ginger ale.

They cuddled on the sofa, her seated between his legs with her back against his chest, as the alcohol helped to return their pulse rates to near normal. Extending her index finger from her glass, she pointed in the direction of her bedroom. "*That*," she said, "That was somethin' else."

"It was," he agreed, careful to cut himself off before adding, *And I could see myself doing that with you for the rest of my life*. Instead, he chose, "A toast to Mark and Kimberly and Jacob, for making this night possible," and tapped his glass against hers.

She sat up and drained the rest of her drink. "Another?" she asked.

"Yes, please. Tell Mark I'll buy him a new bottle." He pulled his guitar from its case while she made him a second, and sat down on the ottoman with the Epiphone in his lap. Returning from the kitchen with a drink for him and a small bowl of butter pecan for herself, she sat crossed-legged on the sofa. She had only fastened the bottom four buttons of his shirt.

"This is one of the first songs I learned to play," he

announced, and strummed the opening chords to "Give a Little Bit" by Supertramp. She recognized it immediately, tossed her head back in laughter, and twirled her spoon in a circle above her head. He borrowed a page from Vic Norton and locked eyes with her as he sang *"There's so much that we need to share."* She sang along with him from the opening chorus on, while gesturing with her hands and dancing in place.

She clapped and whistled when he finished. "I loved it! Will you play another one?"

He had memorized his miniature set list, and reached into his case for the Gordon Lightfoot songbook. Finding the page with the top corner folded down, he propped the open book against the case so he could see the lyrics. "I mainly play the chords on this one. His finger-work is way beyond me."

"Pfft," she scoffed, "Fuck it, then. Why bother?" but she couldn't keep a straight face to the end of the joke. He laughed along with her and began "Carefree Highway." He had always liked how his voice sounded with Lightfoot's songs, particularly when it was a little scratchy after a couple of drinks.

She applauded again, at the song's conclusion, and beamed at him. "One more, maybe? I'm trying not to be too greedy."

"Sure," he replied, and found in his guitar case a hand-written chord and lyrics sheet that was yellowing at the edges. "Some high cheese from the Eighties, perhaps?" He didn't tell her the song was a guilty pleasure, nor that he'd nursed a decade-long crush on Susanna Hoffs. He sang "Eternal Flame" by the Bangles.

She looked almost sad as he played, closing her brown eyes for several measures at a time. She mouthed the words along with him, but he couldn't hear her voice, even though he was playing softly. He almost stopped to check on her, but continued to the end. She still applauded, but not as loudly as before. He moved to put the guitar back in its case, wondering what he might have done wrong, as she stood and unfastened the four bottom buttons. Climbing onto the ottoman, she sat on his lap, facing him. He reached his hands into the open shirt and held her close. "Well, you've done it," she whispered into his ear. "I'm yours."

They kissed, slow and soft, content, and her tongue was cold and sweet. He stood, lifting her, and she wrapped her arms and legs tightly around him. He carried her to her bedroom, laying her gently onto her back. Hovering over her, undressing, his mind raced with all the techniques of his own that he was eager to demonstrate.

✧   ✧   ✧

HE FOUGHT SLEEP after round two, having been on top for the duration before climaxing from behind her, gripping her waist tightly with his thumbs on her Venusian dimples. They had ended up on their right sides in the aftermath, in spoon formation. Only two candles remained lit — the others died of natural causes — and he knew he needed to get up to take out his contacts soon, before the darkness and his exhaustion claimed him. Her hair smelled of rose and coconut. She came at least twice in their second session, as best as he could tell, and he looked forward to learning more about what he did to get her there. He caressed her left thigh, to see if she was still awake. Her voice was hoarse and groggy, and muffled by her pillow.

"Ready again so soon, Murph?"

He laughed. "I need to take my eyes out."

"Okay. I need to get up, too." She clicked her bedside lamp's switch and put his flannel shirt back on. He pulled on his boxers and retrieved his backpack from the living room. Stopping at the hallway bathroom door with his lens case, solution, and toothbrush, he watched as she pulled a couple of cotton pads from a box on the sink and grabbed her bottle of makeup remover. "You take this one," she said with a kiss. "I'll go to their bathroom."

They finished their tasks at the same time. She pointed to her face with both index fingers, on her return to the hall bath. "Me, without makeup." He found her honey irises to be even more striking without the mascara and eye liner. "I already left all my powder either in your hair or on the pillow."

He mimicked her finger-point. "Me, with glasses."

"I see you, professor. Let's go to sleep."

She blew out the candles and shimmied into a

white cotton panty from her dresser. He pulled back the sheet and blanket for her, and she nuzzled backward against him, in the same position they had been before.

"Good night, Chloe," he whispered.

"Mmmmmmm."

The next day was the last day the computer lab would be open and, also, the last day his meal plan card would be honored at Calhoun. He relished every moment with Chloe that morning — sharing coffee while half-dressed on the sofa, snuggles and whispers recounting the night before, showering together with a fresh daytime exploration of each other's bodies — but both of them had a lot to do and he felt it was his duty to keep them focused.

"I shouldn't be long in the lab. I just want to make sure everything is perfect with the handbook before I print a couple of copies and take the disc to Strickland tomorrow morning. Call me when you're done with your laundry and tidying?"

"I will," she said. "But hang on. I have something for you."

He waited at the door with his backpack over his shoulder and guitar case in his hand. She returned from her bedroom with a cassette. "This copy is yours." She pushed it into his breast pocket and kissed him goodbye.

Parking in the nearly-empty lot next to the English building, he took the cassette out of his pocket and smiled. She had written "08 December 1990" on the spine, surrounded by two hearts drawn with a pink pen. The playlist was on the back, in her neatest handwriting, with every word in lower case letters:

jane's addiction - three days / the stone roses - i wanna be adored / the church - under the milky way / terence trent d'arby - sign your name / peter murphy - cuts you up / the cure - lovesong / the smiths - how soon is now? / maria mckee - breathe / crowded house - into temptation / depeche mode - personal jesus / queen - who wants to live forever / inxs - need you tonight

He popped his *Mars Needs Guitars!* Hoodoo Gurus cassette out of the Squareback's player and replaced it with Chloe's.

CHAPTER 14

IMPROV

Thirty minutes into his latest session of pouring over the handbook edits, Royce felt a wave of disgust wash over him. He sat back in his chair and thought about how many hours he'd spent in the computer lab over the past five years, second-guessing himself and making minor changes to his assignments. He realized for the first time that he needed to recognize when good enough was truly good enough. He needed to trust himself. Chloe did. *"I'm yours,"* she'd said. He had never heard those words before, but he was eager to accept the responsibility that came with them. He printed two copies, saved the final version to the disc, and walked to Calhoun.

After lunch, he pulled out a note pad and started another list. He and David had made do with two sauce pans, a couple of rusty baking sheets and a small collection of mismatched plates, bowls, and silverware. Facing a future of planning and cooking his own meals, he catalogued what he thought a true adult would have in his kitchen. Chloe called about an hour later, and asked if he was ready to go on a shopping trip.

There was only one store in Dublin, besides Walmart, that would have everything he was looking for, and he was willing to pay a little extra for a higher-quality product. They walked slowly down the aisles, holding hands, filling his cart with essentials: a cutting board, a proper set of knives, a spice rack, pots and pans, and stainless steel cooking utensils, along with an eight-piece flatware collection and a boxed set of plates and bowls. Chloe suggested something colorful, but Royce opted for brown on brown.

He checked his watch and asked if she would like to join him for his last official dinner at Calhoun as a student. He knew he'd probably eat there at least once a week, paying cash, in order to spend time with his friends. But this meal was special, and he wanted her with him. She enthusiastically agreed. Carlos and Nico had gone back to Atlanta for the remainder of the month, but David and Luke joined them. Neither asked any specific questions about their Saturday date, but the elephant in the room had a seat at their table.

✿   ✿   ✿

ROYCE DROPPED OFF the disc and a printed copy of the handbook with Strickland on his way to work on Monday, and verified they'd be ready for pickup on Thursday. He also stopped by the grocery store and bought a single rose and a glass vase, to leave on Chloe's desk.

The spring tour — for the early dates, anyway — was the easiest to plan. The show had played the same venues, with the same sponsors, for several years. And the same sales rep teams handled the campaigns in roughly the same chronological order. Complicating matters slightly for 1991 was the fact that instead of 12 or 14 sales rep teams, Yawnoc now only had 10, plus whichever dates Darla would deign to handle on her own. Royce knew the Marshalls and the Rosses would be happy to take an additional date or two, as would the Edwards and Thomases. But the teams would not hit the road for their first campaigns until after the new year, so luckily he had weeks to solve potential problems.

Chloe walked into the office looking happy and radiant, but he could tell she had something on her mind. She put away her purse and booted up the computer, then walked over beside him and pointed to his desk calendar. It was a bit of theatre, in case they were being watched from upstairs. "Thank you for the flower. But if we're going to keep this little secret," she said softly, "then I'm really gonna have to work on my poker face."

He pointed to a different date, grazing the back of her hand with his fingertips, and chuckled. "Oh? What do you mean?"

"About thirty minutes after they got home last night, Mark went to the bathroom. Kim waited until he was out of sight and looked at me and asked, 'So, how was he?'"

Royce stifled his laughter. "Oh, shit! I'm sorry that happened." But he couldn't resist a winking follow-up. "Out of curiosity, though, what did you tell her?"

She kissed him on top of his head and walked toward her desk. "I told her he was the best *ever.*"

✧　✧　✧

Royce took elaborate notes during his phone conversation with Joey Vegas on Tuesday morning, and fleshed out the tour on his calendar. Chloe was already finished with the taps for the first dozen dates, but now he could give her the second wave of cities that needed to be completed before the end of the year, to stay well ahead in case they were thrown any curveballs. He called Strickland to get the ticket orders in the pipeline, while Bobby and Darla volunteered to make calls to the sponsors to alert them of the schedule. Royce made contact with the venues and wrote down the security deposits he needed to send. Since the show had done such a good job of taking care of the performance locations, most only required a token deposit of a couple hundred dollars. Over the next few days, he made cash withdrawals from the safe and bought money orders from the bank to send to Florida, a process that would continue for the next several weeks until all the dates were set in stone.

He took Chloe to lunch at the cafe where he used to work. They stopped by a liquor store, so he could replace Mark's bottle, and then visited Strickland's on the way back to the office to collect the bound handbooks for the meeting. They applied label-maker stickers to the covers, to make the presentation as professional as they could.

They also agreed they would not arrive at Saturday's meeting together, though they'd planned to spend the rest of the day afterward comparing observations about what they'd independently seen and heard.

Joey Vegas arrived at the office from Florida on Friday, just before Royce and Chloe were to leave for the day. Royce said goodbye to her, and walked up the steps into the kitchen for some last-minute planning.

"So, I'll do a welcome," Bobby said, "and then I'll bring Royce up to talk about the additions to the handbook and whatever else you wanna say. 'Bout Chloe or whatever. Royce, you can introduce Joey, 'cause I know he's got some updates about the show. Then I'll do a detailed reading of the new book and see what they got to say." Royce and Joey agreed.

Royce drove into The Fifth Quarter's parking lot at 11:00 a.m. on Saturday, an hour ahead of time, and chose a space next to Darla's Mercedes. Darla, Bobby, and Joey had opened the bar, and Bobby already looked a little wobbly. Royce waved to them, but didn't walk over right away.

The conference area that had been reserved for them was as generic as Royce had imagined. Two rows of four-top tables were lined up in front of another table with a small wooden podium on top and four chairs behind it. The drink tokens were in a shallow basket next to the podium, and each of the tables had a menu of three entree choices for lunch.

He didn't notice Darla until she was only a couple of yards from him. She looked troubled, and placed a manicured hand on his shoulder. "Bobby's been up since 4:00 a.m. and he made his first drink around 8:00, I think. He hasn't done one of these without Sal in years, and I don't think he can handle it. Public speaking isn't really his strong suit."

Royce thought for a moment before responding. "Okay, I understand. I'll keep an eye on him and take on whatever I need to." He was not a stranger to performing in front of an audience, but didn't much care for improvisation. He told people he enjoyed being spontaneous, provided he had plenty of time to think about it in advance. Sitting down in one of the chairs behind the podium, he flipped through his handbook and studied the highlighted portions.

Chloe came in a few minutes later. She'd told him she'd borrowed a few things from Kim for the meeting, since hadn't brought her entire wardrobe with her when she moved to Dublin, but she'd certainly put together a fetching ensemble: an ankle-length gray-blue paisley skirt, black leather shoes with a chunky heel, a cream-colored v-neck blouse, and a black sweater. He wanted so much to rush over to her to tell her about Bobby and the situation he was in, but didn't dare. He waved hello to her, and hoped his pained expression would be enough.

He nodded toward the bar. She nodded back, and walked over to greet Darla, Bobby, and Joey.

Chuck and Bess Marshall were the first reps to arrive, just before noon, followed almost immediately by Ken and Sally Ross. Royce found their handbooks at the top of his stack, counted out a dozen drink tokens for the four of them, and walked to the bar to greet them. Chloe intercepted him on his way back to do the same for new arrivals George and Maggie Edwards, and Burt and Gwen Thomas. "Let me get these, love," she said. "Are you okay?"

"I hope so. This is not going to be as easy as I thought it would be."

"I know. Bobby looks like shit."

"Yeah. I could use a beer, myself. Want one?"

"Sure."

He drew as much strength as he could from her smile, but longed for her touch. He overheard Chloe's name as he approached the bar, and bristled. As he got closer, he caught George Edwards' question to Ken Ross. "You think they're fuckin'?"

Their backs were to him, so they didn't see him coming. Royce squeezed between them and rested his elbows on the bar. "I never assume anyone is fucking unless I catch them in the act." He paused for effect. "But who are we talking about?"

George and Ken stammered and took a good look at their shoes. After an awkward pause, George offered, "Oh, nobody. Nobody you know."

Royce took a satisfied swig from his Heineken and scanned the room. "Looks like everyone's here now, if y'all want to find a seat. I'll get the manager to send the wait staff out."

Fueled by a much-needed boost of confidence, he motioned to Chloe with the neck of her beer bottle to join him at an empty table. She wrapped up her greetings with the last of the teams to arrive and slid gracefully into the seat across from him. "Wondering who'll decide to join us here?" she asked, with raised eyebrows.

He handed over her beer. "Yep!" They were outsiders and insiders at the same time. Oddities. Seconds later, the only other member of the group who remotely fit the same description took a chair at their table. After the Marshalls had sat down with Bobby and Darla, Joey Vegas was the odd man out.

"Always a pleasure to see you, Miss Webb," he said, settling down between them.

"Mister Vegas," she replied, with a hand on his forearm.

When their lunch orders arrived, Joey slid an index card to Royce. "I thought of these dates for possible places we could meet during the tour, so you could come down to collect the show's money." All of the dates were Saturdays. He turned to Chloe. "Perhaps you'd be able to accompany Royce on one of these errands, so you could see the show?" It was a clever question, almost certainly meant to gauge her reaction to the prospect of joining Royce for what would be an overnight trip.

She didn't take the bait. "Oh, I'd never think of imposing on him, if he's going to be working through a weekend." Joey looked disappointed. Royce tucked the card into his breast pocket for future reference.

As the wait staff began to clear the empty lunch plates, Darla and Bobby took their seats behind the podium. Royce and Joey excused themselves, as well, to take their own places. Chloe showed two hands with crossed fingers to Royce, and gave him a wink.

As the clinking of ceramic plates and silverware subsided, the reps turned their attention to the empty podium. Joey flipped through his notes, but Bobby made no move to deliver the welcome they'd planned. Royce leaned forward and looked down the row for a signal. Bobby looked at him, shook his head, and remained seated.

Okay, then, Royce thought, gathering his well-annotated handbook and rising to the podium. *Remember what you've learned.*

"Ladies and gentlemen, welcome. We thank you all for giving up your Saturday to come and join us."

Remember theatre. There's no microphone. Project your voice.

"But more than that, thank you all for your hard work with the fall tour. Sales were up seventeen percent over last year, and we all anticipate an even more prosperous 1991." It was a call to applause, and it worked.

Remember mock trial. Shoulders back. Posture. Breathe. Hit your key words.

"There are a lot of additions to the handbook, as you've no doubt noticed by now, since it's about twice as thick as last year's, and we'll go through them in detail shortly. Given the recent personnel changes in the office, we're sure you'll understand the need for a greater emphasis on information gathering. On a personal note, I'm very grateful to Chloe for helping me with this project." In a cruel twist of fate, Chuck Marshall had slid his chair a bit to his left, partially blocking Royce's view of her.

Remember the Toastmasters seminar. Scan the audience. Make eye contact with as many people as you can see.

"But first, I'm proud to welcome everyone's favorite master of ceremonies, our own Joey Vegas." He stepped back and led another round of applause.

Remember your father. Bullshit as necessary.

He wanted very much to listen to Joey's prepared remarks, but instead he dug into his handbook notes. Time was short. He was aware of the audience's reaction, however, as Joey recounted a fish-out-of-water story about the Zhou twins, and spoke enthusiastically about a new juggling act that would be added for the next tour. Joey's primary objective was to keep the sales reps excited about the show, and he emphasized their early rehearsals and the performers' commitment to enhancing their acts. The performances were in small towns that didn't see a lot of touring shows, but it didn't mean sales wouldn't suffer if every year's show was a carbon copy of the one that preceded it.

Once Joey had completed his remarks, Royce again

took the podium, and directed the reps' attention to the new sections of the handbook. "It was a tough task, but we went through your campaign summaries and compiled a master list of contact information for sponsors, phone rooms, and performance locations. They are sorted alphabetically by city name. Sal's ability to keep these details in his head was, I admit, beyond me. So, if you'll take a look at page fifteen, you'll see we made some additions to the information that we're asking you to report, after each sales campaign."

Remember debate club. Be concise. Be economical.

He invited everyone to flip back to page one, and noted the additions and clarifications that had been made. Everything went smoothly until page four, when he got to the line that Bobby had him add, encouraging the reps to make one last call before leaving town to people who had pledged to buy tickets, but had not yet sent in their payments. It seemed like a logical enough suggestion at the time, and he had wondered why it wasn't common policy. He soon got his answer.

Chuck Marshall rose to his feet. "No! Nuh-uh. That's some Sal Russo *bullshit*, right there. He used to have it in his book, but Bobby made him take it out. And now this kid," he pointed at Royce, "This kid, who's never run a campaign, done put it back in!"

Royce felt as though he'd been punched in the chest. The hairs on the back of his neck stood up, and his body temperature abruptly rose. But he was careful not to change his expression.

"If y'all call them again," Chuck continued, pushing his glasses up the bridge of his nose, "Then you're dunning 'em for a donation! For a *donation*! You're dunning people for a *donation*!"

A bead of sweat formed on each of Royce's temples and began a slow trickle toward his ears. He briefly wondered if Bobby had insisted upon the addition to set him up for this conflict. As he shook off the paranoid notion, Chloe leaned sideways, around Chuck's hip, and caught his eye. She placed balled-up fists on the sides of her head, with her index fingers extended, and mouthed to him, "*Tatanka*. Buffalo." He smiled, took a deep breath, and fed on her support.

Chuck found a few interested reps seated near him and attempted to formulate another way to word the same objection he'd already repeated several times. The murmurs were getting louder. Royce raised his hands. "Everyone, please. Everyone." He shifted his weight on his feet as the room quieted. His shirt was stuck with sweat to his lower back.

"Chuck, Bess," he began, "There is not a soul in this room that could possibly argue with your results. I mean, just look at page ten for the sales summaries for the year. Y'all are the all-stars."

He held up his book. "This is a guide. A collection of suggestions. Every single one of you needs to find the plan that works best for you."

Chuck, still standing, attempted to interrupt. "But you said —"

"Please," Royce countered, his hand raised. "May I continue? Please?"

Chuck sat down.

Royce hustled through the final points of emphasis. Within twenty minutes, he was finished with his agenda, and called the meeting to a close.

He walked briskly down the hall beside the bar, staring at the floor, and locked the men's bathroom door behind him. He splashed cold water on his face, adjusted his ponytail, and studied his reflection in the mirror. He was surprised to see that his elevated stress level wasn't written all over it. Chloe was waiting for him outside the bathroom, leaning against the hallway wall beside a pay phone. She leaned in close and spoke softly, with her eyes locked on his.

"You need to take me back to your place, like ASAP," she said, in a low growl.

"I'm sorry. Are you not feeling well?"

She wrinkled her nose. "Am I not *feeling* well? I just watched you rock that entire meeting, off the cuff, and I'm about as turned on as I've ever been in my *life*." She looked over her shoulder for spies. "Give me your key." He did as she asked.

"This works out well," he said. "David's at work this afternoon."

"You think it would make any difference to me if he was home or not?"

He dodged the question. "There's a brick in the

flowerbed to the right of the front door. You can use it to prop it open for me."

She blew a kiss, twirled around, and walked out, pausing only long enough to gather her coat and purse, and to wave goodbye to the few attendees who were still milling around near the bar.

Royce strolled past Darla, Bobby, and Joey without making eye contact, and met briefly with the manager. She looked at her wait staff's checks and confirmed that his pre-payment would be sufficient for the event. He was surprised no one had cheated by putting more drinks on the company's tab or ordering something off the set menu.

Walking back toward the trio he had ignored, he lied, "I need to go. I'm spending the rest of the weekend with a friend in Macon for his birthday. See you Monday." He did not wait for a reply, nor did he acknowledge Chuck and Bess Marshall, who were standing a few feet away.

GIFTS

During drive back to Kingston, Royce thought about Chloe's question. *"You think it would make any difference to me if he was home or not?"* Among David's many quirks was his uneasiness with the discussion of anything of a sexual nature. In spite of all the time they'd spent together, and all of the topics they'd talked about, Royce knew next to nothing of David's romantic history, and he had not been encouraged to speak of his own. For the first six months they had lived together, the subject had been easy enough to avoid, since neither was in a relationship. But now, with Sun and Chloe in the picture, an uncomfortable conversation was imminent.

David had asked Royce point-blank to continue living at Kingston until graduation in May, even though he could afford to move into his own place. And Royce had no desire to move away from the best friend he'd ever had, knowing David would be off to a big city the moment he had his diploma in hand. So, as long as one or both of them was still a member of a couple, it would be almost impossible to schedule sex only for times when one of them would be out. Chloe had made her feelings known, but now he needed to find out how David felt.

He put the brick back in the flowerbed and hustled

up the stairs. Rounding the corner into the hallway, he saw a trail of her clothes on the floor, the last of them in a pile just inside his bedroom door. He closed it behind him and saw that she was already flushed and breathing heavily.

"Sorry," she smiled. "I got started without you."

After a noisy and mutually-fulfilling romp, she collapsed onto her back in the afterglow, and he rested next to her, propped on his left side. With his right index finger, he drew circles around her navel. It was narrow and vertical, like a coin slot. "What do you want for Christmas?" he asked.

"That's a good question." She tapped her chin. "I really want to wear something pretty and sexy for you. Would you pick something out for me, so I'll have an idea of your tastes?"

"I will. And I think you'll find my tastes are... not exotic."

"Okay. What can I get for you?"

"Well, I see a lot of golf in our future, so anything related to that would be thoughtful."

She leaned up and kissed him. "I know just the thing."

✧ ✧ ✧

SHE WENT BACK to her place, not long before David got home from work. *Robocop 2* had just been released and David was eager to see it again. He kicked off his Chucks and flopped into the easy chair with his Video Barn bag.

"How was the meeting?"

Royce chuckled. "Well, the drunk asshole hung me out to dry, and I had to improv the whole thing."

"Shit, seriously? I'm sorry, dude. Good thing you're fast on your feet."

"Yeah. Chloe came back here with me after the meeting, to help me celebrate the accomplishment."

"That was kind of her." He already sounded queasy.

"So, we need to talk about this. We're not always going to luck into those kinds of opportunities. You and Sun. Me and Chloe. I know this isn't your favorite topic, but I'm pretty sure the Jills didn't clear it with you in advance every time they wanted sex."

David shook his head. "I had headphones. I still have headphones."

Royce sat back, relieved. David continued. "But you don't."

"Well, that's the thing. It doesn't bother me. Y'all can do what you want, whenever."

"Are you sure? This hasn't come up before."

"I'm 99% sure. But we can pick this up again later. Once, you know, something happens."

None of the sales rep teams made visits to the office the week before Christmas, leaving Royce to assume they would wait until after Christmas, or maybe even after New Year's, to stop by for the taps and tickets for their first spring tour assignment. Bobby and Darla kept to themselves, as well, and neither said a single word about the sales meeting. Royce made the executive decision to close the office at 2:00 on Friday, so he and Chloe could get a jump on their holiday break. They made plans to return to Dublin as early as possible on the 26th so they'd have a chance to celebrate together and exchange gifts before reopening the office the following day.

Their goodbye hug was long and sad. "Drive safely, please. I'll miss you. Enjoy your family time. I'll see you Wednesday." He didn't want to let go.

"You have a safe trip, too, love," she replied. "I'll be thinking about you. A lot."

✧   ✧   ✧

Jennifer was less than enthusiastic about accompanying her brother on a shopping trip on the Saturday before Christmas, but he managed to charm her into it. He was excited about finally having the money to buy gifts for his family that were more than the token symbols of affection a poor college student could afford, and he had considered several options for each of them. And for Chloe.

He bought his mother a designer purse, and for his father, military-grade binoculars for the lake house. Chloe's lingerie request turned out to be easier than he thought it would be, courtesy of a mannequin in Macy's that mirrored her measurements, wearing exactly the ensemble he'd love to see her in — a white silk lace-front camisole with a matching string bikini panty.

He had a piece of jewelry in mind for Chloe, but had no idea which store might have it. Fortunately, he did know exactly how to describe it, so they didn't waste a lot of time staring at window display cases. At the third store, he saw the perfect piece: a gold Hawaiian sun symbol, with a circular opening in the center that was surrounded by diamonds, and stylized flames extending in all directions.

Jennifer ran her fingers down the string that was attached to the pendant and flipped over the price tag. She flashed him a sour look. "How long have you been dating this girl?"

"Seven weeks, tomorrow. I'm sure they'll throw in a chain, if I pay cash for it."

He led her to believe he was finished, but on their way out pulled her into an electronics store near the entrance. "You said a few weeks ago that you wanted a new boom box. Pick one."

"Really?"

"Yeah. It won't be a surprise gift, but at least I'll know I got you the one you liked best."

Royce and Jennifer enjoyed Christmas Eve dinner at their uncle's house, playing with their cousins as they showed off their new toys, and visiting with their grandparents. His father called him aside to thank him for the binoculars, and to tell him that he and Sun's father had agreed on a sales price for the Squareback. They made plans for the following Saturday.

His mother grumbled that the purse Royce bought for her was too expensive, but did admit it was exactly what she wanted. She and Jennifer checked the news paper and decided they wanted to see a late afternoon showing of the new Cher movie, *Mermaids*. Royce saw his opportunity and took it.

"Y'all go ahead, seriously. It won't take me long to pack up, so I'll split while you're at the movie."

✧　✧　✧

Chloe called from her place just before noon the next day. "You're home already? I expected your machine."

"I am. I came back last night."

"How soon can you leave? I need you."

"About nineteen seconds. I'm already packed."

"Good, thank you. Please come."

He hustled, running through a couple of yellow lights on the way to her apartment. She looked as though she'd driven home in the clothes she'd worn to bed the night before. No makeup and her hair unwashed. He dropped his backpack and opened his arms for her. She cried against his chest.

"Michael called while I was home. He's been re-deployed to the Persian Gulf. He couldn't give details, obviously, but I could hear in his voice that he was worried. I'm so scared for him."

Royce attempted to recall every conversation he'd had with David regarding the Iraqi invasion of Kuwait, as he held her close and tried to offer comfort. David's father had been a Green Beret in Vietnam, and had since served as a consultant for several conflicts and near-conflicts. Dr.

Carson had told his son that he didn't think an armed conflict was imminent, considering how outmatched the Iraqis would be. But no one could know for sure.

"I'm so sorry, sweetheart. Maybe the military build-up and coalition will make them back down before anyone fires a shot." He handed her a tissue from a box on the end table. "What can I do for you?"

She wiped her eyes. "Just be with me. Talk to me."

"I will." He kissed her forehead. "Are you hungry?"

"No, but I do want to take a shower."

He sat on the bathroom floor while she bathed, his back against the sink cabinet and feet pressed to the edge of the tub. The apartment was hot again, and he'd taken off his jeans. He asked her about Jacob's first Christmas. She enjoyed the subject change and spoke animatedly about her family and their holiday traditions.

"There's a bottle of wine in the fridge," she said, turning off the faucet and wrapping a towel around her glistening body. "Would you open it for us? I'll just be a few minutes."

He poured two glasses and retrieved her gifts from his backpack. He sat on the floor in front of their Christmas tree and she joined him a few minutes later. Her hair was still damp, but she'd put on mascara and donned a gray sweater and her black silk panty. Her toenail polish had begun to chip. "Okay, Murph. Who goes first?"

He took a coaster from the coffee table. "Flip you for it? Checkerboard ceramic is you, and skid-free rubber backing is me."

"Do it."

He flipped the coaster into the air and let it fall. "Rubber backing," he said, rubbing his hands together.

"Wait here, then. I wasn't about to wrap this one." She rose and walked to her bedroom, returning with an olive green canvas golf bag with a white bow on top.

"Oh, so nice! I love it!" He looked through all the pockets and zippered compartments.

"If we're going to be playing together, I couldn't let you strap that thread-bare bag of yours next to mine on the back of a cart. It's embarrassing," she joked.

He pulled her toward him with his hand behind her head and kissed her. "Thank you."

"So, which one of these should I open first?"

He pointed toward the larger of the two boxes. "This one, please."

She ripped into the paper and opened the box with the lingerie set. Holding the camisole to her chest by the thin shoulder straps, she studied it. "Gorgeous. I was expecting some elaborate Frederick's of Hollywood bodysuit or something. This is awesome, Royce."

"I'm glad you like it. I told you my tastes weren't exotic. I'm looking forward to seeing that white silk against your tan in the summer."

"I am too," she said, running her fingers along the lace front of the panty.

He reached for the perfectly-wrapped rectangle beside her knee. "What kind of book is this, I wonder?" It was a cookbook, specifically dedicated to recipes for two.

"Yes! Exactly what we need."

"I was thinking we could do a mid-week date night, you know? Dinner and a movie on tape, maybe? I loved cooking with you, a couple of weeks ago, and this should give us lots of ideas."

"It's perfect. And you're exactly right. Let's shoot for Wednesdays."

"Yay! I'm so glad you agree!"

"Okay," he said, "Last one." He handed her the box with the sun pendant inside, and bit down on his cheek. His grand gestures had a way of backfiring.

She opened the lid of the jewelry box and silently examined its contents. Dabbing tears from the corners of her eyes with the sleeves of her sweater, she shook her head. "This is too much. I can't even imagine what this cost you."

"It's not too much. Not for my sun goddess."

She pulled the necklace over her head and centered the pendant on her chest. "You'll be seeing me in this a *lot*. And sometimes *only* this." She climbed onto his lap, kissing him with purpose, and they made love, softly and slowly, on a blanket on the floor beneath the tree.

☼ ☼ ☼

When he got home from work on Thursday, there were two messages on his answering machine, both from Leah. He waited a while to call her back. They hadn't spoken since late October, when he had called to tell her about his new job.

"Royce! I have news!"

"It's good to hear from you! What's happened?"

"I'm *engaged*! I got my RN from Lancaster and now my MRS has come through! He's a second-year resident at Memorial."

He laughed in appreciation of the execution of her plan. Becoming a nurse and marrying a doctor were her number one and two goals, from the time he'd met her. "What's his name, and will he be coming to town with you for graduation?"

"I hope so! His name is *Doctor* Matthew Cohen."

"Leah Cohen. It has a nice ring."

"Oh, my god! And what a ring it is!" she cackled. "I bet it's three carats!"

"I'm happy for you. I've met someone, too. I'll be sure to tell Chloe about your news."

She snorted. "Well, just make sure you don't tell her *everything* about me."

Three sales rep teams, including the Rosses and Thomases, visited the office on Friday, frustrating Royce's thoughts of having a quiet day and maybe slipping out early for the busy weekend ahead of him. He'd packed a small duffel bag that morning, so he could leave Dublin for his mother's house right after work. At least none of them arrived with their hands out for an advance loan.

As the clocked clicked close to five, Chloe offered a stern warning. "When you get back into town on Sunday, you are to come directly to my place. If your weekend bag isn't in the passenger seat, I'll know you went home first, and I will be royally pissed off."

"Understood. I'll call you before I leave." *How do you stuff so much power into such a small package?* he thought.

✧ ✧ ✧

BRIGHT AND EARLY on Saturday morning, Royce Senior met him at Kate's, and followed him on the hour-plus drive to the Choi's home in Alpharetta. Sun's father introduced himself as John. "I'm glad you and my father could come to an agreement," Royce said pleasantly.

"It was not hard," John said, shrugging his shoulders.

"Please, feel free to take a look. I'm sure he described the flaws thoroughly, but I don't want there to be any surprises."

Mr. Choi examined the car, never changing his blank expression, and pulled a small stack of hundred dollar bills from his breast pocket. "It's good."

Royce took the title from the glove box and signed it. He handed over the paper and the two keys and accepted the cash. John shook his hand and held it a few seconds longer than Royce expected. "Tell me of David Carson, please."

Royce grinned. "He's the brightest person I've ever known. And he and Sun seem very happy together." He hoped his face wouldn't convey his worry about might happen in May. David was graduating and likely moving far away, while Sun had another year in school.

Mr. Choi nodded and managed the hint of a smile. "Thank you. I hope the rest of your day goes well."

Royce enjoyed the long drive back down to the south side with his father, and thanked him again for his help with putting both car deals together.

"Well, you're breaking one of my cardinal rules by buying a new car in its first model year. But I did drive the one they held for you, and I have to say it's a lot of fun. It doesn't have anywhere near the horsepower of an American muscle car, but it sure can take a corner."

His contact at the dealership, a tall barrel-chested man of his father's age, greeted Royce with a strong handshake. "Betcha want to drive it some, before signing papers, huh?"

"I do."

Royce and his father found some back roads and put the Miata through a speedy test drive. The narrow range of motion in the gear stick would take some getting used to, but the Squareback felt like a dump truck compared to the responsiveness of this car. He had worried the driver seat's dimensions might be too cramped for his long arms and legs, but the arrangement fit him like a glove.

"Okay, I'm ready," he said, entering the salesman's office. He carefully read through the paperwork, and realized the down payment was $500 short of what he had received from Mr. Choi. His father gently placed five hundred dollar bills on the desk.

"An early graduation present," he said with a proud smile.

"You didn't have to do that." Royce was moved nearly to tears. "But I appreciate it."

They waited in the parking lot while the Miata was washed and detailed. Royce gave his father another bear hug before watching him climb into his red pickup. "I couldn't have done any of this without you, Dad. Thank you so much."

"It was my pleasure. Take care of yourself, son."

He took his mother and sister for drives on Sunday, and both had built-in agendas for him. He and Jennifer met with Eric for buys (one for him and one for her) and, a little later, he drove his mother for a bulk shopping trip. Both gave the new car rave reviews. As promised, he called Chloe before he started the two hour drive back to Dublin. For the first time, she didn't hear him pull up in front of her building.

"This is a sexy car," she said, walking around it and dragging her fingers across its lines.

"And you'll look hot as all get-out behind the wheel." He handed her the keys. "You need to take it down the street behind the movie theater, toward the river. It's the curviest road I could think of near here."

She drove it like a race car, down-shifting into curves and picking up the throttle just past the apex, the acceleration pushing both of them backward into their seats.

He walked her to her door after the test-drive. "So, we should put in a few hours at the office tomorrow, but I'm fine with leaving mid-afternoon. We can go to dinner early, if you'd like. I know you want to get to Sun's to help with the party prep."

"Sounds good. I should tell you something, though. It's that time of the month again, so no shenanigans."

"Copy that. I'll keep a lid on my raw sexual magnetism."

She shook her head and placed her hand on his chest. "You can't. But do try."

CHAPTER 16

ANACONDA

Darla, Bobby, and Mae all came outside to check out the Miata on Monday morning, but only Darla asked for a ride. Royce considered talking to her about the sales meeting debacle while they were out, but she didn't bring it up and he decided not to. There weren't many curvy roads near the office, but he did his best to show her what the car could do.

"Thank you," she said upon their return to the office. "I didn't get to enjoy too many sports car rides with boys, when I was your age. Nobody wanted to be seen with the little fat girl."

He smiled. "It was my pleasure." Since he didn't know what had happened between her and Sal at Bobby's birthday party, he was not completely comfortable being alone with her. But he was afraid that refusing to take her for a ride, in front of Bobby and Mae, would look even worse.

The afternoon was quiet — not surprising, for New Year's Eve — so they closed the office around 4:00 p.m. After dinner, Chloe drove the Miata to Sun's so she could help with preparations. Royce would come later with David.

Sun had warned her guests that her neighbors would

also be hosting a New Year's Eve party, so stepping out back with a joint would be inadvisable. Royce and David compensated by sharing a bowl at the apartment before stopping by the grocery store for the supplies they'd volunteered to bring. Royce had already bought an inflatable air mattress and a sheet set so he and Chloe could crash in the living room, but they also needed some fruit and cheese, chips and salsa, and a bottle of tequila.

At the liquor store, David read the words Baby Blue on a wine bottle, prompting him to launch into his Bob Dylan imitation, which ruined Royce's efforts to appear sober among the crowd of holiday shoppers. It was a quality impersonation, and it always broke him. After a clumsy transaction, they were back on the road. The car ahead of them was slow to respond at the traffic light and in his best Dylan voice David yelled, "It don't get no greenah! Go!" Royce doubled over with laughter, but managed to compose himself as they pulled up to Sun and her roommate Heather's place. They found the three girls in the kitchen, preparing snacks and dancing to Disc 1 of *Boingo Alive*.

Chloe wore a navy cardigan, a short black skirt, and thigh-high black socks. The three inches of exposed skin between the top of her socks and the bottom of her skirt were mesmerizing. Sun wore a short boyfriend dress and leggings, and gray wool socks with white snowflakes embroidered on them. Her roommate, Heather Jameson, a delightfully curvy young woman with strawberry-blonde curly hair, wore a strategically-unbuttoned maroon blouse and a short denim skirt, with tan stockings. None of them wore shoes, allowing them to slide gracefully across the hardwood floor as they danced. Royce wished he and David had given as much thought to their own attire, though David's Velvet Underground tribute T-shirt was maybe his best work.

Sun and Chloe greeted their dates with hugs, as Heather looked on. "Happy couples," she said, wistfully. Her BBH had broken up with her over Thanksgiving break, citing his frustration with their long-distance arrangement. She wasn't over it, but her planned career in counseling taught her to observe, and studying non-verbal communication was one of her favorite things to do. Royce had been warned that he might feel he was being analyzed.

He made it a point to meet Sun at the fridge, while she checked the sliced beef in her marinade. "I'm sorry I didn't get to meet your mother last weekend."

"Oh, thank you. She missed meeting you, too. I hope my father behaved himself."

"He was fine. Everything went perfectly."

"Listen," she said, almost in a whisper, "Chloe told me about your plan to do a dinner-and-a-movie night during the week. Would it be okay if David and I joined you, from time to time? Please tell me if I'm imposing. I don't mean to."

"Oh, no, not at all! If it's okay with Chloe, it's okay with me."

She reached out and took his hand. "Thank you. We all know David is leaving soon, and he can tell the Video Barn manager he has an evening workshop on Wednesdays and can't work those nights. I'm hoping to spend as much time with him as I can before we have to say goodbye."

Royce was taken aback by her frank acknowledgement that their relationship had an expiration date. He hoped the following months would allow himself to prepare for the same kind of closure. But he didn't want to think about it right then. Heather playfully hip-bumped him out of the way and pulled four ice trays out of the fridge. "Sorry, y'all. Gotta get my Jello shots out!"

Heather's enthusiasm for coaxing her guests into eating the snacks and sucking down Jello shots paled in comparison to her desire to get the poker game underway. As they stood around the marble-topped island in the kitchen, she re-counted the poker chips she had arranged in stacks of eighty, and conducted elaborate shuffles of her favorite deck. Her father was a serious poker enthusiast, spending several weekends a year at any casino within driving distance to play in weekend tournaments. Apparently, he had taught his daughter everything he knew. Royce intently watched her hands as she manipulated the cards.

The doorbell rang, and Sun left to answer it, returning with Carlos. "Sorry," he said. "Nico flaked on me at the last minute. He's staying in town and going to a high school friend's party."

Heather tapped a spoon to a shot glass. "Okay, everyone! This party has officially begun!" She and Sun had invited several of their other friends, as well, but didn't expect any of them until much later in the evening. Heather poured tequila into six shot glasses and topped them with a lime wedge before passing them out. Everyone licked their hand and poured salt onto the wet spot, then clinked their glasses together. Before Royce could lick the salt from his hand, Chloe grabbed it and licked it for him, then offered hers to him. They downed their shots and bit their limes along with the others.

Heather called for the buy-ins. Everyone had been instructed to bring twenty dollars in singles, and in return they were handed eighty poker chips, valued at twenty-five cents each. They all sat at the kitchen table, with Sun and Carlos pulling over bar stools, so they sat a few inches higher than the others. Heather cycled through another complex shuffling routine before dealing a few five-card draw hands with fifty cent antes. Royce was surprised to see how conservatively she played, folding all of her hands before the final round of betting. Then, she introduced everyone to the diabolical but incredibly fun variation known as Anaconda.

Seven cards were dealt face down to every player, after the ante, with the instruction to build the best five card hand they could assemble from the seven cards. The twist came after the first round of betting, when everyone had to pass three cards to the player on their right. If you had a shit hand, this was a great opportunity to add to your pool of cards. If your initial seven cards contained a straight, a flush, or a full house, however, you were fucked, and you had to break it to make the pass. David was the first to suffer this fate, surrendering a flush and losing a large pot with his resulting two-pair hand to Heather's trio of tens. He pulled off his ivy cap and tossed it in the air, combing his hands through his hair in frustration.

Around 10:30, four more of Sun and Heather's friends arrived, announced that they were starving, and batted their eyes at their hostesses, who had promised to feed them. As the new guests introduced themselves to people they didn't already know, Sun heated a wok and began to cook her mother's beef bulgogi dish, while Chloe rolled sausages into pigs-in-a-blanket. Heather force-fed more Jello shots and poured two more rounds of tequila before refilling her serving bowls with snacks. Royce counted the poker chips and settled up the winnings. Carlos and David were the biggest losers, while Chloe and Royce nearly broke even. Heather and Sun both turned a tidy profit.

Sun presented her bulgogi strips with sheets of lettuce to wrap them in, and two different dipping sauces, which Royce named in his head "gut inferno" and "damned near inedible." His palate would need to adjust, and quickly, if Sun would be offering recipes for their Wednesday dinner gatherings.

After another round of tequila shots, the group staggered into the living room to watch the final countdown on MTV's New Year's Eve special. As the clock on the screen struck midnight, Royce grabbed Chloe and pulled her tight to him. She was unsteady on her feet from the alcohol, but he held her straight and true. Their celebratory kiss was deep and intimate, and he couldn't imagine, in the moment, that any future year would be ushered in without the two of them together.

The sound of rushing footsteps from next door, and the first window-rattling explosion, confirmed that Sun and Heather's neighbors had made good on their pledge to drive to South Carolina to buy mortar-style fireworks that were illegal in Georgia. The group hastily put on their shoes and coats and filed out the front door to watch the show. In addition to the artillery, the neighbors had carried their keg to the front yard, and invited them to fill a cup.

Heather decided that the only thing missing was music, and ducked back inside to retrieve her boom box. She pulled the girls together to sing and dance with her in the grass, beneath the showers of dying sparks from the brocade and waterfall shells. Royce was surprised that it took more than an hour for the first police car to arrive. Fortunately, the officer was good-natured and exhausted, and only stopped long enough to warn them about the noise.

The neighbors waited a few minutes before lighting any more fireworks but, determined not to let their long drive for supplies go to waste, reloaded their canisters and quickly launched the final dozen or so rounds. They were stuffing the spent tubes into garbage bags when a second police car pulled up with his red-and-blues flashing. One of the neighbors walked back to the street to assure the officer that they'd made all the noise they'd planned to make. Sun and Heather's foursome of friends said their farewells once the fireworks show was over.

Carlos was not much of a drinker, and was the first to grab a spare blanket and crash on the sofa, barely taking the time to kick off his shoes. Royce slid the coffee table against the wall to clear floor space, and asked Sun for her hair dryer so he could use the cool setting to inflate the air mattress. Returning from the bathroom after taking off her makeup, Chloe sat on the recliner and checked to make sure Carlos was out before she undressed. She traded her sweater and bra for an oversized t-shirt, but Royce most enjoyed watching her slowly slide her thigh-high socks down her long legs and off of her pretty feet. Putting on a sexy show for him apparently did not violate her *no shenanigans* rule.

Royce settled onto his back as she curled up against him. She stroked his face with her fingertips and a whispered, "Happy New Year, Murph. I like you."

"Happy New Year. Something tells me 1991 will be the best ever."

✧   ✧   ✧

Monday, January 7, was a day of milestones. David, Nico, and Carlos all began their final semester at Lancaster, while Chloe started her first. When she arrived at work shortly after eleven, Royce asked in a sing-song voice, "So, how was your first day of school?"

"It was good, thanks! Nico and I have a class in the same building at ten, so we'll be seeing each other every day, probably. He wanted me to ask you if he should kick the ass of anyone he sees sniffing around me."

Royce chuckled. "I'm pretty sure that won't be necessary, but I'll let him know I appreciate the offer."

Bobby called him upstairs later in the afternoon. "I need you to put together one of those neat little summary sheets you do for Daughtry. Last year's numbers and this year's projections. Chuck and I are goin' up there Wednesday."

"Wait, what? Why aren't Chuck and Bess in Florida?"

"Their phone room space won't be available 'til next week. So he's drivin' me to Atlanta."

Royce frowned. He felt he should have been included in the meeting that Sal had normally conducted with Daughtry every January. But he did as Bobby asked, and left a bit early to stop by the computer lab to type up a document that would look as professional as possible. He had already gathered the numbers, because he'd used them for the handbook.

After printing a few copies of his work, he joined the guys for dinner at Calhoun. Since Wednesdays would be date nights at Kingston, he decided Mondays were ideal for a weekly meal with his friends. He looked forward to hearing about their weekends, and what they might have planned for the week ahead. He was not surprised to see a look of despair from Nico and Carlos. In spite of warnings from classmates, both of them had waited until their final semester to take the most feared and notorious required course in their respective majors, leaving them no margin for error.

For Nico's degree in Business Administration, his mandatory course was Policy, a heavy and dense investigation of corporate law that required dozens of hours of outside reading. Carlos faced Analytics, for his major in Sports Management. No course outside of mathematics or computer science demanded such a thorough grasp of numbers and statistics. Neither of them would be able to coast their way to the finish line.

◇ ◇ ◇

THE MARSHALLS CAME to the office mid-morning on Wednesday, so Chuck and Bobby could set out for Daughtry around noon. Royce and Chloe had settled on a red beans and rice dish for their first mid-week dinner-and-a-movie date, and spent some time in the afternoon planning their shopping trip to double the recipe, since Sun and David would be joining them. He looked forward to a screening of *Fandango*. It was one of Royce and David's favorite films, a little-known gem from 1985, with a brand of humor that was perfectly suited to the two of them.

Just before three o'clock, Wendy Smith, the CEO of Daughtry Village, called the office. She and Royce had first spoken back in October, when he called to tell her about Sal's firing and his new position, and they had talked a couple of times since then about the tour schedules and sales figures. She sounded furious.

He did his best to piece together the day's series of events, based on Wendy's emotional description of the meeting. Apparently, Bobby and Chuck had packed thermoses of cocktails for their drive, and drank their way to Atlanta. They had sexually harassed the eighteen-year-old receptionist as they waited in the lobby, and then did the same to Wendy and her assistant once their meeting began.

He fumbled through rushed apologies, careful not to interrupt, as Chloe covered her face with her hands, listening to his side of the conversation. "I am so sorry, Wendy," he said, "I can't even begin to imagine how awful this was for you and your staff."

Wendy explained that she had called security, and had Bobby and Chuck escorted from the building. Royce thought fast, checking his desk calendar. "Could you meet with me on Friday afternoon, maybe? If you have some time? It's a lot to ask, I know, given what happened, but I value our business relationship and I want you to know you would never have to deal with anyone but me or Chloe again, going forward."

"Let me think on that," she said. "The money is important to us, but I need assurances that the members of my team will be safe from this kind of thing. I'd like to meet you and Chloe, though. I'll sleep on it and call you tomorrow."

"Thank you. I look forward to talking with you again tomorrow. Please give my sincere apologies to your assistant and receptionist." He wrote their names onto his calendar after hanging up the phone, and slumped back into his chair. Chloe rushed over and took his face in her hands. "Fucking Christ, Royce! Again?"

"Again." He summarized the conversation for her while she sat on his desk. "So, do you have any plans for the weekend?"

"Well, it sounds like I might be heading to the big city with my man." The prospect of making a weekend out of it with her was intriguing. But he didn't want to get too far over his skis.

He stole a quick kiss and walked upstairs to find the ladies in the living room, watching a movie. "Have either of you heard from Chuck or Bobby today? 'Cause things did *not* go well in Atlanta."

Bess shook her head. "What happened?"

"I'm gonna let them explain themselves to you when they get back. And I need not to be here when that happens." He looked at Darla. "I'll see you tomorrow."

CHAPTER 17

DAUGHTRY

Royce followed Chloe to the grocery store, trying his best to shake off the day's shit-storm so he could enjoy the evening. He had been looking forward to the date night idea since she had proposed it, and had become even more enthusiastic after Sun asked if it could be a double date. Sun was already at the apartment when they arrived, and the three of them squeezed into the tiny kitchen and set to work on dinner. David had brought out his plastic bong, and said that he'd handle the dessert preparations.

Royce cringed as Sun nearly doubled the chili powder and red pepper flakes on the recipe, hoping he still had antacids in the medicine cabinet. The apartment lacked any dining room furniture, so Royce and David were used to eating their meals off the coffee table, hunched over like cavemen on the sofa. Sun and Chloe preferred to sit on the floor pillows, with the table at a far more agreeable height for a dinner service.

David and Royce washed and dried the dishes, as they listened to Chloe's description to Sun of the latest Yawnoc fiasco. They passed around the bong, and David pushed the movie into the VCR. All four somehow managed to curl themselves up onto the three-seat sofa.

Royce was happy to see that Chloe and Sun laughed at *Fandango's* big comedic set-pieces and snappy dialogue, but he was unprepared for their reaction to the wedding scene at the end. Sun brushed away tears as Gardner and Debbie danced together after her marriage to Kenneth. "So sexy, and so sad," she said.

Chloe nodded. "That's how she tells him goodbye. And she'll probably never see him again."

She had spoken spontaneously, without thinking about how her comment might apply to David and Sun, and her words hung in the air, unanswered. As the closing credits rolled to "Can't Find My Way Home," the girls put on their coats, and the guys walked them downstairs to their cars.

✧   ✧   ✧

Royce set his alarm an hour early on Thursday, hoping to catch Mae in the kitchen before the rest of the house woke up. He opened the door from the office to the kitchen and saw Darla sleeping on the living room sofa under an Amish quilt. He motioned for Mae to join him downstairs. She pointed to a ceramic cup, and he gave a thumbs up. She closed the door behind her and handed him a coffee.

"So," he said, "What did I miss yesterday?"

She laughed. "A whole bunch of ugly! Bess asked

Chuck what happened, and he didn't want to talk about it. All he said was they got kicked out of the office. She slapped him across the face so hard that she knocked his glasses off!"

"Good for her!"

"And Darla, she just curled up in a little ball on the floor and wouldn't even talk to Bobby. He tried to explain himself, like bein' drunk was some kind of excuse for actin' shitty, but she just sat there and cried."

"Damn. I have a lot of work to do."

"Yeah, but you can do it. Get 'em some flowers or something, and say you're sorry. Hell, they can't hold it against *you*. You didn't do anything."

✧   ✧   ✧

WENDY CALLED AT 10:30 and agreed to meet with Royce and Chloe on Friday, whenever they could get there. He went upstairs and asked Bobby if he still had the paperwork he'd prepared for their aborted meeting. Bobby slid him the manila folder, but the pages inside were crumpled and stained with cranberry juice.

"Never mind," Royce said in disgust. "I'll print some fresh copies."

"I tried to tell you about split-tails," Bobby began, but Royce interrupted him.

"Don't, Bobby. Just don't. I'm going up there tomorrow afternoon, and I'm taking Chloe with me."

"You're takin' *Chloe*?"

"I am. Don't you think it might be wise to have a woman with me, given what happened yesterday?"

"So y'all are spendin' the weekend together?" His sad blue eyes begged for details.

"You need to be thinking about how I'm gonna fix this. Anything else is a waste of time." He never dreamed that this would be the way his relationship with Chloe would be revealed, but here he was.

He wheeled around and slammed the door behind him, cutting off Bobby's attempts at follow-up questions. He searched for an Atlanta Yellow Pages, but couldn't find one in the office, so he called Jennifer's work number and left a voice message for her to call him when she got to work after her morning class.

He needed to make arrangements, and his sister could read off some phone numbers to give him a head start on them. He could have called his mother, but he knew she'd give him a guilt trip about not coming by, if he was going to be in town. To him, it was a little early for meeting-the-parents, and he was sure Chloe would agree.

Chloe came in a few minutes later, and demanded a thorough briefing on what he'd learned. He told her about his conversations with Mae, Bobby, and Wendy, and concluded by saying, "I don't want to cause any trouble, if Mark and Kim need you. But I'd really appreciate it if you could come with me. We can come back Saturday, if you need to."

She pinched his cheeks. "I'm in for the whole weekend. I talked to them last night."

✧   ✧   ✧

JENNIFER CALLED BACK around lunchtime, and he asked her for the phone numbers of his favorite steak house and his preferred hotel in Buckhead, as well as a couple of fall-back options if they were booked. He also needed the name and address of the florist that he thought he remembered being on the same street as Daughtry's office. He scribbled everything down on a note pad. "Thanks so much, Jen! I'll be in touch."

He made a dinner reservation and gave his credit card number to the hotel to reserve a room on an upper floor for Friday and Saturday nights. He knew Chloe was watching him as he made his calls, and tried in vain to ignore her. When he hung up, she brushed her hair behind her ears, winked, and whispered, "I am already wet," before spinning quickly around and returning to work on the taps.

Later, at his apartment, he held the phone receiver and stared at a scrap of paper with Sal's phone number. He felt horribly that he hadn't reached out once in the last three months, and even worse that he was making this call because he needed help. But Sal immediately put him at ease.

"So good to hear from you, Royce! I'm doing well, thank you. The missus and I spent time with all ten of our grandkids over the holidays, and I don't think I've ever been happier. But how are you doing?"

Royce told him about the December sales meeting, and about the Daughtry fiasco, and asked his advice on dealing with Wendy Smith.

"Wendy's tough, I won't lie. She has zero tolerance for bullshit, so be direct and stick to the facts. Flattery will get you nowhere with her. And don't promise her anything you can't deliver, 'cause she will absolutely call you out on it."

"Thank you, Sal. I'll let you know how it goes."

✧   ✧   ✧

HE WORKED FOR a couple of hours on Friday, and then met Chloe at her place when she'd returned home after her classes. They tossed her weekend bags in the trunk beside his, and he made a beeline south to I-16. He had asked her to bring some cassettes for the drive, and her road-trip-specific mix tapes did not disappoint. He looked down at the speedometer several times to remind himself to slow down.

She turned down the radio soon after they'd merged onto I-75 North in Macon. "Gotta hand it to you on your wardrobe choice," she complimented. "Freshly pressed khakis and a non-threatening yellow Oxford."

She wore the same borrowed skirt from the sales meeting, and the same chunky heels, but with a different blouse and sweater combination. And of course, her sun pendant necklace. "Yours, too," he said. "About as professional as a couple of children can look. I mean, I can't do much about the ponytail and the earring, but I can at least pay attention to what I'm wearing."

They had put another thirty miles behind them, singing along with her tapes all the way, before he spoke again. "So I was thinking about things to do tomorrow. Since you haven't spent much time in Atlanta, maybe we could go to the High Museum, and then over to Little Five Points." He kept to himself that he'd named the idea *culture and counter-culture.*

She shifted in her seat to face him and said simply, "I'm yours. I told you. You can take me anywhere you want. I'm down for whatever you want to do."

His heart swelled. She seemed to find a way to surprise him nearly every day.

She turned toward the passenger window and continued. "I'm still processing my feelings about Bobby Lee Conway knowing that we're *fornicating,* though."

He laughed. "Well, it was gonna come out, sooner or later. I'm not thrilled with it, either."

He exited I-85 at North Druid Hills Road. In the flower shop, he wrote personal notes to Wendy, her assistant, Dorothy, and Cara, the receptionist, while Chloe and the florist put together identical arrangements with red carnations, white asters, and assorted greens. He handed Chloe his pen to sign the notes. He thought it would be important to have no mention of the company on the cards, but rather just their two signatures.

Just after 2:00 p.m., he parked in Daughtry's lot and shut off the engine. He took a deep breath. "Are you ready?"

"Are *you* ready is the better question," she replied with raised eyebrows.

"I hope so."

They entered Daughtry's spacious lobby area and approached the receptionist's desk. "Cara?" he asked. She nodded. "These are for you. I understand our colleagues behaved unforgivably to you a couple of days ago, and I wanted to offer my most sincere apologies. I'm Royce, and this is Chloe. We're here to see Ms. Smith."

Cara rose and accepted the glass vase with a broad smile. "These are beautiful! Thank you! I'll take you to the conference room and tell them you're here." They followed her, and placed the other two vases on the large maple table. The walls were decorated with framed prints of Daughtry's properties, and artistic renderings of houses that were still under construction. He was studying a picture of an expansive location in Augusta when Wendy and Dorothy entered the room.

They all exchanged introductions and handshakes, and then Royce pointed to the portrait. "This is near Memorial, isn't it? My former roommate is a pediatric nurse there. She loves her job."

"It is," Wendy replied. "That facility and the one here in town are our busiest locations."

Royce offered them the flowers. "We are so very sorry for Bobby and Chuck's behavior. I hope you'll accept this as a small token of our regret. I've enjoyed working with you, and Chloe and I admire the work you do here. We want to continue to help."

They all sat down and Royce distributed the papers. "The 1990 dates showed a 12% increase over '89, and I'm sure we can do better with the upcoming tours. We have added one new date for the spring that is a Daughtry exclusive. I believe Covington is as close to the Metro area as we have ever come for a show. It's new ground, but it has a lot of potential. And if you or anyone on your staff could come to the performance, I'll make sure that Chloe and I are the only ones from the office at the show. You would be our honored guests."

Wendy did not change her expression. He estimated that she was roughly twice his age, and he concentrated on meeting her gray-eyed stare. "I appreciate the time you put into this," she said, rather coldly. "And I'm willing to give the show another tour to see how the numbers come out. But you must understand our public perception is in part tied to the circus. And, frankly, we cannot continue this partnership if there is another... *incident*. I'd also like to request that Chuck Marshall not be allowed to do any sales for our dates." This wouldn't be a problem, since the Marshalls hated doing campaigns for anything but local sponsors.

"I do understand. And if you ever have a need to call the office, and the phone is answered by anyone other than Chloe or me, just hang up and call back later. Please leave it to the two of us to take care of your concerns."

"Thank you for coming all the way up here," she said, managing the faintest hint of a smile. "And thank you for the flowers. I can see you both are thoughtful and professional, and you certainly make a handsome couple. I know you're aware of my concerns, and I appreciate that, too." He felt his cheeks flush. He didn't dare make eye contact with Chloe.

They talked a little while longer, about Daughtry's support from various charitable foundations in the area, along with particulars of the circus and its acts, though *handsome couple* kept ricocheting across the back of his mind.

Wendy checked her watch and rose abruptly. Dorothy followed suit. "I need to make some calls, before the afternoon completely gets away from me. It was a pleasure meeting you both, and I hope you have a safe trip home."

"Thank you for your time," Royce replied. "I will do a much better job of keeping in touch with you."

Royce and Chloe walked silently to the car, and neither spoke until they had both closed their doors. "Oh, my fucking god," he said. "We are *terrible* at keeping this secret, apparently."

"It looks that way, doesn't it?" she giggled.

He drove to their hotel, checked them in and sent her upstairs with their bags and a bellman while he found a spot in the parking garage. When he got to the room, she had kicked off her shoes and cranked the heat insanely high.

"Dinner reservation's at six-thirty, right?" she asked. He nodded. "Okay, love. Relax for a bit. I know today has been super stressful for you."

"Thank you." They snuggled on the bed for a while and flipped absently through the TV channels before freshening up for dinner.

They both ordered filets, cooked medium, and chose grit fritters and sautéed broccoli as their sides. Chloe loved the unique decor and the attentive staff. Their waiter seemed particularly taken with her, and patiently answered all of her wide-eyed questions about the menu and his experiences. (The most famous person he'd ever served was Robert Redford, who left a $100 tip.) They glanced around the room over dinner and wine to see if they could identify any local VIPs.

Picking up the car afterward, he asked if there was anything else she'd like to do or see before going to back to the hotel. "I'm beat, actually, and I know you must be, too. Let's just go and chill." It was music to his ears. He took out his Zippo and lit one of the two joints he'd stashed in the glove box for the weekend. They only had time for a couple of drags apiece before carefully extinguishing the cherry in the parking garage and saving the rest for later.

The thermostat in the room was still set to her tropical temperature, so he stripped to his boxers while she disappeared to the bathroom with her overnight bag. He opened the curtains, admiring the southern view of downtown, with its tallest buildings firing their lights into the low-lying clouds and creating halos. It was not a perspective he could enjoy in Dublin. He turned off all the lamps except for the small one on the desk, and found his favorite Atlanta station on the clock radio. Sitting upright against the headboard, he stretched his legs out in front of him and tried to relax.

She opened the door and posed for him with her hands on the frame, backlit by the bathroom light. The white silk camisole and panty combination he'd given her fit even better than he'd hoped. She flicked off the light and walked slowly toward him.

"You are so unbelievably sexy," he sighed. "May I see the back?"

She turned slowly in a circle, with her arms out-stretched, and bent over at the waist when her back was to him. "I'll tell my wardrobe consultant that you approve of his choices."

She climbed on the bed and onto his lap, straddling him. "I was so proud of you today," she said, with a gentle kiss. "Until you said whatever you did to tip Wendy off about us."

He scoffed, brushing her hair behind her ears. "Oh, really? You're sure it was me? I think maybe your expressions betrayed us. What about that?" He was learning to give as well as he got.

She tapped her chin. "Okay, maybe I did. But like I said, I don't care anymore. I'm dropping this burden, effective right fucking *now*."

He undressed her slowly and reverently, and the

encounter that followed reminded him very much of their first time, though on a much larger bed. Tender, passionate, and best of all, unhurried.

✧　✧　✧

THEY VISITED THE High Museum on Saturday, after having lunch at one of his favorite Buckhead delis. As she stood in the atrium and looked upward at the white spiral ramp that led to the upper floors, he asked if she'd ever seen the 1986 film *Manhunter*, and briefly described the plot. "It sounds familiar," she said. "Maybe I watched it on video." He told her the film was so stylized that the asylum where the protagonist goes to visit Dr. Lecktor was filmed there, inside the museum.

They held hands and walked slowly through the exhibition areas, pointing out things that caught their attention. A popular temporary exhibit on the ground floor drew most of the foot traffic that day, so they didn't have to fight a crowd to tour at their own pace.

When they made their way back down to the lobby, he noticed a pair of pay phones near the restrooms. He had a dangerous question to ask, and prefaced it with a caveat. "If it's too soon, please tell me, okay? No pressure at all. But I wanted to ask what you thought about having an early lunch with Jennifer tomorrow, on our way out of town."

She raised her eyebrows and blinked a few times. Stepping closer and wrapping her arms around the back of his neck, she beamed at him. "I would love to meet your sister. Yes."

He held her close and whispered, "Thank you," before feeding a quarter into the slot and dialing his mother's number. He could only hope Jennifer would be the one to answer. She did, and they set up an 11:00 date at the Bennigan's across from Southlake Mall. She kept her voice low, so as not to arouse any suspicions from their mother. They hoped the early meeting time would allow them to beat the busy after-church crowd.

CHAPTER 18

WAR

Royce and Chloe left the museum and he took her to the neighborhood known as Little Five Points. The day was bright and sunny, but bitterly cold, with a steady wind blowing in from the north. He indulged her every whim as she excitedly entered record shops, vintage clothing stores, and a couple of specialty boutiques. They agreed to head back to Ponce for dinner at Fellini's Pizza.

On the way back to the hotel, he lit the remains of the joint they'd abandoned the night before and passed it to her. From the corner of his eye, he noticed her staring at him, and waited thirty seconds or so to see if she'd speak first. She didn't.

"Something on your mind?" he asked.

"Yeah. I wanted to apologize in advance for this mood I'm in, in case you don't share it."

He took a long drag at a red light and blew the smoke through the crack at the top of his window. "Well, that's either promising or terrifying. Which is it?"

"The prospect of sex in hotels sometimes makes me, um, *rowdy.*"

"Rowdy, you say? You have my full and undivided attention."

"Well, you know." She shifted uncomfortably in her seat. "We've never done it, but I was thinking that sometimes it might be fun to… play rough."

He nodded, but didn't reply, and they were both silent for the remainder of the drive. At the last traffic light before turning into the parking garage, she took a final, carefully-pinched drag and flicked the tiny roach out the window. They caught an empty elevator from the lobby to their room on the thirtieth floor. As the floor counter chimed, he turned abruptly and stepped toward her, pressing her back against the wall with his hands on her hips.

He opened his mouth wide and bared his teeth on her neck, while sliding his right hand between her legs and pressing his fingers against her. She gasped, closing her eyes. "Are you sure about this, mister?"

"I am very sure."

Before the door to their room had fully closed behind them, they began undressing themselves and each other, with clothes flying in all directions. She quickly stepped sideways, with her hands on his chest, and pushed him backward onto the bed. She retreated to the bathroom and took a condom from his shaving kit. He raised himself up onto his elbows so he could watch her. His knees were bent over the base of the mattress, with the balls of his feet barely touching the carpet. He watched as she tossed the wrapper aside and rolled the condom onto him. She drew him inside of her slowly, but soon sat upright and began to ride him, fast and deep.

He reached up to her breasts, but she grabbed his wrists and guided his hands back down. The fire in her brown eyes wordlessly confirmed the challenge: his agenda would have to be implemented by force. He attempted to sit up, but she slapped her hands to his shoulders and pushed him back onto the bed, following him down and pressing her chest to his. Pinning his forearms over his head with a surprisingly strong grip, she climaxed, loudly and triumphantly.

He lacked leverage, since his feet weren't firmly on the floor, but knew he needed to act quickly to turn the game in his favor. There was plenty of room on the bed to his right, so he raised his left leg high enough to get his foot onto the mattress. Quickly extricating his arms from her grip, he wrapped them around her back tightly, pushed down hard with his left leg and rolled them both over until he was on top of her. She giggled at how swiftly her fortunes had reversed, but almost immediately began to squirm beneath him, trying to push him back over.

He would have none of it, easily securing her hands with his and restraining them on the mattress above her head. She struggled in vain for a few more seconds before surrendering. "Okay, then," she whispered. "Fuck me."

He did, as if his very life depended on it. She had ignited a segment of his psyche he had rarely explored, but always knew was there. He shifted his grip to secure both of her wrists with only his left hand, and used his right to collect a handful of hair at the base of her neck. Biting down on her shoulder, he increased the pace and depth of his thrusts until she wrapped her legs around his back and cried out. The intensity of her orgasm sent him over the edge, and he came with heat and fury.

When he released her hands, she took the back of his head and pulled his mouth to hers. She kissed him wickedly, her tongue wild and busy. Stopping suddenly, she pressed her forehead to his and said, "*God*, yes."

They rested on their backs, still breathing heavily, side by side in the darkness. She raised her hands near her face and flipped her wrists back and forth, examining them. "I'm meeting your sister for the first time tomorrow. You better not have left any bruises on me, fucker."

He chuckled. "Sex bruises don't count. Besides, you still like me."

"No." She rolled onto her left side, facing him. "I love you."

Hearing the words he had been waiting for and had longed to say, he felt as though all the air in his lungs had been sucked out. He rolled onto his side and gently cradled her face in his hand. "I love you, too." He inched closer and they wrapped their bare arms and legs around each other. Both of them were trembling.

✧   ✧   ✧

THEY CHECKED OUT of the hotel at 10:30 on Sunday morning and drove south. Jennifer was standing near the restaurant's hostess station when they came through the door, and Royce greeted his sister with a warm hug before making introductions.

"May I?" Jennifer asked, reaching tentatively for the sun pendant. Chloe nodded. "I was with him when he bought this. It's beautiful on you."

"Thank you! I love it, but I told him it was too much."

They were shown to a table, but barely glanced at the menus. The conversation was fast and animated. Jennifer asked how their weekend had gone, and Chloe excitedly recounted their visit to the High and Little Five Points. "And the business meeting?" Jennifer asked.

"It went okay," Royce offered with a shrug. "They didn't fire us."

Chloe reached over and took his hand. Looking at Jennifer, she said, "He's being modest. He kicked ass."

"So this circus company is not at all like a standard business?"

Chloe threw her head back and laughed, "Ha! Yeah, you could say that. I blame this one," she said, pointing her thumb toward Royce. She adopted a phony deep voice, mocking him. *"Five dollars an hour, cash on Fridays. Just a simple data entry program. Just need twenty hours a week.* He conveniently left out the part about the owner being an unpredictable raging alcoholic, and that most of the sales reps are ne'er-do-wells at best, and criminals at worst."

Jennifer cackled. "Wow! Good thing y'all have each other, at least!"

Chloe asked about Jennifer's weekend, and she said she'd had a date the night before with a guy from her class. Royce pointed the tines of his fork toward Chloe. "I would never have heard about this if you weren't here." Jennifer stuck her tongue out at him.

They told tales about their families and laughed at one another's funny stories until well after the plates had been cleared. Royce took note of the dining area filling with patrons who stopped for lunch on their way home from church, and suggested they give up their table.

Chloe and Jennifer hugged goodbye, and said they hoped they would see each other again soon. Royce walked Jennifer to her car while Chloe started the Miata and turned on the heater. Jennifer embraced her brother warmly and smiled broadly. "I love her!" she said.

"I do, too."

✿ ✿ ✿

They were mostly quiet on their way back to Dublin. They had shared what amounted to a 48-hour high, packed with milestone moments and important words, and the impending return to routine weighed heavily on both of them. For his part, he recognized the significance of her meeting with Jennifer, and vowed to himself to spend more time with her family when he picked her up or dropped her off. He didn't have to wait long for the opportunity.

When they entered Chloe's apartment, Mark was working on a new arrangement of photos of Jacob and he and Kim were trying to figure out where they should hang on the wall. Jacob was fussy, but lit up when he saw Chloe. "Give me a few minutes, please? I'll be right back." She hustled to her bedroom with her suitcase.

Royce stepped forward. "I'd be happy to take him," he offered, and walked over to sit on the sofa with Jacob. He kicked off his shoes and put his feet on the base of the coffee table to let the baby sit on his lap and rest backward against his thighs. He offered his index fingers, which Jacob gripped tightly in his tiny hands. He and Chloe had been listening to the B-52's *Cosmic Thing* cassette in the car, so he sang "Roam" and had Jacob do the hand-claps in the chorus by tapping his fingers together.

Chloe hustled back into the living room, stopping in her tracks and pursing her lips at Royce. "You're singing the B-52's. To a baby."

"Well, first of all, he doesn't seem to mind. And I couldn't think of any baby songs off the top of my head."

Kim called from across the room, "Those are nice, happy lyrics, Chloe. I would have said something if he was singing Metallica to him."

Chloe stuck her tongue out at him.

ON MONDAY MORNING, Royce conducted the weekly audit of his desk calendar and Chloe's task list, making sure they were in sync and matched the tap print-outs and tickets that waited in the shoeboxes for the reps to pick up or to have mailed to them. All of the teams, save for the Marshalls, had begun their second campaign for the spring tour, and Chloe was nearly finished with the taps for their third. The tickets for these were already in the boxes, with another round to be finished by Strickland on Friday.

Bobby came down to the office with a lit cigarette as Royce was finishing the audit. He took a long drag before asking with a smirk, "So, how was your weekend?"

"It was good. We had a good time."

"I bet you did!" Bobby replied lasciviously, with a laugh so long and hearty that it ended with wheezing and coughing. He continued, when he managed to get air back into his lungs. "What about Daughtry?"

"They're going to give us the spring tour, at least, and take a look at the numbers again, afterward. But they don't want any contact from anyone here, except for Chloe or me."

"Fine with me! Buncha tight-asses."

"Are we done? I have a lot of work to do."

"Then you'd best get to it," Bobby said, dropping an inch of ash onto the carpet as he turned and went back to the kitchen. Royce waited until the door closed to do an audit of the petty cash and the money in the safe. *You should have asked me if the hotel room was nice,* Royce thought with satisfaction, *since you paid for it.*

✧   ✧   ✧

ROYCE WAS SHUT out of the planning for Wednesday's

dinner double-date, which was to be a surprise from the girls, so he and David played *Bad Dudes* on the Nintendo while Sun and Chloe put together their ingredients and cooked. Royce shuddered to think about how many quarters he and David had shoved into the *Bad Dudes* arcade game at the mall, so David had bought the game the day it was released for the home platform. Sun and Chloe came into the living room, each carrying two plates. They had made gyoza, along with a fried rice side and steamed broccoli. They both were beaming with pride, and offered plates to their guys. "Wow," David said, "This looks and smells amazing!"

"It does!" Royce offered. "Thank y'all so much for doing this."

As they were finishing dinner, David's father called. David took the phone into his bedroom, but quickly returned to the living room. Cupping his hand over the microphone, he said, "Dude, put it on CNN. We're at war."

Royce scrambled to find the remote and change the channel, while Chloe pulled her feet onto the sofa and said, "Oh, shit." He positioned himself behind her and wrapped her in his arms. They watched the grainy footage for half an hour without saying a word. He combed her hair with his fingers as she listened to the reports. "I'd feel a lot better if I only knew what ship Michael was on."

"Not sure it would matter, at the moment," David replied. "Looks like cruise missile strikes and Apache helicopters, for now. Dad said they'll send in A-10

Warthogs and other bombers to hit the tanks and ground forces, once their radar and anti-aircraft sites have been disabled."

"But they've been bragging about those Scud missiles, and threatening chemical weapons," Chloe said, wiping tears with her napkin.

David shook his head. "The Scuds are mostly junk, and even if they find targets, they'll be in Saudi Arabia and Israel, to try to bust the coalition. Every one of those explosions you see is one fewer piece of what meager offense they had." He looked at Chloe and tried to comfort her. "This will be over soon."

Sun put her hand on Chloe's knee and squeezed. "I'm so sorry. Your brother and your family will be in my thoughts."

"Mark!" Chloe exclaimed. Royce handed her the phone. "I should call him and see if he's watching this." She took the phone into Royce's bedroom.

Royce asked David, "Do you really believe everything you just said to her?"

"Yeah, I do. But I'm a little worried about the chemical warfare, too. No telling what they'll do, once they're forced to retreat."

Chloe came back from the bedroom and said, "I called my parents, too." She returned to the sofa and curled up under Royce's arm. He kissed the back of her head and held her tight.

✧   ✧   ✧

Over the next couple of weeks, Royce tried to memorize every conversation he had with David, as they watched CNN for nightly updates, and paid particular attention to anything David learned from his father. Dr. Carson's name was already being mentioned as someone who might be part of the team to help restore public utilities to Kuwait, once it was liberated and a cease-fire was established.

Royce spent the next two weekends at Chloe's, passing along anything comforting he had heard and trying to explain what might happen next, based on what David and his father had discussed. Fortunately, Michael had been able to call their parents a couple of times. He couldn't reveal many details, but assured everyone he was fine. He was not on a carrier, he said, but he was part of a strike group and on call to the carrier if needed. He was a hospital corpsman, so he joked that he had treated two crew members who had fallen down the stairs on the ship while hustling to their duty assignment, and another sailor who'd gotten his hand crushed between two heavy ordnance boxes while moving them. "Same thing I'd be doing in Japan."

Chloe was not feeling particularly amorous on those weekends, with Mark, Kim, and Jacob at home, and with all of them worried about Michael. But Royce was content simply to sleep with her, and to comfort her as best as he could. It was a different kind of intimacy, and one he had not felt in a long time. Every shared "I love you" before she turned off her bedside lamp brought them closer, and he was happy to be able to support her and her family as she had supported him in his work.

✿   ✿   ✿

Sun's birthday was on a Thursday in early February, so Wednesday's dinner-and-a-movie date was moved in her honor. Royce and David attempted a baked ziti with spicy Italian sausage, though David was only trusted with the garlic bread, pasta, and salad. Royce didn't want to poison their guests with undercooked meat, fearing that David's thirst for instant gratification might be dangerous to their health. He thought about his first brush with David's impatience, when they'd gone on a trip to Athens to see a band of Lancaster graduates play. They were stopped on Highway 441 due to an accident, and David grew more frustrated by the minute. After nearly an hour, he exploded. "When we get up there, I'd better see body parts scattered all over the fucking highway!"

Chloe and Sun competed in a spirited game of UNO on the coffee table while the men tried to plate an appetizing dish. After dinner, Royce and Chloe presented Sun with their gift; a matching pearl necklace and earring set. She was overjoyed, put them on immediately. David gave her a collection of CDs and VHS movies he had specifically selected for her, though the implication that these were titles to remember him by was not lost on anyone, and hung in the air like a fog. Fortunately, they'd chosen a light comedy, *The Princess Bride,* for their movie that night, so any lingering tension was soon forgotten.

As Chloe was putting on her coat and saying good-bye to Sun, David leaned over to Royce and whispered, "Okay with you if she stays tonight?"

"Of course. Y'all have a good night."

He walked Chloe to her car, then turned on CNN to see if there were any new updates from Kuwait. Neither David nor Sun were very vocal in bed, perhaps because they knew they weren't alone in the apartment, but David's squeaky bed frame delivered a play-by-play through the living room wall. Royce smiled. He was happy for them, and had come to love Sun like a sister, but couldn't help but feel sad that David had waited until six months before graduation to make his play for her. He went to bed and pulled the bookmark from his new copy of *L.A. Confidential* by James Ellroy to read before bedtime. Glancing at his wall calendar, he realized the spring tour would open in Homosassa Springs, Florida the next day.

CHAPTER 19

DESTIN

At work, the tension that had been building between Darla and Bobby since the unpleasantness at Daughtry had become unsustainable. Their arguments had spilled from the bedroom into the kitchen throne area, causing Royce and Chloe to exchange cringes when raised voices and harsh words bled through the door into the office, to the point that Royce actively encouraged the reps to give him PO Box addresses so he could send the taps and tickets for their next campaign, rather than having anyone come by the office.

On the day before Valentine's, during another heated argument in the kitchen, Royce overheard that Darla's daughter, Bridget, was bringing a van to the house around noon. He met Chloe at the door when she rolled up at 11:00 and said, "We should go and take a long lunch." She nodded and followed him to his car. As they pulled out of the circular driveway, Mae was dragging Bobby into the passenger seat of her Ranger to get him out of the house for a while.

They passed by Sammy's Bar on their return from lunch, and Royce was happy to see that Mae's truck was still in the parking lot. He parked alongside a white

Chevy conversion van with its back doors open. Several moving boxes were on the ground behind it, and Darla and a younger version of herself were struggling to drag a wooden steamer trunk down the brick steps from the kitchen door.

"Let me help you, please," he said, and extended his hand to Darla's daughter. "You must be Bridget." She had her mother's blue eyes, and paired them with a sunny disposition and the exuberance of youth. She couldn't have been more than eighteen years old.

"Thanks," she replied in a Deep South drawl. "We can barely lift these. We slid 'em on the floor most of the way."

He looked at Darla. "Is this the last of it, or is there more downstairs?"

"This is it. We saved the trunk 'til last. Not smart."

He packed the boxes into the van and made sure everything was loaded in a way that would be easiest to get out. He assumed they were bound for Darla's home in Tifton. "Would you talk with me, for a few minutes, before y'all head out? I have questions," said Royce. Darla nodded, and led them into the kitchen.

Bridget turned on the TV in the living room and curled up on the sofa while Darla, Royce, and Chloe sat around the bar. Darla spoke first, pulling a box of tissues toward her and gripping one in her fist. "You want to know about Sal."

"Yeah, I do."

She nodded, dabbing at tears that had already started

to form in the corners of her eyes. "I'm so sorry about this. I am. I know you won't believe it. But I went along with Chuck."

"So, Sal wasn't stealing from the company?"

"No. Chuck and Sal never got along, and Chuck had been wanting him gone for a long time. He'd been talking to Bobby for weeks, about trips that Sal and his wife had taken, trying to convince Bobby the Russos were living well beyond what he was being paid. Planting a seed, you know?"

"I understand. But what happened at the birthday party? And how?"

She smiled. "Well, it had a lot to do with *you*, actually." Chloe was seated behind him at the bar, and felt him bristle at Darla's comment. She dragged her fingernails back and forth across his shoulders, trying to comfort him. He reached back and rested his left hand on her thigh.

Darla continued. "At the party, Chuck walked Bobby around Sal's house, over-valuing every collectible and piece of furniture in the place, trying to reinforce the idea that he was stealing. Bobby was finally drunk enough to believe him."

"And then it was your turn," Royce said, his tone surprisingly calm.

Darla reached for another tissue. "Yes. Chuck took me aside and told me this was the day to strike. I followed Sal to the kitchen and kept him in there, talking, for twenty minutes or so. Bobby was stewing on the back porch. Every now and again, Chuck would wonder out loud where I was."

Royce shook his head. "This is unbelievable. But, oddly, it's also pretty close to what I figured. And it's why I wasn't crazy about taking you for a ride in the Miata. Being alone with you."

"That's fair. I get it." She dabbed more tears. "So I went to the porch and told my lie, Bobby screamed at Sal and fired him, then stormed out. I grabbed Mae as fast as I could, so we could follow him back here."

"And everything changed, just like that." Royce snapped his fingers. Chloe leaned forward to rest her forehead on his back.

"I couldn't face Sal the next day. When Bobby and the deputy went down to the office, I ran to the bedroom and hid. I was so ashamed. I still am." Her slow tears dissolved into sobs, but Royce wasn't willing to let her off the hook.

"You said the timing was about me. What do you mean?"

Darla gathered herself. "Ever since Sal hired you, Bobby's been talking about how smart you are. Chuck figured he would offer you the job first, and said you'd be competent enough to keep things from turnin' to complete shit, but young enough to be intimidated into doin' whatever we wanted."

Royce felt cold. He checked to make sure he was still

breathing. The thought of being talked about this way, behind his back, was nauseating.

Darla shrugged her shoulders. "Chuck and I were right about the first part, but wrong about the second."

He squeezed Chloe's thigh, silently begging that this was the end of the conversation and Darla and Bridget would leave soon. Instead, Darla walked back to the master bedroom to check one more time that she had collected all of her belongings. He took Chloe's hand and led her downstairs to the office.

"Just damn," she said, shaking her head. "Are you sure you want to stay here?"

It was a valid question, and one he'd thought a lot about, especially after the sales meeting fiasco and the Daughtry kerfuffle. As he was collecting his thoughts, Darla and Bridget walked out, climbed into the van, and drove away. Neither of them looked back.

He flopped in his chair and motioned for Chloe to join him. She sat on his desk, facing him, and put her feet on the seat between his legs. He slipped off her Keds and moved her sock feet to his thighs, taking her ankles in his hands.

"Yes, I'm sure I want to stay here. And as much as I hate to lead off with the money, it's important. If I went back to Atlanta and found an entry-level job related to my degree, I'd be lucky to get thirty grand a year. And with the lower standard of living, forty thousand here is probably the equivalent of forty-five or maybe fifty, in the city. You watched me drop a few hundred dollars on kitchen supplies I needed. Well, I'm about to have to spend ten times that amount to furnish my own place. And I'm looking forward to it. I've struggled long enough, and now I want to see what it's like to have a little spending power."

She nodded and flexed her toes, pushing them down against his legs.

"Besides, even if I did find a job in Atlanta that paid well, who's to say my boss there wouldn't also be an unpredictable alcoholic with a brain full of backwards views? The devil I know against the one I don't, you know?"

She laughed, inching forward on the desk and leaning close to stroke his face with her hands. He pulled himself as close as he could, until the arm rests of his chair hit the desk.

"Secondly," he continued, "I enjoy the work, and I feel like I'm good at it. A few months ago I didn't think either of those would be the case, but it's true. It's gratifying. I watched Sal for months, marveling at all the balls he kept in the air, and now I'm doing the same thing. Plus, I faced down Chuck at the sales meeting, and maybe even rescued the Daughtry relationship."

She kissed him, soft and tender. "You're right. You're doing great."

He blushed, but wanted to add one more point. "And I have other people to consider. You have become so important to me in such a short time, and it would kill me to face any kind of uncertainty with us if I were to leave here. I wake up every day with a smile, because I know I'll get to spend the afternoon here with you."

She tilted her head, a little confused. "There's no uncertainty. We're a team, now. I love you."

He took a deep breath as a broad smile stretched across his face. "I can't wait for you to see the expressions from the children who come to the shows. Joey and Gloria do such a great job of making it a big event for the audience, and I love helping them."

She edged herself off of the desk and stood up, taking his hands in hers. "This would normally be the point where I would ask you to take me to your bed. But Mark is still out of town until tomorrow afternoon, and I'm needed at home."

He stood and pulled her into his arms. "I know. Remind me to find us a hotel for the 23rd. *Silence of the Lambs* tomorrow night?"

"A horror movie for Valentine's Day? How could I resist?"

He watched her leave, balancing her sarcastic parting words against the knowledge that a dozen roses were waiting for her at her place. Fortunately, he was already on his way home before Mae and Bobby came back from the bar.

He had failed to call Sal back after the meeting at Daughtry, but did reach out that evening to report Darla's confession and departure from Dublin. Sal snickered and said, "Well, I'm glad she finally came clean."

"It went down pretty much how I had suspected, back in October," Royce said. "I never believed any of their shit for a second, and I have been wary of them, just like you said."

"I knew you wouldn't fall for it, Royce. And I want to thank you for doing such a good job with the show. Joey tells me he trusts you, and that you're doing fine. I appreciate that."

"I won't let you down, Sal."

He had no idea why Orion Pictures would choose to release an intense psychological thriller on Valentine's Day, but he had been looking forward to a possible film adaptation ever since he'd read the book two years prior. David was green with envy that Royce would get to see the movie first. He would be working at the Video Barn, but made plans to see it with Sun the following evening. He threatened to smother Royce in his sleep if he gave away any spoilers.

He took Chloe to the most expensive restaurant in Dublin for dinner, a steak and seafood place called Quint's, as a thank you for indulging his choice of movie. Without giving away too much, he tried to prepare her for the story and what he thought might be the most disturbing scenes. And he had another surprise: he'd booked a room in a small beachside hotel in Destin, Florida, for their trip to Niceville to meet the show. It would only be a thirty minute drive between the two locations and, even though it was February, he was excited to spend some time at the shore with his sun goddess.

She watched much of the film through her fingers, curled up against him as tightly as the armrest would allow. Even though he knew the story, the screen adaptation chilled his bones with its ferocity and brutality. They walked out of the theatre toward the end of the closing credits behind a trio of high-school girls. Chloe snaked her hand through the bend in his elbow, sighed, and put on a sarcastically loving and breathy tone. "You know, I just can't decide which was more romantic. That time when the crazy guy in the prison slung his spunk in her face, or the other guy telling his prisoner to put the lotion on her skin."

The girls stopped in their tracks and turned in unison to laugh at her commentary. Royce could only shrug his shoulders. "I know. She kills me like that pretty much every day."

They took full advantage of David's work schedule, and went back to Kingston after the movie. He lit a couple of candles in his bedroom, and they shared a prolonged and gentle period of foreplay, teasing each other with every touch of their fingers and tongues as they undressed one another slowly. He heard David enter the living room, just as Chloe climbed on top of him, and he pictured his roommate hustling to his bedroom for his headphones. Chloe was not quiet.

✧   ✧   ✧

NINE DAYS LATER, they were off on another adventure. The show had only been on the road for a couple of weeks, but the two Homosassa Springs dates that opened the tour were traditionally the most lucrative events on the spring schedule, and Joey Vegas was flush with cash and anxious to be relieved of most of it. Royce picked Chloe up on Saturday morning, and they sped southwest toward the coast. Had it not been so cloudy, with rain in the forecast, he would have dropped the convertible top once they hit the Florida line.

They checked into the hotel in the afternoon, and Chloe flung open the windows to allow the warm sea air to blow into their room as she took a deep breath. She pulled an oversized towel from her overnight bag, traded her flats for sandals, and pulled him out the door and down to the beach. The tide was receding, so she picked a spot where the dry sand met the distinctive gray saturation from high tide, and spread out her towel. They sat without speaking for nearly an hour, with his arm around her waist and her head on his shoulder. People walked by, both in front and behind them, but neither acknowledged the presence of anyone else in the world.

He checked his watch and spoke, reluctantly. "Do you want to go back to the room and freshen up before we need to leave?"

"I probably should. I'm sure my hair's a disaster."

He stood behind her, with his hands around her waist, as she fiddled with her hair in the bathroom mirror. The agreeable dark brown mess reminded him of the photo of her with her brothers on Tybee's North Beach. "Do you think I have time to shower?" she asked his reflection.

He pulled the shoulder strap of her powder blue tank top down to her bicep and kissed the skin he'd exposed. "I wish you wouldn't. You smell like a combination of coconut oil and sea air. Like what I thought the beautiful girl in the photo with the lighthouse would smell like. We became a couple in the winter, and I know it's not your preferred season."

She smiled and shook her head. "It's really not."

✿　✿　✿

They made it to the parking lot of the National Guard armory in Niceville a few minutes after five, and Royce parked the Miata beside Joey's RV. They climbed the steps and knocked. Joey answered, wearing a gold track suit. His toupee sat sideways, and Royce wondered if they had interrupted his preparations. Joey was gracious and welcoming. "Come in, please! I am happy to see you both!"

He opened the gate to Lord Connelly's cage, and the little horse bounded out to meet Chloe. She dropped to her knees and hugged his neck. "How beautiful you are!"

"I'm sure he could use a brushing," Joey offered, nodding to an array of supplies on his sofa's end table. Chloe took the brush and set to work on his ivory mane and tail, cooing at her new four-legged friend.

Joey handed Royce a zippered vinyl bank bag of cash,

with a receipt page on the inside noting the total, and a breakdown of each tour date. Royce counted carefully, and verified the numbers. He slipped the bag into Chloe's purse.

"Now, I really should be backstage," Joey said. "Y'all are welcome to walk with me." He led Lord Connelly back into his cage, and pulled a hanging bag containing his tuxedo from his small closet. Chloe kissed the horse on his forehead and told him she'd see him later. Joey asked a couple of stage-hands to bring Lord Connelly to the dressing room.

They followed Joey to the bustling backstage area and found an out-of-the-way spot to sit and watch the preparations. Royce pointed out everything he could remember about the individual acts as they hustled past, as Chloe listened intently, until Lady Gloria entered the area with a handler carrying Ashanti in her cage. "You have to see this," he said, "I hope she remembers me." He led Chloe to the leopard.

He introduced Chloe to Lady Gloria and, with her permission, he lowered a small metal panel on the door of Ashanti's cage and offered the back of his hand for her to sniff. The black cat nuzzled him and accepted his caresses.

"Put your hand on his," Lady Gloria instructed Chloe. "Slowly. Let her smell you, too." She interlaced her fingers with his, and they rubbed the big cat's fur together.

Chloe rested her head on his shoulder and whispered, "This is unreal." He knew the feeling, exactly.

He looked at his watch again. "We should probably go and find something to eat, before the show." The sound tech Sal introduced him to at the Dublin show in September walked up, overhearing Royce's comment.

"Hey," he said, speaking to Royce but looking at Chloe, "There's a good barbecue place a couple of blocks north of here. A bunch of us had dinner there yesterday when we got into town."

"That sounds good!" Chloe replied enthusiastically. "What are those?" She pointed to the two orange traffic cones the tech held in his hands. The word RESERVED was written on them in a thick black marker.

"Oh, yeah. Joey said I should put these on the top bleacher at stage left, to save y'all a place."

"How sweet of you! Thank you!" She beamed at him and he blushed a deep crimson. Royce took her hand and they left to find the restaurant.

He studied the menu, but glanced up to see her looking at him. "Are you okay?" he asked.

"Well, let's see," she replied with a tap to her chin. "My man has driven me to the coast, where I have VIP seating to a show. In the meantime, I have brushed a tiny miniature horse, and rubbed the ears of a black panther. I'm a little overwhelmed."

He smiled and nodded. "I had the same reaction when Sal introduced me to everyone in Dublin. We don't have many perks in this job, but there are a few."

✧   ✧   ✧

THEY ATE DINNER quickly, and returned to take their seats a few minutes before the show began. Royce surveyed the crowd, which appeared to have far more groups of chaperoned children than families, in contrast to the Dublin performance. He suspected this was a more affluent area, and that local businesses and residents had purchased tickets and donated them, rather than attending themselves.

Joey's welcome was roughly the same, and the Zhou twins again opened the show with their act, but their costumes were new and the order of their formations had been altered. Royce paid far more attention to Chloe than to the show itself, taking great pleasure in watching her reactions to the acts. She sat on the edge of her seat, gripping his hand, laughing at the clowns and marveling at the monkey act.

Lady Gloria led Ashanti through her routine, the black cat fiercely baring her teeth and lashing at the air with her claws. "Yikes!" Chloe said, "That's not the big kitten I met!"

And a little later, when Lord Connelly pranced through his obstacles, she squealed and clapped, "Oh, wow! Look at him go!"

She stood and applauded, as Joey brought all of the performers out for one last reception. "Can we go back-stage, just for a few minutes?"

They stepped down the bleachers and found an open path through the curtain to the back of the house. "I'll be right here," he said, kissing her cheek and taking her purse. "I'll keep this. There's a lot of money in it." He found a seat on a bench along the side wall and watched. Chloe found the Zhou twins first and, though he couldn't hear what she said, he loved watching her animated hand movements and bright smile. The twins blushed and nodded.

She also found Nazir, the monkey trainer, and then the clowns, charming them all with her effusive praise. He so enjoyed studying her from afar, this way, warmed by her infectious enthusiasm and naked sincerity. He wondered what good deeds he had done in his past to have been rewarded by fate to have her waltz into his life.

As he pondered the machinations of the universe, Joey approached him from behind and leaned near his right ear. "She is something special, isn't she?"

"You have no idea." He was both proud and relieved to have their relationship out in the open. She walked over and offered Joey a big hug.

"Thank you so much, Mr. Vegas. I had such a great time!"

"I am pleased you enjoyed the performance, Miss Webb, and I hope you will come again."

"I certainly will." She took Royce's hand and waved goodbye to everyone she could make eye contact with on their way out the back door.

CHAPTER 20

RESEARCH

Royce took the key from inside the hotel's wall safe and pocketed it, placing the vinyl bag inside and closing the door. Looking over his shoulder, he watched Chloe as she pulled off her cardigan, unhooked her bra, and pulled it out from underneath her tank top. He smiled at the realization that she'd worn capri pants to the show in anticipation of a moonlight walk on the beach afterward. Lacking her foresight, he was forced to take a few minutes to roll up the cuffs of his jeans.

They walked barefoot along the shoreline, holding hands and letting the cool surf lap at their feet and ankles. It was a clear night, so even the gibbous moon was sufficient to light their path with its blue glow on the sand. She spoke, with a distinct vulnerability in her voice. "Would you do something for me, when we get back to the room?"

"Anything."

"Would you go down on me?"

He stopped walking, squeezing her hand and gently pulling her closer. "Beggin' your pardon, but didn't you tell me in no uncertain terms you didn't like that?"

"I did." She wrapped her arms around his waist, resting her head on his chest. "But I've been wondering if it might be different with you. I mean, every *other* damn thing has been, so far."

He smiled and stroked her back. "I can trust that you'll stop me, right, if you're in any way uncomfortable or not enjoying yourself?"

"I promise." She raised herself onto her tiptoes and kissed him. He turned around and bent down a bit at the knees, with his hands extended behind him. She took the hint, and leapt onto his back so he could carry her piggyback to the hotel. She nibbled his ears and pawed at his chest as he walked.

Crossing the walkover that connected the beach to the hotel's property, she found an outdoor shower and they washed the sand from their feet. She pulled him by the hand with a purposeful stride, and unlocked the door to their room. As he locked it behind them, she stripped in a matter of seconds and rested on her back on the big bed. He pulled off his jeans and crawled slowly over her, from her feet to her head, finally finding her eager lips with his own.

She kissed him hungrily, pausing only to pull his T-shirt over his head so she could scratch his bare back as their tongues resumed the feverish dance. His thoughts returned to his disappointment that night at the Waffle House, when she confessed she didn't enjoy oral sex, and he hoped she wouldn't stop him. He hoped it *would* be different with him.

He moved to her neck and shoulders, biting, licking, savoring her. The sweet scent of her coconut body oil was now mixed with the salty flavor of the ocean air. Then further down, between her breasts, snaking his hands around her waist and then lower, spreading his fingers and gripping her ass tightly, roughly. Her breath came in gasps, her chest heaving as he closed his mouth around each swollen nipple, in turn, pulling them with his lips and teeth.

Backing his way off the end of the bed, his knees on the floor, he grabbed her narrow waist and tugged her to him. She reached above her to grab a pillow and put it beneath her head. "Hold my hands," he urged, and she interlaced her fingers with his. Parting her thighs for him, she draped her legs over his shoulders and crossed her ankles at the center of his back.

He was gentle, but deliberate, understanding that she could call for an end to this at any time, and that he would respect her wishes. Using the tip of his tongue, he traced the folds of her silky pink flesh, up and down, again and again. Her low moans grew louder with each stroke, and she tightened her grip on his hands. Spreading his knees a few inches, he adjusted his center of gravity a bit higher and flattened his tongue against her clit, making steady clockwise circles.

Walking the thin line of interpreting non-verbal clues as cautiously as possible, while keeping his intensity, his spirit soared as she rocked her hips forward, urging more pressure from his mouth. He didn't even realize she was stroking the base of his thumbs with hers, in the exact rhythm and force of his tongue, until she pulled her hands free and began to undo the thin black band that held his ponytail.

He stopped abruptly. "Are you okay?"

"Yes," she breathed, her voice soft and hoarse. "Don't stop. Please. You're fixing to make a quivering mess out of me, and this is the only way I can make a mess back."

True to her word, she came less than thirty seconds later, her fingers tangled in his hair, her hips bucking and grinding against him, her heels digging into his back. He held her tight, reaching his hands up to her chest and splaying his fingers across her breasts, guiding her as best as he could through the receding spasms of her orgasm.

He climbed onto the bed beside her and pulled the bedsheet across them. Her eyes were closed, and her hands were folded across her chest. "I take it that was different?" he asked with a wry grin.

She smiled. "*Way* different. Thank you."

After resting for a few minutes, she snaked her right hand under the sheet and began to stroke him, quickly coaxing his erection to full mast. He glanced to the floor, and hoped he could reach his overnight bag without leaving the bed. Rolling onto his side, he stretched his left hand as far as he could, and fumbled through the bag for a condom. She took advantage of his vulnerable position and slapped her hand down hard on his butt with a loud thwack.

He clenched a foil wrapper in his fist and flipped back over quickly to find her propped on her right elbow with her left hand covering her mouth and a guilty look on her face. "Sorry! That was a lot harder than I meant it to be!"

He climbed on top of her, pinching his knees tight to her hips and drawing his face to within an inch of hers. His unleashed hair fell down the sides of his face and brushed against her cheeks. "Feeling rowdy, are you?"

She shook her head. "Only about a two, on my one-to-ten rowdy scale. But I will let you know in advance, when I'm ticking around an eight. It's only fair to give you warning."

"Please do."

She leaned up, kissing him softly. "Take me slow and easy tonight."

✿   ✿   ✿

He felt his contact lenses drying out, lying tangled with her in the afterglow, and forced himself to sit up. Gathering the condom he'd had the good sense to remove and tie off, he kissed her and made his way to the bathroom. He heard the TV click on as he brushed his teeth. "Damn, Royce!" she called.

With his toothbrush still in his mouth, he stepped back into the bedroom and saw the CNN footage of the beginning of the ground war in Kuwait. They watched more grainy footage of tanks and troops, which were apparently facing little resistance as they made their way to Kuwait City. "I need to hurry," she said, hustling to the bathroom.

He studied the crawler at the base of the screen, memorizing as many details as he could, before she returned, wearing a white cotton panty and the same heather gray Navy T-shirt Michael had given her a few years earlier. She'd slept in it every night since the first sorties and cruise missiles had been launched.

She sat on the edge of the bed, staring at the screen, with the TV remote in her hands. He snuggled up behind her, wrapping his arms around her waist like a seatbelt. He waited until after midnight, before taking the remote from her hands and pressing the Off button. She wiped tears from the corners of her eyes. "I just want to talk to Michael," she said, barely above a whisper.

"I know. Please, let's get some sleep."

✧ ✧ ✧

THEY WERE UP and out early on Sunday morning, packing and checking out of the hotel with the kind of efficiency that would be more expected from couples who had been traveling together for years. They took a last stroll across the walkover and watched for a few minutes as the gulf tide rolled in, grabbed a couple of coffees from the deli next door to the hotel, and headed home.

An hour into the trip, she turned down the radio. "I meant to tell you I won't be in on Friday."

"Is everything okay?"

"Yeah, everything's fine. I have an appointment with my gyno in Savannah on Friday afternoon, and I need to stay in town to visit with Mom and Dad for a while.

I haven't been down since Christmas, and Mom's not happy with me. Somebody's been monopolizing my weekends."

"So it's a routine appointment?"

"Sorta. If everything checks out okay, I'm going on the pill."

He suddenly felt guilty. "This isn't on my account, is it? I don't have a problem with condoms."

She reached over and took his hand. "No. There are benefits for me, physically. But it would allow us to be more, um, spontaneous. It's a win-win."

She pulled a textbook from her bag and spent most of the ride home studying for her upcoming midterm exams. He kept the volume on the radio low.

On their way into Dublin, he stopped at the office to put the money in the safe. She stayed in the car and Royce almost made it back without being confronted by Bobby, but as he was turning off the lights, the kitchen door opened. "What was the total?"

"About thirty-four thousand."

"That's a good number! And you and Chloe had fun, I bet."

"We have nothing *but* fun, Bobby. And she loved the show." He even managed a smile. "See you tomorrow morning."

On Monday, Royce drove to Calhoun for his weekly dinner with the guys and pulled up beside Luke's Chevy.

After dinner, he walked with Luke to the parking lot. He had been putting off the conversation, but hoped he could count on his friend to be discreet. Luke possessed an extensive and legendary bootlegged collection of porn, initially inherited from his brother, but then added onto by him.

"What can I do for you?" Luke asked.

"Okay, so Chloe has this thing where she likes to play rough, sometimes, when she's in hotel rooms. I'm totally cool with doing that, but I want to do a little research, you know? Like, ideas on positions and transitions and stuff. I don't want to be fumbling around, when she's in a mood, but I don't have a lot of practical experience. I was hoping you might let me borrow a few tapes, so I could take mental notes."

Luke offered a sideways grin. "Follow me." They parted and Royce followed Luke to his parents' house, where he had also inherited the finished basement suite. Royce followed him through the private entrance. The overhead beams were exposed, but the rest of the area was professionally finished and well-appointed. Thick shag carpet in the living area, along with a full-sized refrigerator, microwave, and electric hot plate in the kitchenette. The bookshelves were packed with alphabet-ized VHS tapes, with the names of at least three movies scratched on handwritten spines. Luke dragged the tip of his index finger along the tapes, and pulled four cas-settes from the shelves. "These should get you started."

Royce checked out the titles. "*Naughty Nurses 13*? If I

haven't seen the first twelve, will I even be able to follow the plot of this?"

Luke smiled at the obvious joke. "It's the second movie on that tape you want to see. Good luck! Chloe's a pistol."

☼   ☼   ☼

As MUCH AS Royce knew he'd miss Chloe during her trip home, he was also coming to grips with the fact that he didn't have too many more weekends with David before graduation. David hadn't revealed any details of his plans, but Royce had overheard phone conversations. It sounded for all the world like a big move was in the works.

He had stashed a note pad and pen on the coffee table to help him record David's spontaneous observations, as they happened. Since many of them arrived while they were both baked to the gills, he knew he couldn't rely on his next-day memory to recall them accurately. On the back pages, he had already begun to write down some of his favorite memories and conversations with David and his other friends, so time wouldn't rob him of his recollections. His foresight was rewarded within the first week.

On Tuesday, he was watching a PBS show about the 1950s, while choking down a failed roasted chicken breast and broccoli recipe. David walked in and silently studied the show. "Can you even imagine," he asked, "living in an America so innocent that Elvis fuckin' Presley was the most controversial public figure in the country? An America where a white-bread guy like that could literally destroy families, driving a wedge between parents and their children? That's nuts, man." And after a quick change of clothes, he was off to work.

✧   ✧   ✧

Chloe called when she got back into town on Sunday. He was eager for news.

"How'd your doctor's appointment go?"

"Good! Everything checked out, and I got my pills. Took the first two yesterday and today, so we should be able to ditch the condoms in a couple of weeks."

The prospect aroused him, but he tried to play it off. "So y'all had a good visit?"

"We did. Though I have to tell you I have been ordered to produce you for inspection. Mom and Dad said if you're so important that I stay here instead of visiting them, then you're important enough to bring you down to meet them."

He laughed quietly. "That sounds serious. And when would this happen?"

"Well, you're in luck, mister. Saint Patrick's Day is so huge in Savannah that the inn doesn't have any open reservations on Fridays or Saturdays until the last weekend of the month."

"Okay. So when would you be available to come to Atlanta with me?"

"Anytime, honestly. I'm looking forward to it. I love you."

"I love you, too." He hung up the phone and made calls to his mother and father. He had plans of his own to put in place.

✧   ✧   ✧

Sun and Chloe prepared a baked salmon dish for Wednesday's double date, while Royce worked on sides of roasted carrots and fingerling potatoes. David checked into the kitchen a few times, but didn't have much to say and seemed uncomfortable. He remained preoccupied as he and Royce washed up after dinner. Then, after sliding a copy of Bill Murray's *Quick Change* into the VCR, he stood and addressed them.

"I have an announcement." He brushed his loose wiry hair with his hands and shuffled his feet. "A high school friend of mine hooked me up with a software development company in New York, and I have accepted an entry-level position. They have more work than they can manage, and they're bringin' in as many new graduates as they can recruit."

Sun didn't change her expression, as Chloe reached over to hold her hand. "You can afford to live in Manhattan on an entry-level salary?"

David tugged at the hem of his homemade T-shirt, which celebrated the crazy Sam Raimi film *Crimewave*. "Brooklyn. The company partnered with a real estate firm, and they've helped place us new arrivals into housing we can handle. I'll struggle, I know, but I'll be in New York." He smiled a crooked smile.

The phone rang, breaking a few seconds of awkward silence, and David took the receiver into his room. Sun blotted tears from her cheeks with a napkin as Chloe wrapped her in a hug. "Are you okay?"

Sun nodded. "Yeah, I'm fine. I knew this was coming. We all did. I was holding out a little hope it would be Atlanta. Or Charlotte. Someplace close enough that we could at least try to do a long-distance thing." She laughed and shrugged her shoulders. "But I can't compete with New York."

David returned from his bedroom and took his seat next to Sun on the sofa. She climbed into his lap and pressed 'Play.' A silly comedy was exactly what they all needed.

✿　✿　✿

CHLOE PRACTICALLY SKIPPED into the office on Thursday, with an ear-to-ear grin. "Look at you!" Royce said. "What's going on?"

She wrapped her arms around him. "We got a call from my parents late last night. Michael is being rotated back to Japan sometime in the next week or so! The cease fire made it unnecessary to have extra medical staff in the Gulf, so he and a bunch of others are being redeployed."

He kissed her forehead. "I'm so happy to hear it! That's great news!"

She took a long, deep breath, with her head on his chest, and patted his butt before turning to click on the computer.

He waited an hour or so before asking if she'd thought any more about getting away that weekend for a trip to Atlanta. They had already planned their Savannah visit for the end of March, and had penciled in a final road trip to meet the circus in Thomasville, GA for the weekend before that. Between all that and finding and furnishing his own apartment, he felt as though he was booked up every weekend until graduation. It almost made him want to return to being an aimless college student. Almost.

"Yes, I'm ready. And I'm looking forward to it," she said, clapping her hands silently. "And yes, I'll remember to pretend I'm meeting Jennifer for the first time."

"Good. I need to call and remind her tonight."

Soon after, Sun's roommate Heather called. Sun had told her about David leaving and Heather wondered if Royce wanted to consider moving into one of the duplex units on their street. She said that current tenants were being offered a $100 bonus for referring new tenants, and if Royce was interested, he could stop by later that night to check out their monthly bills to see if it worked with his budget.

CHAPTER 21

SOUTHSIDE

Royce met Chloe at her apartment after class on Friday. They worked for three hours or so before shutting down and driving north to his childhood home. He was surprised that she didn't seem as nervous as he knew he would be when their roles would reverse in two weeks.

They stopped at a traffic light between two county government buildings, a few miles shy of their destination. She looked at the directories, which were full of abbreviations for the departments located there. "What's DHUD?" she asked.

"That's, uh, Delicate Heroine Under Duress, I think."

"Hmmm, you're probably right."

"What about FACS?" he asked, expecting her best.

She tapped her chin twice before offering, "Oh, a Facial Acne Cooling Shed."

He laughed with his head on the steering wheel before a horn from behind them suggested he should resume driving. "Gross," he said.

They stashed their bags in his old bedroom, as he braced for her withering commentary about his posters and collection of vinyl LPs. Instead, she focused on his bargain-basement electric guitar and monitor, which sat just inside the closet door. "Royce Murphy, is that a knockoff Flying V guitar I see?" She fanned herself. "Well, my underwear just might fall apart this very instant!" As she giggled at her own joke, his mother pulled into the driveway, followed by Jennifer.

Royce made the introductions, and Chloe and Jennifer did a fine job of pretending they'd just met. Kate was aloof, as he assumed she would be. She had always kept an emotional distance from his girlfriends, at least at first, but had warmed to several of them over time. It used to bother him, until David broke him of it with *"Dude. Ask."* Besides, he'd never been with anyone as strong as Chloe, and he knew she wouldn't feel threatened by his mother's remote nature. Both his mother and sister were dressed for casual Friday at the office, so they didn't need to change clothes before dinner. Jennifer broke a heavy silence with, "El Sombrero?"

Royce nodded. "I'll drive."

They had discovered the restaurant during his sophomore year of high school, and had dined there at least one Friday night a month, ever since. The food would never win any awards, but it was inexpensive and tasty, and the margaritas were potent. Plus, a mariachi band performed on weekends, and they could sit beneath the party lights on the patio and sing along.

Royce poured margaritas from the pitcher as Chloe and Jennifer chatted loudly about school and work and their upcoming plans. His mother listened intently to Chloe's description of the inn, and at her excitement about taking Royce there on a trip in a couple of weeks. Savannah was one of Kate's favorite local cities to visit, and her envy that the young lovers would be spending a weekend there was written on her face.

As the second pitcher of margaritas arrived, the mariachi band made its way onto the patio. They opened their set with "Guantanamera," which Jennifer quickly advised Chloe to sing as *One Ton Tomato*. To Royce's amusement, his mother clapped and sang along with them. After a few more songs, the pitcher was emptied and Royce settled the bill before driving his tipsy companions back home.

Jennifer pulled Royce's high school yearbooks from his hiding place and sat on the sofa with Chloe to giggle at his teenage awkwardness. He did his best to ignore them as he talked with his mother in the kitchen about his plans for moving into his own place. "Please let me know if you need help or advice," she said. "You did a great job setting aside money for your taxes. You pretty much broke even."

Royce and Chloe went to bed just after midnight, maneuvering to get comfortable on the twin mattress. "I'm sorry, my mother can be cold, sometimes."

She interlaced her fingers with his. "But you're not. Nothing else matters to me."

✧ ✧ ✧

He got up early and cooked breakfast. They said their goodbyes to Kate, and Jennifer followed him and Chloe in her car to Royce Senior's lake house. They stopped along the way to buy food for dinner and picked up four sandwiches from a deli for lunch. When they pulled into the gravel driveway, they could see his father fiddling with his pontoon boat.

Royce Sr. greeted Chloe warmly, and she hugged him. He shared her authentic and friendly demeanor, and Royce had a feeling they'd hit it off right away.

"Need help with the boat?" Royce asked.

His father nodded. "Yeah, just working on the fuel line, as usual."

Royce turned to Chloe and Jennifer. "Can y'all take the stuff inside for me?" Chloe raised herself on her tiptoes and kissed him.

His father knew that Royce had no particular expertise in motor repairs, but Royce suspected his father wanted a few minutes alone with him. "How'd it go with your mother?"

Royce sighed. "You know. She was distant, but not outwardly hostile. I gave Chloe a briefing, so she knew what to expect." He held the line in place while his father tightened the connectors, then squeezed the primer bulb a few times.

"Well, let's see how it goes." He climbed forward and settled into the pilot's chair. He turned the key and the motor roared to life, spewing a bit of blue smoke but otherwise humming nicely. He walked back to the stern and leaned over the rear bench to check the new parts and, satisfied with his work, walked forward again and shut down the motor.

"Come up and have some lunch, Dad. We brought sandwiches. You've gotta be hungry."

Chloe placed Royce Senior's sandwich and some chips on a plate and put it down in front of him at the small kitchen table. She mussed his hair and looked at Royce. "Is this what I'm looking forward to?" Royce's father had gone fully gray just after his thirtieth birthday.

Royce smiled. "Yep. Ask her," he said, pointing his thumb to Jennifer.

"I've been dying my hair for two years!" Jennifer motioned toward her temples.

An afternoon thunderstorm confined them to the screened porch, where they talked about everything under the sun and the conversation moved smoothly from one topic to the next.

They watched as the wind blew ripples across the rust-colored surface of the shallow cove, often diagonally intersected by schools of shad darting just below the water line, with catfish and bass breaching the surface to attack their prey.

When the weather cleared, Senior prepared the pontoon for launch while Royce stacked charcoal briquets into a pyramid on the grill and lit them. Chloe seasoned the chops and set them out on the kitchen counter before pulling on her fleece hoodie and making her way to the dock. Royce wrapped her in his arms and pointed out his favorite lakeside houses and landmarks during a brief ride on the boat.

After dinner, they baited hooks with minnows and played catch-and-release with some unlucky bream and crappie. The mosquitoes began to swarm, right around the time it got too dark on the dock to see, so they retired to the screened porch and played poker to the loud soundtrack of frogs and crickets. Chloe and Royce taught them to play Anaconda, which Royce Senior particularly enjoyed until he suffered the night's first cruel twist. He'd been dealt a full house, within his seven cards, which he had to break. He bet his remaining two pair heavily, but lost a large pot to Chloe's trio of eights.

They said their goodbyes to his father and Jennifer on Sunday and began the ninety minute drive back to Dublin. Royce took back roads and enjoyed testing the Miata's limits on the big curves and elevation changes. Chloe cranked the Indigo Girls' *Nomads Indians Saints* cassette and they sang loudly along as he drove. She could easily handle Amy's alto range, so he took Emily's melodies down an octave. When the cassette ended, he turned down the radio. "So, your first impressions of my family?"

She smiled. "Your father's a big ol' teddy bear, isn't he? And you already know how fond I am of Jennifer." She paused and looked out the window. "I'll win your mom over."

"I know you will. She's only like that for the first few times I bring someone home. She's funny and engaging, once she allows herself to be. I don't know why it's such a struggle."

✧   ✧   ✧

He walked her up to her apartment and visited with Kim and Jacob while she unpacked. Mark had left earlier in the day for a week-long visit to check on a project in Denver, but would be back before Royce whisked her away to Thomasville the following weekend.

When he got to his place, David and Sun were curled up on the sofa watching a show about World War II. Or rather, David was watching the show, while Sun practiced one of Heather's intricate shuffles with their worn deck of cards, giggling every time she made a false move and spilled them to the floor. The bowl in David's bong was still smoking, but he packed a fresh one and handed it to Royce. "How'd it go, man? That had to have been intense."

Royce took a deep drag. "It was. But it was good. Chloe will fit right in." Sun formed an awkward smile. She and David had not met one another's parents, and now there was little reason to, so Royce was relieved when David looked back at the show and changed the subject.

"I'd loved to have seen the look on Hitler's face when he learned about Pearl Harbor. I mean, the Japanese didn't exactly fit his vision of the master race, and the U.S. was pretty content to sit it out up until then. So they found this big sleeping bear in a cave and poked it with a stick. He had already watched us join a war late and turn the tide of it from the fucking trenches. He must have been *pissed*. It took about two seconds for us to declare war on Japan and then say, *You know what? Fuck a bunch of Nazis, too.*"

Royce grinned and reached for his note pad.

✧   ✧   ✧

AT WORK, ALL of the sales rep teams had begun their second to last campaign for the spring tour. He had talked a big game to Wendy Smith about the Covington campaign for Daughtry, which would be the final performance of the spring tour, and kept his fingers crossed that the numbers would be good enough to keep their statewide sponsor on board. He'd tried to talk Ken and Sally Ross into tackling the Covington date, but they were unwilling to trade it for a different town they'd worked successfully before. His second choice was Burt and Gwen Thomas, and he had high hopes for them. He held onto his grudge against George Edwards, whom he'd caught speculating about his sex life at the winter sales meeting, and would be damned before he offered him and Maggie such a significant assignment.

Royce and Chloe had taken to referring to the spring campaign as "our tour," since it was the first one they would handle beginning to end, by themselves. They kept expecting to be blindsided by an error: a ticket order or taps update that they'd missed, or a miscommunication with Joey about the route or the tour dates. But the Ides of March had come and gone without incident, and they had begun to relax a bit. Royce booked a chain hotel for their Thomasville trip, having found no unique place for them to stay, and used his alone time in the apartment during David's evening shifts to review the tapes he'd borrowed from Luke. He suspected Chloe might have something interesting in mind, with the work excursion sandwiched between their visits to meet each other's parents.

✿ ✿ ✿

WHEN HE ARRIVED to pick her up for the three-hour drive to Thomasville, she was not in the living room waiting for him. He wondered briefly about the change of plan, but greeted Jacob and Kim before knocking on Chloe's door.

"Entrez-vous!"

She wore a gray Henley-style top, with the sleeves pushed up to her elbows, but was bottomless save for a leopard-print panty in a sexy low-rise bikini cut. His eyes were drawn to it immediately.

"Do you like it?" she cooed, offering views of the front and back. "I went shopping last week."

"You could say that," he replied, swallowing hard.

He drove southwest on side roads before merging onto I-75 near Cordele. When he shifted into fifth gear, Chloe reclined her seat back, slipped off her flats, and propped her bare feet on the dash. She had dressed her nails in a fresh cherry red, and flexed and splayed her toes in case he didn't notice right away. He had.

"Very lovely." He was a ball of yarn between her paws, and they both knew it.

She pulled a textbook from her backpack, along with a highlighter, and studied silently as he drove. He'd worn gym shorts for the trip, in the interest of comfort, and from time to time she grazed her fingernails along the inside of his thigh. Sometimes, accidentally on purpose, her fingers wandered too high and her pinkie touched his genitals through the cotton fabric. She made overly dramatic corrections of these transgressions, clutching her book in both hands, as he bit the inside of his cheek and willed himself to remain flaccid.

On the main drag into Thomasville, a mile or so short of their hotel, he caught sight of Joey and Gloria's RVs parked facing each other in a car dealership's parking lot and quickly downshifted to make a risky left turn. He parked the Miata near the entrance, which was festooned with yellow and blue streamers and balloons.

He took Chloe's hand and they weaved their way through a crowd of fifty or so onlookers to find Joey with Lord Connelly, and Gloria with Ashanti, behind a yellow rope beneath a banner that read "Grand Re-Opening!" Joey and Gloria led a procession of children through the ropes so they could pet the animals, while parents who had the foresight to bring cameras to the event snapped photos. Joey looked up and noticed them in the crowd, then spread his fingers and mouthed *"five minutes"* to Royce.

The owner of the dealership thanked everyone for coming, and reminded them of the time and location of the circus performance. "I'm beginning to understand how the circus manages to operate on less than 25 percent of the phone sales," Royce said.

She squeezed his hand. "How's that?"

"How much do you figure the dealership paid them for this appearance? And they keep all the concessions money."

A couple of stagehands appeared, seemingly from nowhere, and helped harness the animals and lead them to the trailers. Royce and Chloe followed Joey, waving goodbye to Gloria and Ashanti, and climbed the steps to Joey's RV.

"We're good, Jason. Thank you," Joey said to the young man who carried Lord Connelly up the stairs and inside. "I'll be a few minutes here, if you'd like to catch a ride back with Gloria."

"Yes, sir," Jason replied, and bowed a farewell, closing the door behind him.

"Such a good lad," Joey said.

Chloe sat on the floor, petting the tiny horse, and looked up at Joey. "Where do you find them, the stagehands?"

"Well, Miss Webb, they certainly aren't drawn to us for the money!" Joey laughed. "Like most traveling performers, we aren't looking to get rich. We are happy to get by, and to bring joy to people with our acts. The kids who come along to help, sadly, often come from less than happy homes. They only make minimum wage, but they get to travel and to be away from home for months at a time. Their basic needs are met, they are learning useful skills, and the scenery changes. For most of them, that's enough."

Royce thought for a moment before chiming in with a question of his own. "So, the walk-up ticket sales. Those don't go to the sponsors, right?"

Joey shook his head. "No, they don't. It's eight dollars a ticket at the gate, and all of those proceeds stay with the show. Another incentive for Gloria and me to do these appearances whenever we can arrange them."

He pulled the bankers bag from his safe and handed it to Royce, who counted the contents twice and verified the numbers. "Now, if y'all will excuse me, I need to head back to the venue and get myself ready for the show. Oh, and I understand from Bobby that you both have been involved with theatre?"

They nodded in unison.

"Good! I thought you might enjoy watching the show from backstage, then. I'll have the boys set up a couple of stools for you, behind the curtain at stage left. It's a comprehensive view."

They thanked him and left. With only a couple of hours to showtime, they hustled to their hotel, stashed the cash in the wall safe, and began freshening up for the evening. Royce had assumed she'd planned to wear the denim skirt and Henley to the show, so there was no reason for her to emerge from the bathroom wearing only her leopard panty and sun pendant, but there she was. She hardly spoke, which was unusual unto itself, but she bumped against him repeatedly as they crossed paths in the small space, with more exaggerated gestures of apology. If her long game for the day was to drive him bananas with desire, she was succeeding.

They grabbed a quick dinner at a fried chicken place, and then hustled to the performance, which was being held in the gymnasium of a private high school. The sound tech immediately recognized Chloe and blushed, and escorted them backstage to their stools. Chloe positioned hers in front of Royce's, since he could see over the top of her head. Backstage was bustling, though it appeared to be a controlled chaos. Within a few minutes of their arrival, the stage manager, a young woman with hazel eyes and a thick black ponytail, whom Royce had met only briefly, made walkie-talkie calls to the spotlight operators and the two techs at the front of the house, advising that everyone was in their places.

Joey Vegas stood just behind the curtain, with his feet set wide apart, his head down, and his hands folded in front of him. At the conclusion of the pre-recorded introduction, he snapped immediately from prayerful to gregarious, stepped through the curtain and commanded the stage. Royce and Chloe watched as each act queued in place and, in the case of the clowns and the Zhou twins, whispered quick words of encouragement to one another, much like a band or an athletic team, just before taking the spotlight.

They waved to Gloria as she led Ashanti to her waiting place, bending to one knee and rubbing the big cat under her chin before rising and smoothing wrinkles from her costume. They both stood and applauded as Gloria walked out with Ashanti, and craned their necks to get a better look. Chloe pushed her stool away and backed up between his legs, twisting her hips to the beat of Ashanti's music and pressing herself against him. He took her waist in his hands and, at first, enjoyed the sensations.

As her grinding intensified, however, the discomfort of a growing erection confined within the double layer of underwear and jeans set in. He gave her the benefit of the doubt, and assumed she didn't know how painful this might be for him, and he didn't want to scold her or undercut her playful mood. So he played along with her, tightening his grip on her waist and spinning her around to face him. "You're ticking around an eight on your rowdy scale, aren't you?"

She looked up to the ceiling and tapped her chin. She shook her head. "No. A niner."

He pulled her stool back over and patted the seat. As the final few acts took to the ring, his mind raced as he replayed as many of his favorite scenes from Luke's videos as he could remember.

C H A P T E R   2 2

DEMON

They made their rounds after the show and chatted with the performers. It was the final spring tour performance they would attend, and they both made it a point to speak to as many people as they could, to thank them for their hard work, since they had no way of knowing which acts would return for the next tour. Chloe hugged Gloria and Joey, and patted Ashanti and Lord Connelly again before waving goodbye.

As they drove back to the hotel, Royce suddenly remembered there was a sports bar in a small strip mall nearby. Without a word to Chloe, he flicked on his left turn signal, and found a parking space near the entrance. "I feel like having a drink or two. Are you with me?"

"Yes," she replied, careful not to indicate that she knew he was hijacking her agenda. "But I need to go to the bathroom."

"What can I get you?"

"Seven and Seven?"

"Will do."

He brought their drinks to a high-top next to an open coin-operated pool table, and nodded to the two guys in truckers' hats at the next table. When she joined him, he noticed right away that she'd unfastened a couple of buttons on her Henley and brushed her hair behind her ears. She fished two quarters from her purse, fed them into the coin slots, and racked the balls that rolled loudly toward her end of the table.

"You break, love," she said, and he scattered the rack, pocketing a solid ball. He drained two more, as she walked around the table opposite him and stood in his sight-line for each shot, leaning forward to offer views of her cleavage. He missed his third attempt, and left her set up for at least two of the striped balls.

She hitched up her skirt and stretched her legs to line up the shots, which were far easier than she made them out to be, and sank two balls before a third target rattled out and sat on the lip of the pocket. "Fuck!" They both noticed that the two large men had not taken their eyes off of her while she shot, but quickly looked away when they were caught.

Royce sank two more solids, but couldn't continue the run, and finished off his drink. He took their empty glasses back to the bar for a refill, glancing over his shoulder to watch her circle the table and push several striped balls into pockets with her hands. He was still thirty feet away from her, walking back with their drinks, when she locked eyes with him and began seductively stroking the top fifteen inches of her cue with her fingertips. He handed over her drink and glanced at the table. "What did I miss?"

"I put in four in a row!" she squealed with delight.

"Is that so?" They looked over to the truckers, who nodded sheepishly.

Royce missed his next shot on purpose, leaving the cue ball in prime position for her final striped ball, which she buried, and then pocketed the eight ball on her first try. She twirled in a circle and spun her cue above her head like a helicopter rotor in celebration. Her Henley crept up her torso, revealing her flat belly and coin-slot navel.

"A rematch, if you please?" he asked. She pulled two more quarters from her purse and re-racked the balls. The truckers seemed pleased that there would be another game.

Royce sank a striped ball on his break, and pocketed three more quickly before he found himself without an open shot. He made it a point to leave her without anything decent to shoot at, and followed her miss by sinking two more. She made one before missing an easy shot, and mentally checked out on the game, which had become a lost cause. But she found another opportunity to torment him, when Alannah Myles' "Black Velvet" began playing through the bar's speakers.

They both despised the song, but she gripped her cue like a microphone and sang loudly along, swishing her hips to the beat and rubbing against him as he closed out the game with a couple of well-planned leaves to set up easy finishes. Before the eight ball had settled into the well of the table, she took his cue and placed it on the wall mount beside hers. He sat down on a stool, his knees apart, and finished his drink. She spread her legs and straddled his left thigh, snaking her arms around his neck.

She spoke softly, in a girlish voice. "I know I've been a merciless tease today." And then, leaning in closer, whispered in his ear. "I should probably be... *punished.*"

He felt his ears burn. "Yes, you should."

She waved goodbye to the truckers on their way out to the car, and the brief ride to the hotel was mostly silent. She pulled him by the hand from the elevator, and ducked into the bathroom with her overnight bag as soon as he'd unlocked the door to their room. He stripped to his boxers and pulled the tie from his hair, combing it with his fingers as he studied himself in the hallway mirror.

As always, he thought about his good fortune at having met her, and briefly questioned his worthiness of her love. But, shaking his head, he forced himself to concentrate on the moment. Every exploration of the darker side of their sexual nature offered him another opportunity to show her he could be everything she wanted. That he was game for whatever scenarios she chose to present, and that he would participate with an enthusiasm that equaled her own. He turned off all the lamps and opened the curtains, allowing the ambient glow from the parking lot's blue streetlights to fill the fifth floor room. He suddenly realized this would be the first time they would have sex without a condom, and wondered if the added stimulation might cause him to lose control too quickly. But the click of the knob on the bathroom door interrupted his worrying.

She rounded the corner wearing her white silk camisole and the leopard panty, blinking her brown eyes to adjust to the dim light. With his hands on her shoulders, he backed her against the wall beside the bed, and studied her expression for any sign that she had changed her mind. He found only playfulness and desire. Taking her face in his hands, he kissed her, deep and long and tenderly, the evening's final display of his preferred *modus operandi*.

He reached down to his hips and seized her hands, pinning her wrists to the wall above her head. He encountered only token resistance, and crossed her arms so that she could be restrained by only his left hand. Brushing her hair behind her left ear, he trailed his fingers downward and wrapped them around her neck. Her body tensed at the sensation, but her eyes urged him onward. She licked her lips.

Sliding his fingers downward still, he found the swollen nub of her left nipple pressing through the thin fabric, and pinched and pulled it harder than he ever had before. She gasped, leaving her mouth open for a kiss that he refused to provide. Instead, he released her breast and pushed his index and middle fingers between her lips, and she sucked on them eagerly, rolling her tongue under them, back and forth. She dug her toes into the carpet and closed her eyes.

With his right foot against the instep of her left, he

pushed her stance wider. He leaned forward, resting his forehead against hers, and slipped his hand into the front of her panty. Her saliva on his fingers, combined with her slick arousal, provided a warm, silky playground for his touch. She pressed her hips forward as he worked his fingers inside her, and struggled against the tightening grip of his left hand. He did not release her wrists, nor did he allow her to climax, abruptly staying his fingers when he sensed she was close. The anger and frustration in her eyes was obvious, and doubled in intensity when he again brought her to the brink and denied her.

He clutched her hips and turned her around. "Hands on the wall," he commanded, in a voice that he barely recognized. She complied, as he pulled the waistband of her panty down past her thighs and allowed it to drop to her feet. He grabbed a fist-full of her hair with his left hand and pulled, stroking her exposed neck with his right. Taking a half-step backward, he lined up his strike and brought his hand down against her right butt cheek. It was a harder slap than he had intended, but he delivered another right behind it without thinking. The sound that escaped her lips was a cross between a growl and a purr.

He bit down on her neck and shoulder, roughly rubbing the reddening hand-prints on her ass. Her breath came hoarsely, as he reached around her waist and pressed his fingers into her again. She came almost immediately, grinding against his hand and whispering, *"Please."* He stepped backward again and, looking down, frowned at the asymmetrical coloring. The distinction between what was left of her tan and the fairer skin that had been covered by her bikini bottom was delightful, but only the right side bore a red print in the shape of his hand. He decided this would not do, and administered two quick strikes to the other side with his left hand. She cried out in surprise and repeated her growl-purr.

He leaned close to her right ear. "I want you. Now."

She spun around to face him, her eyes smoldering and her smile wide, as she pulled off her camisole and dropped it to the floor. She climbed onto the bed on all fours, pulling two pillows and stacking them beneath her chest, the tops of her feet against the side of the mattress. Arching her back to raise her ass up high, she wiggled her hips back and forth.

He pulled off his boxers and positioned himself behind her, guiding himself into her to his full depth in one smooth motion. He paused briefly, to savor the feeling of her flesh without the latex barrier, before taking her waist tightly in his grasp and beginning a steady, rhythmic thrusting. She bucked backward against him, harder and faster than his chosen pace, and he responded by lifting his left leg and placing his foot on the bed, to drive into her at an upward angle. She shrieked into the pillows as she came, coating his shaft in her warm wetness and, as her climax subsided, he slapped her ass hard, twice more, triggering another.

She must have sensed that her second nearly sent him over the edge, because she pulled her hips forward, releasing him, and flipped over onto her back. "Come here. I want to see your face when you come inside me." He climbed up between her legs, and pushed himself back into her. She raised her arms above her head, and he interlaced his fingers with hers. They shared a long, passionate kiss, as he found the depth and angle that he knew would unravel him, and surrendered to his passion. He locked eyes with her, and erupted. "Oh, fuck!" she gasped, pushing her pelvis upward and spiraling again into orgasm as the heat of his climax filled her.

He rolled to his right, settling on his back, and pulled her onto him. She slung her right leg across his, and they both giggled at the unfamiliar tickling sensation of their mingled fluids leaking out of her and onto his thigh.

"I hope I didn't hurt you," he said, softly.

"You did," she replied, nuzzling against his neck. "Thank you."

She stroked his bare chest with her fingertips and whispered, "I love you, but I'm beginning to wonder if you're not some sort of demon."

"A demon? Shit, that sounds awful! What do you mean?"

She shifted her hips. "Well, from our first time together, up until tonight, I've had at least ten silent thoughts in my head during sex where I said, *I hope he does so-and-so.* And then, within just a few minutes, you did the so-and-so."

He smiled. "That's called sexual compatibility. Besides, why am I a demon? I might be an angel."

She reached down to rub her sore right cheek. "No. Angels don't fuck like that." She pulled the bed sheet over her head and disappeared beneath it. Taking him into her mouth, she quickly coaxed another thick erection and climbed aboard. She was slow and gentle and wonderful.

✧   ✧   ✧

THEY HAD DEPOSITS to tackle the following week, and checks coming back from the sponsors, but no taps to enter or tickets to order. Royce was putting together his thoughts and numbers for the summer sales meeting, and keeping a particular eye on the Covington campaign for Daughtry, but the meeting was months away, and they welcomed the unusual absence of urgency.

Chloe talked a lot about her parents, and he smiled silently at her obvious enthusiasm for his first meeting with them. When she told him that they would be staying in room one at the inn, he said, "I'm a little surprised they'd set just one room aside for us. I assumed we'd be sleeping separately."

"They know we're lovers, Royce. It's the same as it was with your parents. They accepted our relationship and let us sleep together, and we repaid their kindness by not fucking under their roof. It's a fair arrangement, and easy for both sides." There was no way he'd argue the logic of her statement, even if she hadn't concluded it by blowing him a kiss.

On Thursday afternoon, Bobby was feeling restless

behind his kitchen throne and tagged along with Mae on her errands. Assuming the errands would end with an extended stay at Sammy's, as they usually did, Chloe walked behind Royce's desk, kicked off her shoes, and curled up into his lap. "Tell me why you love me," she cooed, wrapping her arms around his neck.

It was a conversation he had come to refer to as The Talk, and he understood very well the significance of it. Growing up in a house with two women, he felt he had a different sensibility for their need to experience validation, plainly spoken and expressed. This would be especially important with Chloe, who had an unrivaled bullshit detector.

"You mean, besides the fact you're as hot as seven hells?"

She smiled. "Yes, besides that."

"We make a great team. We complement each other. Anyone who has spent any time around us will tell you the same thing. We share so many of the same interests and tastes, and our life priorities align: family, work, education. I'm proud of you, and I'm proud of myself for being with you."

She kissed him, hard, and smiled broadly. "That will do, thank you."

"Okay, your turn. Why do you love me?"

She tapped her chin. "Well, you're cute and you have a big dick." She cackled at her own joke. He expected nothing less than an initial dodge of the question.

"I don't trust easily," she continued, far more seriously,

"but I trust you completely. I mean, I'd never be able to ask the things I ask of you if I didn't know one hundred percent that we were meant to be together. You treat me like a princess and a partner, and you make me happy every day. I told my mother…" She shook her head and bit her bottom lip.

"Hey, now. You can't start something like that and not finish it."

"It might be too much."

"I can promise you it won't be."

She rested her head on his shoulder. "I told my mother that I thought this was what a *forever* kind of love was supposed to feel like."

His stomach turned a cartwheel in his gut, and he squeezed her with all his might. "I agree with you."

They held each other silently for a minute or more, before he lightened the mood with another probing question. "So, when did you start to think this might be a possibility for us? I mean, I'm sure I didn't do a very good job of hiding the fact that I was into you from the moment you arrived for your interview."

"Honestly? I never let myself think about it. I mean, I thought you were handsome and funny and kind, and that I'd be happy sharing a two-person office with you."

"Oh? So when did you realize things might be different? On the golf course? Before?"

She shook her head. "No, it was after. I knew you were being playful with me that day, but I still wrote it off as just you being nice to the new girl. But there was something in your voice when you asked me to dinner afterward. I had a little panic attack and thought, *Shit, I've been on a date for the last three hours*! Then things really got serious at the Hound, during Vic's show. And especially afterward, when you knocked my feet out from underneath me with that kiss."

He felt his face flush. "Well, I'm glad we finally got on the same page."

CHAPTER 23

MADISON

"It's this one on the right." Chloe pointed to a four-story red brick building with a wrap-around porch that sat a few steps above street level. He found a parking spot just past the inn on the tree-lined street. They had closed the office early Friday and arrived in Savannah just after six, blasting Faith No More's *The Real Thing* all the way down I-16. He pulled their suitcases from the trunk and carried them up the concrete steps. The porch had wooden rocking chairs and palm-leaf ceiling fans, and planter boxes filled with blooming pansies, zinnias, and violas.

She held the door open for him and he entered the lobby area. On the right was a small unmanned reception desk at the entrance to a sitting room with a plush pastel sofa, a wide-screen TV, and several wingback chairs. Chloe turned left, however, into the dining room. It had long buffet cabinets on two walls, topped with a couple of coffee dispensers, tidy containers of condiments, and a basket of silverware wrapped neatly in table linen and tied with string. Three high-top bistro tables with four chairs at each were staggered near the front windows, overlooking the street. She pushed open a swinging door marked Staff Only and called, "Mama? We're here!"

He left their bags next to one of the buffet tables and followed her through the door into a well-appointed chef's kitchen. Mary Webb released her daughter from her embrace when Royce entered, and offered him a warm smile. "Royce, I am very happy to meet you!" She shook his right hand with both of hers clasped around it.

"It's my pleasure," he said. "Thank you so much for having me."

She was a couple of inches shorter than Chloe, with broader hips, but they were otherwise built similarly. Her black hair was piled in a bun on top of her head, and her rosy cheeks were dotted with dark brown freckles. She studied his eyes silently for a few seconds before turning back to Chloe. "Do go downstairs and open the gate for him, darling." Turning back to Royce, she continued. "There's a driveway behind the building on the side street over here. You can park beside our car." He followed the motion of her arm and nodded.

Chloe stood at the chain-link gate, her hand on her cocked hip in a posture of mock impatience. She opened the gate, and he parked alongside her parents' white Pathfinder. She hustled to the car as he exited it and took his hand. Pulling him toward an awning at the back corner of the building, she introduced him. "Daddy, this is Royce."

The sweet smells of cape jasmine and honeysuckle that lined the privacy fence hung heavy in the humid air, but the curry marinade on the chicken breasts Paul Webb was cooking on his tabletop hibachi grill carried an even stronger aroma. He offered Royce a wide and genuine smile, flashing the gold crowns on his canine teeth. "I have heard a lot about you," he said with a wink.

"All good, I hope," Royce replied, offering his hand. Paul wore a floral print short-sleeved shirt, revealing an anchor tattoo on his right forearm. He moved gingerly because of the arthritis, much like Bobby Conway, but he was far more stoic in hiding his grimaces.

Royce nodded toward the grill. "These smell delicious. Anything I can do to help?"

Paul shook his head. "It's all under control. Y'all go on and get settled. I'll be up in about ten minutes."

Chloe took his hand and led him through the back door of her parents' basement suite. Their living area was small, but laid out with an emphasis on efficiency, with curtains in lieu of walls to separate different living areas. He only got a glimpse as she pulled him to the far end of the area and up the stairs to the kitchen. She whispered, "Most of their belongings are still at the big house on Whitemarsh, but they brought their favorite things here. I need to bring you back down again over the summer, so we can get the stuff I left behind."

She opened the door into the kitchen, where her mother was arranging four place-settings at a simple wooden table in front of a bay window that overlooked the back yard. The Webbs took their dinner at the table every night but, on this occasion, two additional mismatched chairs had been added for Chloe and Royce. Mary filled two ceramic bowls with a fragrant rice side and a mixed green salad, and left a spot on the table for Paul's chicken breasts.

Over dinner, Royce didn't speak unless directly spoken to, but listened intently to the family chatter about Michael, Mark, Kimberly, and Jacob. Chloe had an easy rapport with her parents, and spoke with them as a near-equal, as Royce did with his own. Paul, who had been a logistics specialist with the Navy in Vietnam, asked about the particulars of the circus movements from town to town.

Royce chuckled. "Well, it isn't exactly Operation Overlord, and the ringmaster is the primary engineer of the mechanics of the tour, so I'm more of a support staffer. But we do a good job of making sure the campaigns are set up well in advance, with everything they need to be successful." Chloe smiled and squeezed his thigh under the table.

"And what's it like, working together?" asked Chloe's mother. She winked at Paul. "We have a bit of experience with this."

Royce blushed and made eye contact with Chloe. "We work well together. And spending several hours in the office every day certainly gives us the chance to learn about each other. The getting-to-know-you phase of our relationship has been fast, but thorough." He weighed his next words carefully, shifting his eyes from Mary to Paul and back again, before snaking his fingers through hers. "She means the world to me. And I'm very happy to have met you both, finally." All three Webbs nodded in appreciation, and he felt relief that he hadn't said too much, and hadn't made anyone uncomfortable.

After dinner, Mary gathered the plates and bowls. Royce offered to help, but she shook her head and waved her hand. "This is a simple clean-up. Take your bags upstairs and freshen up, if you'd like. We always take a walk after dinner, and you're welcome to join us." He nodded and grabbed their suitcases from beside the buffet table, and followed Chloe up the stairs to room one.

It was simply furnished, but was both elegant and cozy; a dark wood four-poster bed, a bedside table with a Tiffany-style lamp and clock radio, a matching dresser, and two small chairs that flanked a wooden table in front of the window. Beside the dresser, a narrow doorway opened to a compact bathroom with a pedestal sink, toilet, and stall shower.

"It's getting chilly, so I'm gonna change before we go out," said Chloe, pulling some things from her bag and walking into the bathroom. Royce opened the curtains and looked out onto the street. The sun was setting, filtering orange light through the Spanish moss that hung from the oaks along the avenue.

"Murph!" she barked. "Come and look at this."

He stepped cautiously to the bathroom door, and watched as she struggled to look over her shoulder at the mirror. She had pulled her panty down past her shapely cheeks, revealing several fading splotchy purple marks on her skin. He opened his mouth to offer an apology, but she interrupted him.

"I love them," she purred. "They're yours." She kissed his cheek and pulled on her jeans.

They walked with her parents to Columbia Square, strolled around its perimeter, then approached the Wormsloe Fountain. Chloe fished a coin from her pocket and reached for his hand. Closing her eyes tightly, she squeezed his hand and flipped the coin into the fountain.

He smiled. "What did you wish for?"

She cocked her head to the side, smiled a wry smile, and pressed her index finger to his lips. Silently, she turned and snaked her hand through her mother's bent elbow as they made their way back to the inn.

He chatted with her father along the way, answering questions about his immediate family. Paul seemed particularly interested in his father's lake house, and Royce took pleasure in providing additional details and extending an invitation on Senior's behalf, anytime Mary and Paul wanted to visit.

When they arrived at the inn, Chloe and her mother sprang into action, and Royce was encouraged to join them in the kitchen. While Mary put away the dinner dishes, Chloe opened cupboards and pulled out a kettle, a hot plate, and wicker baskets containing tea bags and sweeteners, along with a honey dispenser and a lemon. He followed her into the dining area and together they arranged everything on one of the buffet tables before returning to the kitchen for cups and saucers. Paul had retrieved Scrabble and Trivial Pursuit from the sitting room and had taken a seat at the center table in the dining room.

Mary was the last to settle into a chair at the four-top, pausing to take a quick look at Chloe's set-up before nodding her approval. "Four of our guests are in town for a class reunion," she said. "Four others are here for a concert and, sadly, the other two have come for a memorial service." She looked at Royce. "We try to be here when guests return in the evenings, in case there's anything we can do for them before they retire."

"I understand," he said with a smile, taking seven tiles from the Scrabble bag and passing it to Chloe.

It was easy for him to throw the Scrabble game, since no one could see the letters in his rack, though Chloe did narrow her eyes at him a few times when he laid down low-scoring words. He bit his finger to keep from laughing as she and her father battled spiritedly to the last few letters before Paul edged her with his final word to take the win. As they were clearing the board and preparing the Trivial Pursuit set-up, the two couples who had been at the concert walked in.

Mary stood to greet them, and directed them to the tea service. One couple took advantage of the offer and then boarded a tiny elevator behind the stairwell to take them with their tea cups to their room on the third floor.

Royce took an early lead in Trivial Pursuit, correctly answering eight consecutive questions on his second turn, and moving his token deftly up and down the spokes on the game board, choosing mostly Arts & Literature and Entertainment squares. He had collected three scoring wedges before any of the others had obtained their first. Chloe rolled her eyes at him, and drummed her fingers on the table in mock boredom. He knew the answer to his next question, as well, but purposely answered incorrectly.

As Chloe's mother rolled the die and began to move her game piece, they were interrupted by the sound of two women laughing loudly and the clip-clop of high heels staggering up the front steps. Mary rose again and greeted both couples in the foyer. The women pulled off their shoes as their husbands steadied them, and in loud drunken voices told Mary about their fun at their twentieth reunion. Mary asked if she might prepare her favorite hangover remedy for them — a strong chamomile tea with a shot of heavy cream, honey, and a squeeze of lemon juice — and the ladies agreed. The two couples took seats at the table beside Royce and the Webbs and continued to gossip about the classmates they'd seen at the reunion. The mention of chamomile brought daisies to Royce's mind, and for the first time in months he thought of Dr. Dalton's blue sundress. He closed his eyes tightly until the image faded.

Royce closed out his victory two turns later. Knowing that breakfast would come early, they put the games and tea service away, and Chloe helped her mother wash the cups and saucers. As they were saying their good-nights, the inn's final couple returned. Paul had been acquainted with the deceased, from high school, and stayed downstairs to have a beer with them while the other three went to bed.

With the arrival of spring, Chloe had taken to wearing only a short black silk boxer to bed, and made a show of stripping down and pulling it on before climbing into bed. He was sitting up and reading a hardback copy of Michael Crichton's *Jurassic Park*, which David had read over the winter and insisted that he read it, too. She curled up against him and wrapped her leg over his, caressing his shin with the arch of her bare foot. She spoke softly. "Are you happy with how tonight went? 'Cause I'm happy with how tonight went."

He grinned. "I'm very happy with how tonight went. I love you."

She rolled to her left and set the alarm clock for 6:00 a.m. "Get some sleep. I love you, too."

✧   ✧   ✧

THE NEXT MORNING, they hustled downstairs to help her parents in the kitchen. After pouring himself an over-sized cup of coffee, Royce asked Mary what station he could tackle. "Bacon?" she offered.

"I'm on it." He pulled on a hair net and apron, and preheated the flat top. Paul worked the gas range station next to him. Saturday's special was biscuits and gravy, and Paul tweaked his recipe constantly as the gravy simmered in a stainless steel pot. He also had a cutting board to his right, and prepared an array of fresh fruit when he wasn't stirring and tasting.

Mary grated a frozen stick of butter as the final in-gredient of her biscuit dough mixture, then tossed a bit of flour on the counter and gave half of the dough to Chloe. "Just do what I do, dear," her mother said, kneading and folding the dough.

Royce laid a full package of thick raw bacon strips onto the flat top and clicked his tongs to get Chloe's attention. She looked up from her dough and blew her bangs out of her eyes. She looked at her father, then back to him, smiled, and mouthed the words *I love you so much.*

Breakfast hours were from 7 to 10 a.m., so they used warming trays, foil wraps, and chafing dishes to present each new arrival with a plate that tasted fresh from the kitchen. They thanked the guests who were checking out and gave the most efficient directions back to I-16. Royce and Chloe stayed in the kitchen, cleaning up the breakfast dishes and rinsing out the coffee pots, so her parents could spend a few extra minutes with their guests. All but the couple who was in town for the memorial service checked out on Saturday.

At ten, the inn's assistant manager, Josefina, arrived. She was bright and bubbly, and always smiling, with dyed dark red hair that was almost maroon. She was fluent in English, Spanish, and French, with a demeanor that struck a perfect balance between friendly and professional. She greeted Royce warmly and offered Chloe a wink as she shook his hand. "Juana will be here in a few, to turn over the rooms," she said to Mary and Paul, "and Gladys is coming in at noon. Y'all go rest for a bit and enjoy your afternoon! I've got this."

CHAPTER 24

CLICK

Chloe took Royce's hand and led him back upstairs to their room. "We have an hour, probably, before they're ready to go, if you want to nap or read or whatever."

He pulled her onto the bed with him and into his lap. "And what will you be doing?"

She kissed him, lightly and playfully. "I'm going to give myself a quick mani-pedi, in case Cassie calls. I'd really like for you to meet her."

"I'd like that, too."

She sat on one of the chairs in front of the window and spread her tools on the table as he stretched out on the bed and returned to his book. He glanced up from time to time and grinned at the look of concentration on her face as she dragged the brush across her fingertips. By the time she threw her legs onto the table to decorate her pretty toes, however, the battle between man and velociraptor suddenly became secondary, and he let the open book fall to his chest.

She used a folding fan to help dry the blood-red polish and, after a while, noticed his interest. With a coy smile, she shifted her position on the chair to tease him with a better view. But she wasn't finished. She walked on her heels toward the bathroom, her toes pointed upward and splayed to protect the wet polish, and closed the door behind her. Her mother called and said, "Come down and make a sandwich. We are about ready to go."

"Thank you, Mary. We'll be down soon."

Chloe emerged from the bathroom wearing denim cut-off shorts and nothing else, and carrying a bottle of her favorite suntan lotion. "Would you put this on my back?"

She sat on the bed, between his legs, with her back to him. He reached around her waist and gently slid his hands upward, cradling and caressing her breasts. "Can I do the front, too?"

She giggled and squirmed. "I've already done the front. Maybe next time."

Squeezing a bit of the oil into his palm, he rubbed his hands together and began smoothing the thick coconut-scented liquid onto her shoulders and down her back. The oil smelled dense and sweet, and he inhaled deeply. Her signature aroma. Even during the winter, when she wasn't tanning with the lotion, she chose body wash and perfume that was similarly scented. He had become skilled at calling it to mind when he drifted off to sleep alone in the bedroom of his apartment.

He tied the rear string of her bikini top for her, and she pulled on a gray Lancaster Cardinals sweatshirt and her sandals before taking his hand and pulling him downstairs to the kitchen. The foursome made sandwiches and packed them into a picnic basket. Chloe helped her father into the passenger seat of the Pathfinder and took the seat behind him. They set out on the twenty-minute drive to Tybee Island.

After passing Fort Pulaski, they crossed the bridge over Lazaretto Creek, and Royce looked to his left to see the Cockspur Lighthouse. The tide was high, so most of the island's oyster and mussel beds were underwater. But he had heard it was accessible by kayak at low tide, and that there was a visitors' book on the top level, for those who were adventurous enough to paddle out and make the climb. He added this to his mental list of things he wanted to do with Chloe.

Mary parked in the lot at North Beach, near the Tybee Lighthouse, and they crossed the walkover and found a good spot to spread a blanket. Chloe peeled off her sweatshirt, folded it into a square and sat down on it. He had studied her tan lines thoroughly, but he'd never seen her wearing the bikini until today. The black tri-angles were smaller than he'd imagined, and he had to make a conscious effort not to stare. Instead, he made eye contact with her parents and asked, "So, what was Chloe like as a child?"

She scowled at him, but her father leaned backward and laughed. "This one," he said, pointing his thumb toward her, "She was a firecracker straight out of the womb. Michael and Mark thought they could get the best of her, but she was giving back better than she got from the time she could walk."

Royce smiled. "I can imagine."

"That's his perspective, mind you," Mary added. "They knew their father would foster and egg on their rivalries, so they went to him for it. I saw three very close siblings who loved and looked out for each other."

Paul put his hand on Royce's shoulder and said, in his own defense, "Iron sharpens iron."

Mary continued, with a smile for her daughter. "She's always been deliberate about choosing her passions. But when she commits, she goes in with her whole heart."

Chloe had heard enough and, with quick hands, gathered the remnants of everyone's lunches and walked them to a trash can. "I would like to take a walk. Are you feeling up to it, Daddy?" Paul nodded, and they folded the blanket and set out for a slow stroll along the water's edge.

Royce snaked his arm around her waist and grinned at the thought of her going in with her whole heart. She cast him a knowing smile. "They didn't scare you away from me, did they?"

He shook his head. "They confirmed what I already knew. I love you."

They walked as far as the Big Anchor monument at the island's ninety-degree turn, and doubled back toward the parking lot. The Atlantic coast water was much chillier than the Gulf had been during their Destin trip.

Paul was stiff and sore, when Mary stopped at her favorite market on Whitemarsh Island, so Chloe stayed in the car with him while Royce went inside to help. Mary had planned a tempura dish for dinner, and carefully selected two pounds of freshly-caught shrimp, along with seasonal fruits for breakfast the next morning. "So," Royce asked, "What's on tomorrow's menu?"

She smiled. "Sundays are for pancakes, with my secret batter recipe. Can I count on your help on the flat top?"

"Of course. But only if you'll tell me one of your secrets."

She reached into her bag and pulled out an orange. "Zest. Zest is the best."

✧   ✧   ✧

Josefina waved Chloe over to the front desk when they returned to the inn. "There was a call for you. Cassie."

"Oh, yay! Thank you, Jo!" She dashed into the kitchen and returned the call from a wall-mounted phone, while Royce and Mary put away the groceries. Paul only made it as far as the center table in the dining room before he had to sit down.

Royce gathered, from Chloe's side of the conversation, that they were to meet after dinner at a bar called Farley's on Bay Street. She smiled broadly and did a little dance when she hung up the phone. She helped her father walk from the dining room into the kitchen, and sat him down at the table beside the bay window, before putting on an apron and joining her mother to help with dinner. Royce took particular interest in watching Mary prepare the shrimp and the tempura batter, with the hope he could duplicate her technique in his own kitchen.

He took the lead in washing the dinner dishes

afterward, nudging Chloe upstairs to get ready and her parents out for their walk. When he walked into their room, he caught her examining herself in a very short pale-yellow sundress he'd never seen before. "Too little? I can't decide."

He shook his head, looking her up and down. "Perfect. God, that's perfect."

She put on her sun pendant necklace, then wrapped her arms around his neck and worked the hair tie out of his ponytail. "Wear your hair down for me tonight? Cassie likes long hair on guys."

"Wait, are you showing me off?"

She offered a mischievous grin. "Uh-huh. You okay with that?"

He shrugged. "Why not? I haven't been objectified in a long time."

✧   ✧   ✧

SHE CALLED CASSIE from the front desk to tell her they were leaving, and they walked arm-in-arm to Farley's. They settled into a booth near the front of the bar, and ordered a pitcher of Killian's Red. The wood paneling and the burgundy and forest green accent colors reminded him of the Hound.

Cassie arrived ten minutes later, wearing a pumpkin-colored silk blouse and jeans so tight that Royce thought they must have been melted onto her. She was lovely, though, with chestnut brown wavy hair that was parted in the middle and landed in waves at her shoulders, and green-gray eyes that sparkled when she spotted Chloe.

The girls nearly went airborne when they embraced, twirling around each other and squealing. He knew they had not seen each other since Chloe's visit to Savannah for Christmas, and stood back as they talked over each other in voices that increased in pitch until he could barely make out the words. He extended his hand. "It's a pleasure to meet you." She wrapped him in a surprise bear hug.

"I've been dying to meet you, too! Chloe raves so sweetly about you that she's giving all of us diabetes!" Chloe playfully slapped her shoulder and blushed.

"Well, it's good to put a face with the name. She has entertained me with so many stories about her friends that I feel like I already know you all."

As they took their seats and Royce poured Cassie a beer, she reached across the table and touched Chloe's necklace. "Oh, this is the pendant you told me about on the phone! It's so gorgeous!"

Chloe beamed. "Isn't it? I still think it's too much, but I'm learning to let him spoil me."

They knew they didn't have much time to catch up, given the ungodly early hour Royce and Chloe would have to be up the next morning to help with breakfast, so the girls gave each other an outline, of sorts, of the biggest events in their lives since the last time they had seen each other. What followed was a rapid-fire turn-based conversation, where one would flesh out her story with as much detail as possible before yielding the floor to the other. He thought the only thing missing was a chess clock on the table between them, so he entertained himself by imagining one. *Click*.

Cassie unraveled the story of her latest break-up. She admitted she became bored easily, and lamented that she seemed to be stuck in a rut where every relationship she had lasted somewhere between three and four months before it flamed out. She sighed and looked at Royce. "I'm a serial monogamist."

Click. Chloe talked about Michael's experiences during the Gulf War, and how worried she had been for him while he was there. He was next scheduled for leave late in the summer, and she looked forward to seeing the photos he had taken during the conflict. He was something of a shutterbug, and enjoyed preserving records of his travels with the Navy. Royce excused himself to get a refill of their pitcher, but mentally recorded a *Click* when he got up.

Upon his return, Cassie was fretting about her upcoming senior year at SCAD, the Savannah College of Art and Design. She was studying Illustration, and had two exhibitions of her work scheduled for the fall semester. She was very interested in a graphic novel production house in Miami, and desperately hoped they would have a representative on campus for at least one of her displays.

Click. He refilled their mugs as Chloe provided details from her first trip to see the circus. She recounted every detail she could recall about Joey Vegas, Ashanti, and Lord Connelly, with an enthusiasm in her voice that warmed Royce's heart. He had never known a joy quite as profound as seeing Chloe excited about something. When she finished, she sat back and rested her head on his right shoulder, reaching across him to comb his hair with her left hand. "Stop it," Cassie said, pointing her finger.

Click. Cassie divulged the latest drama with her sisters. She was the oldest of three and, despite her own reputation for hell-raising, her sisters were taking their disobedience to unprecedented levels. She denied, of course, giving them a model of what teenage rebellion looked like.

Click. Chloe surprised him with her next topic, explaining how thrilled she was about their plans for the following weekend. They would be meeting with Sun and Heather's leasing agent to tour some of the duplexes that were available. She turned to him. "You know I love David, but you could have moved out months ago, and I think you'll be happy with a change of scenery." He nodded. He was excited about having his own place, it was true, but he looked forward to the time he had left with David, too.

Click. Cassie closed out her recaps by offering up all of the gossip she had heard about Key Academy's graduating class of 1987. There had been a couple of arrests, a couple of unplanned pregnancies, and at least one serious illness. Chloe put her head back on his shoulder and brushed his hair again, prompting a more forceful response from Cassie. "*Stop. It.*" Chloe tossed her head backward and laughed.

Click. She gave glowing reviews to her own classes at Lancaster, and reported that she'd already chosen courses for the summer semester. She was eager to catch up, as best as she could, with an eye on graduating in two more years.

They drained the rest of the pitcher, offering a toast with whatever remained in their last glass, and made promises to get back together again over the summer. Cassie's father had a boat docked at a Bull River marina, and volunteered Royce to drive it so she and Chloe could relax on the bow and sunbathe as they enjoyed the scenery.

Once they were assured that she was okay to drive, they walked Cassie to her car. "It's like five whole miles, *Mom,*" she said in exasperation. With hugs and waves goodbye, she put her car in gear and disappeared around the corner.

✹ ✹ ✹

ON SUNDAY MORNING, Royce found himself on the flat top again, this time armed with Mary's batter dispenser so he could measure out pancakes of exactly the same shape and size. Chloe worked the range next to him, with two cast iron skillets filled with sausage patties. "Two and half minutes per side, Royce," Mary advised. "The grill temperature is perfect, and I've let the batter rest for twenty minutes. No need to put them on until people arrive in the dining room."

He raised his spatula to his forehead and, with a wink, saluted her. Paul and Mary cut fruit and prepared sauce boats with melted butter and a few different syrups, while Royce playfully harassed Chloe with exaggerated assistance she neither needed nor requested. As she alternated between slapping his hands away and kissing him, he felt her parents' eyes on them.

Paul watched the dining room through the window in the kitchen door so he could signal whenever he saw new guests come down. Royce responded by dropping batter for pancakes until everyone had been served. He smiled to himself at how well he'd fit in with their team, as he turned off the griddle and began washing up the pots and pans.

After the last of the guests had finished breakfast, Royce and Chloe went upstairs to pack. "It's warm and sunny out," she said. "Can we put the top down for the drive home?"

"Of course we can. Are you thinking of wearing your bikini top for the ride?"

She gasped and clutched at an imaginary strand of pearls. "How lewd!" After a giggle, she continued. "No, but I do have this itty-bitty tank top." She put it on, without a bra underneath, and pulled her sweatshirt over the top. They gave the room a final scan, picked up their suitcases, and made their way downstairs to the kitchen.

Mary frowned at their bags. "Are you sure you can't stay a little longer?"

Chloe hugged her hard. "Sorry, Mama. Kim will be back from her airport run right about the time we get there."

"Where is Mark off to this week?" Paul asked, shaking his head.

"New Orleans, I think." She hugged her father tightly, and they all walked out to the car.

Royce stowed their suitcases in the trunk and lowered the Miata's top. He hadn't had much practice, and worked deliberately while Paul watched. Royce offered an embarrassed grin. "This is why it's probably unwise to buy a convertible in the dead of winter. You forget all those helpful instructions before it's warm enough to need them."

"Well, Royce," Paul said, "I hope we'll be seeing you again soon. And please, tell your family they're welcome here anytime. Just give us a call and we'll reserve a room or two."

"That's very kind of you, and I'll certainly let them know."

Mary walked over to the driver's side and embraced him warmly. "It was wonderful to meet you. Please come back whenever you can."

"We will. Thank you so much for your hospitality."

"No need to thank me. You more than earned your keep, and I enjoyed sharing my kitchen with you."

CHAPTER 25

ROSEWOOD

On the drive home, Royce confessed, "I'm a little disappointed we won't have any alone time at your place before Kimberly gets back."

"Oh, we will," she replied, pulling off her sweatshirt and tucking it beside her. "I fibbed a little. We should have an hour, at least."

He looked at her and wiggled his eyebrows.

"I know," she continued, "All weekend, I've been nursing a strong need for you to completely tear me apart."

He allowed her words to hang in the air between them, and used the surge of adrenalin to wind fourth gear nearly to the redline before finding fifth as he merged onto the interstate. She pushed her copy of The Replacements' *All Shook Down* into the cassette player, and cranked the volume to compensate for the wind. He would have nearly two hours to contemplate *completely tear me apart*, but he also had a serious topic to discuss with her. He decided to wait until the album ended, because her elaborate seat-dancing and exuberant sing-along with Paul Westerberg were exactly the distractions he needed for an otherwise boring drive.

As "The Last" faded through the speakers, he reached over and turned down the volume. "So, for a little over a year, David has been trying to get me to take an acid trip with him. Ever since he learned that I'd never done it. I've decided I'm going to, and I wanted to let you know."

She pulled her blue-mirrored sunglasses up to the top of her head and shifted in her seat to face him. "Are you sure? I've never done it, either, but I've heard some horror stories."

"I have, too, but I'm sure. And we're running out of time. You and I are busy next Saturday, but I'm hoping the weekend after that would be good for him. I was planning to talk to him tonight when he gets home from work."

She leaned over and kissed his cheek. "Thank you for telling me ahead of time. I mean that. Promise you'll always talk to me about things. I'll try not to worry."

When they arrived at her apartment, she disappeared into the bathroom, so he took her suitcase into her bedroom and undressed. She joined him in her bed, and he took control immediately. He was forceful, though not particularly rough, manipulating her body with confidence and authority, and using four months of collected knowledge of her desires and responses to make her melt beneath him. He reveled in every clench and spasm of her muscles, and every dig of her nails into his skin, moving relentlessly and without pause, until both of them were spent. The teeth marks on his chest and shoulders, and the scratches on his back, were a testament to her pleasure. They fell asleep in each other's arms, and were awakened half an hour later by the sounds of Jacob's babbling.

Dressing quickly, if not completely, they moved to the living room. Royce took Jacob in his lap and played with him while Kimberly and Chloe talked about the weekend and made a list of things they wanted to accomplish for the rest of the day. Chloe had schoolwork to do, as well, so Royce said a quick goodbye and headed home.

He packed the bong tightly and left it on the coffee table, and made himself a quick dinner before David got home from work. "Dude! How was Savannah?"

"It went better than I could have hoped. Her parents are awesome, the inn is gorgeous, and we had a great time."

David murdered a bag of Chinese takeout, and took a massive rip for dessert. They passed the Dutch bong until the bowl was empty. Royce changed the channel to MTV and lowered the volume. "So, I've been thinking, and I want to drop acid with you sometime before graduation."

David leaned forward in the easy chair. "Seriously? That's big news! I only trust two guys with their product, but I'm sure I can meet one of them in Macon next weekend. When do you want to do it?"

"Two weeks? On Saturday the 13th? I'm going apartment shopping next weekend, but if I find a place, I'm free the Saturday after."

"Can do."

Royce settled comfortably onto the sofa and cracked *Jurassic Park* back open, while David did the same with his own current interest. He only looked up once, when a Joe Cocker video began. "If I could trade my voice for someone else's, I'd take his. Who's your choice?"

Without hesitation, Royce replied, "Michael Wincott."

David slapped his forehead. "You son of a bitch! Why didn't I think of him?"

Royce laughed. "No take-backs. I got Wincott."

✧ ✧ ✧

FOR WEDNESDAY'S DOUBLE-date, Sun and Chloe made mandu — Korean-style dumplings — but given the difficulty of the dish, they also wanted to choose the movie. David and Royce agreed to let them choose but dreaded the decision, and were not surprised when they picked *Ghost*, one of the Video Barn's latest releases. Royce wanted to watch the meal prep, so he jumped onto the counter beside the sink and studied Sun's technique.

As she combined the filling ingredients into a mixing bowl, she looked up at him and asked, "Have you thought about where you're going to get furniture? Wallace's on the bypass north of town has twelve months same as cash. Heather and I have bought a few things from them."

Twelve months same as cash. Royce had never heard the term before, but it instantly became his favorite five-word phrase.

Over dinner, Sun asked David for more details about the upcoming acid trip. Like Chloe, she had no interest in doing something like that herself, and only wanted to make sure he and Royce would be safe.

David shook off her concerns. "People who have bad trips either take too much or they aren't properly prepared for the experience. I know better. It'll be something to remember."

"As long as it's not like the Robo night, I'll be good," Royce said, taking the bong from Chloe. She sputtered on her exhale and covered her mouth with her hand.

"You did *not* do that."

"We did," he replied. "We were bored, and out of weed. It was about a year ago, before I moved in here." After a long drag, he passed off to Sun. She was pouting.

"Okay, I'm going to need someone to explain to me what this means."

David put his arm around her. "You drink an entire bottle of Robitussin, and then hallucinate like a motherfucker."

"But doesn't it make you sick?"

Royce chuckled. "Yeah. Yes, it does. But you hold it down for as long as you can, before throwing it up."

Chloe leaned forward and took his hand. "Okay, so what happened? What was it like?"

"Well, after I puked for what seemed like half an hour, I only made it as far as his bedroom floor before I had to lie down. The Jills' bedroom light was on, and I remember the rectangle of light through their doorway slowly getting farther and farther away. And every sound was muffled, like I was underwater."

"I remember that," David added. "I was on the bed, on my back, watching these thin leafy vines climbing the walls and spreading across the ceiling. I have no idea how long we were both frozen in place. It seemed like hours."

"That's… disturbing," Sun said, after a few seconds of silence.

"Well," Royce replied with a wry smile, "Now you see why it took me so long to agree to drop with him."

David countered, "I can almost guarantee the acid won't make you throw up."

☼   ☼   ☼

ROYCE HAD MADE an appointment to meet with the leasing agent the following Saturday morning, and picked up Chloe on the way. She was giddy. The first vacancy they toured was in the same development as Sun and Heather's place, at the dead end of their street. Like the other buildings, it was an unremarkable ranch-style house, with a covered entrance in the center that had entry doors to the two units on either side of it. The front yard was flat, but the property sloped in the rear, creating the paved parking area in back well below street level.

He parked on the street behind a late-model Audi, and took Chloe's hand as they walked the pave-stone path to the front door. Tanya, the leasing agent, answered the bell and handed both of them her business card. She was a tall and slender Black woman, with closely cropped hair and a killer smile. They knew what to expect from the floor plan, since it would be nearly identical to Sun's unit, but Royce immediately appreciated the simplicity of the color scheme. The walls were taupe, and the baseboards, moldings, door and window frames were painted a glossy white, with white blinds on the windows. Chloe went to check out the kitchen, while he stopped at the bathroom, which had both a stall shower and a garden tub, with plenty of counter space on either side of the sink.

"Murph! Come in here!"

He joined Chloe in the kitchen to find her posing like a model from *The Price is Right* in front of open louvered doors. "How much extra would you pay," she asked, in the voice of a game show host, "for a space that included a nearly new washer and dryer set?"

He laughed and turned to Tanya. "I think I'll take those rental application documents from you now."

"I figured as much," she replied. "That's why we started here. It's about a hundred dollars more a month than your friends' place, but the foreman of the development lived here during the construction phase, so it has upgrades the other units don't."

Chloe had gone out to the back deck, overlooking the paved parking area. When Royce joined her, she was moving from one side of the deck to the other and craning to look around the corners of the building. "I don't think anyone besides your neighbor would see me, if I did some sunbathing out here. Maybe I could even get some of my tan lines to fade, up top."

He added an outdoor lounge chair to his mental shopping list.

They had budgeted the time to view three or four places that morning, so the decision to take the first one gave them the time to do some shopping. They thanked Tanya for her help, and Royce promised to bring the application to her office on Monday. After a stop for an early lunch, they arrived at Wallace's Furniture.

The showroom was cavernous, like an airplane hangar, and within his first ten steps Royce came to a sobering realization. While he had made a comprehensive list of what he needed — a dinette set, coordinating bedroom and living room pieces — he had given very little thought to his own personal aesthetic. He saw styles that he knew he didn't like, which was a start, of sorts. Black lacquer and country motifs were definitely out, but the other assemblies blended together into a cluster of confusion. Chloe recognized the look on his face and snaked her hand through the bend of his elbow. "I've learned a few things from Mark, if you'll let me help you."

He looked down into her brown eyes and smiled. "Yes, please. I'm making a financial commitment, and I'm gonna be sitting on these things for years, so I'm afraid of buying something I'll end up hating in six months."

"I understand," she replied with a grin. "Walk with me and show me what you like."

As they strolled through the living room set displays, he discovered that he had an affection for the Lawson style of sofa, and directed her attention to a couple of options in neutral colors.

"Gotcha. But I feel the need to mention that there's an ass-load of brown in the place, between the walls and the carpet. Let's think about colors, okay? Here, look at these." She directed his attention to an arrangement with a navy blue recliner and a matching sofa with navy and cream vertical stripes. He nodded and smiled broadly. They found a coffee table and end table made of maple that paired perfectly with the sofa and chair.

Moving to the bedroom displays, he quickly noticed several collections in the Craftsman style, and he was particularly attracted to a set in distressed pine. The bedside tables were simple and small, and the measuring tape he carried in his pocket confirmed they would fit beside the bed on the wall where he envisioned them. She studied the dresser, which had a wide mirror mounted on it. "This would sit against the wall opposite the bed?"

"That was my idea, yes."

"Good! I'm looking forward to watching us in that mirror while you fuck me," she whispered.

He was surprised to feel himself blush after so many months of her stabs at shocking him and pressing his buttons.

"We could brighten the room with some pastels for the bed linens," she continued.

"A pale green?" he offered.

"Write it down!" She stepped closer to him and patted his left butt cheek. "I know you have your note pad back here."

"You know so much?"

"Your keys are in your right front pocket, with your wallet in the back. You already showed me your measuring tape in the left front, so that means your note pad is back here. Don't think I don't know you, lover."

Determined to make Wallace's a one-stop shop for everything he needed — the simplicity appealed to him — he wasted no time in selecting a farmhouse-style oak dinette set, with four chairs and a rectangular table with white tile on its surface. "We'll get placemats and towels to add color to this, right? Maybe red?"

She smiled and wrapped her arms around his waist. "Red. Yes. Exactly what I was going to say. In a checkerboard pattern, if we can find them."

She flagged down a fortunate sales associate, who walked with them and recorded the SKUs of every piece they had chosen, before they settled around a desk at the rear of the store. Royce wrote a check for five hundred dollars as a downpayment, to compensate for his limited credit history, and scheduled delivery for three weeks later, on the afternoon of the day he would move out of Kingston. He was due to receive his $7,000 end-of-tour payment in two weeks — he bristled every time Bobby referred to it as a "bonus" — so he knew he could cover any expenses if his applications for the furniture or the duplex took a wrong turn.

When the salesman's attention was diverted, she turned toward him, and spoke softly. "What are you going to do with the other bedroom? I just thought of that."

"I'll furnish the second bedroom with my shitty twin bed and dresser, and make it a replica of every bedroom I've had since I moved out of the dorms. If I ever start to feel too big for my britches, I can walk in there and remember the lean times."

He dropped Chloe off at her place, and thanked her again for her invaluable assistance. When he got back to his apartment, David was at work, but he had obviously made his run to Macon earlier in the afternoon. Royce found two blotter tabs on the coffee table, sitting on an index card, and smiled at the *Simpsons* artwork on them. On the index card, David had written *100 micrograms on each. Itchy or Scratchy?*

CHAPTER 26

TRIPPING

The following Saturday, Royce slept in for as late as his body would allow, knowing that he would be awake until God knows when on Sunday. He decided to push the battle between his nerves and his excitement to the back of his mind, dropping the Miata's top and running mundane errands in the early afternoon. Rain was not expected until late that evening, but heavy gray clouds were already gathering. He wondered if Chloe was poolside in her black bikini.

As he put away his groceries, David walked him through his plan for getting the most out of their trip while keeping them as safe as possible, and Royce agreed that it made perfect sense. He trusted his friend completely, and knew David would be looking out for them both. He called Chloe a few minutes before 5:00, just before they left the apartment. "Well, we're doing it!"

"You call me if you need to, please. Even if it's late. Enjoy yourself, and try to remember as much as you can. I'll see you tomorrow. I love you." She did not allow herself to sound concerned.

He tapped his tab to David's, like a champagne toast. They tucked the squares underneath their tongues, walked down Kingston's stairwell, and exited through the rear door. As they made their way past the fire pit, heading in the direction of the abandoned cracker factory, Royce asked, "How long again, do you think?"

"Thirty minutes or so, before we start feeling it. Maybe Connie's won't be crowded. But we'll be in and out of there before the effects get real serious. I hope." Royce checked his watch. David had explained that they would probably lose their appetite, so their favorite deli would be a good first stop.

They cut through the long narrow stretch of pine trees that separated Lancaster from the cracker plant's property, and made their way around the tall chain link fence surrounding its employee parking lot. At the far corner, they found the old railroad spur that had served the factory when it was in operation, but was now over-grown with weeds and wildflowers. Following the spur until its junction point with an active line, they turned north and walked along the tracks toward Connie's.

As they entered the deli, Royce was definitely be-ginning to feel different, but he couldn't identify what, exactly, was off. He didn't feel drunk or stoned, though. He was certain of that. He ordered two Italian sub spe-cials while David filled plastic cups with ice and water from the fountain. They took a booth in the corner of the near-empty seating area.

"Is it really loud in here?" Royce asked. "It's really loud in here."

"It's a little loud in here," David agreed, but Royce had already turned his attention to the condensation on the outside of his cup. He put his right index finger on it and used his left hand to rotate it. He turned the cup slowly, moving his finger down to make a spiral. Upon reaching the bottom, he sat back and stared at it. He checked his watch, then slapped his right hand against its face to hide it.

"What time do you think it is?"

"Quarter after six," David replied, confidently.

"So I'm the only one with a fucked-up sense of time passing? I thought it was a lot later."

"That's not it," David replied. "There's a clock on the wall behind you."

✿ ✿ ✿

THEY EACH MANAGED to eat at least half of their sandwich but, as David had predicted, Royce didn't feel like eating. He really wanted to *walk*. The sun was already beginning to cast long shadows, and he felt a deep need to be outdoors. "Can we go?" he asked, drumming his fingers on the table. "I'm getting antsy."

David nodded and gathered their trash. They walked out to the railroad tracks and headed south, back toward the apartment. Royce extended his arms for balance and tiptoed along one rail, for as long as he could, but felt a quick surge of panic when he saw he was lagging behind. He rushed to catch up, but found he so enjoyed the exhilaration of jogging that he broke into a sprint, flying past David while imitating the Road Runner's "Meep meep!" He looked up and ahead as he ran, watching the tops of the towering pines on either side of the tracks bend toward one another, forming a tunnel for him as though he was seeing through a fisheye lens.

He stopped when he got to the spur that led to the factory and waited for David, who was laughing as he approached. "You're running, and I'm out here without my Acme catapult." His hand-made T-shirt celebrated an obscure 80s horror movie called *The Sender*. He pointed down at the tracks. "Let's keep going. I wanna go to the bridge." Royce agreed and followed him.

Half a mile later, they came upon the simple steel structure, spanning a creek. On the right side of the sleeper beams was a width of diamond plate walkway and a black handrail. They walked to the center point of the bridge and faced west.

Royce couldn't remember seeing anything so beautiful. Dappled orange sunlight filtered through the leaves of the tall hardwoods at a bend in the creek, fifty yards or so in front of him. With every hint of a breeze, pollen from the pines drifted into the air and became tiny electric sparkles, flashing yellow when passing through the rays of light. Half a dozen dragonflies hovered above the surface of the creek, darting at mosquitoes and gnats. One thing was missing, however. He walked back to the end of the bridge and collected as much gravel from the ballast bed as he could carry.

Returning to the center, he sat down and let his feet hang over the edge. He neatly stacked the gravel into a pyramid beside him, and selected one rock to lob into the creek. He watched intently as it landed, sending drops of water upward that glinted like diamonds in the glow of the setting sun. The creek was only a few feet deep, and moved as slowly as lava. It might as well have been stagnant. Its surface was covered in a layer of smelly yellow pollen, except for those places where Royce's rocks broke the slow progression and sent ripples of brownish-yellow water toward the banks. In his mind, however, he was creating a kinetic foreground to nature's impressionist painting.

He heard his father's voice, as he stood on the bank of a lake. Royce was six years old, and learning how to skip rocks on the water. He turned to see his mother, breaking small pieces of cheese and bread for Jennifer, then a toddler. Black smoke that smelled of coal and lighter fluid drifted from the campsite's grill.

Royce closed his eyes tightly and then opened them to find that the painting was growing dark around the edges. The light was nearly gone. He tossed his remaining rocks two at a time, sending more diamonds skyward. Resting his head against the metal handrail, he said, "It will never be like this again."

"What?" David replied, from halfway up a small tree on the other side of the bridge. Royce had no memory of him leaving his side.

Royce shook his head. "I don't know."

David hopped down and walked back toward him. "We should get moving, while we still have some daylight."

Before they reached the spur, they felt a rumbling beneath their feet and heard the distant approach of a train, and then the whistle. They began to walk more quickly, but simultaneously realized the train was approaching from behind them. For safety's sake, they left the tracks and scrambled up a small hill to sit and wait. The ground shook beneath them and the noise seemed to be coming from all around, as the beam from the locomotive's headlight cut through the encroaching darkness. When the train finally arrived, David was shocked to see that the engineer was leaning against his open window and appeared to have his eyes closed. When the final car passed and the noise began to fade, he asked, "Was that dude asleep? Should we call somebody?" He cackled and rose to his feet.

By the time they reached the cracker factory, it was completely dark, except for the half-dozen street lamps in the parking lot that still worked. They walked back around the fence, and Royce noticed the portion that connected the wire structure to the building had been cut and pulled back, leaving a triangular opening large enough for a person to crawl through. He worked his way through the hole and examined the lot. It was flat and expansive, big enough for at least a hundred cars, and free from concrete parking blocks or large cracks. Between the edge of the asphalt and the building was a stretch of dormant sod, about five feet wide, that had a few dead azalea bushes planted beside the brick steps leading to the two entrances.

"I have an idea," Royce said. "Wait here."

"Where are you going?"

"The apt. I'll run."

He sprinted the entire way, with a youthful exuberance he hadn't felt in years, through the narrow strip of pines, past the fire pit, and entering Kingston through the back door with his card key. Taking the steps two at a time, he reached the top floor in seconds and burst through the door. He pulled the sand wedge from his golf bag and found the box of novelty golf balls — the kind that float if you hit them into a water hazard — under his bed. He snickered at the memory of how funny his uncle thought it would be to give him those for Christmas, instead of balls he could actually use.

Suddenly aware of how thirsty he was, he stopped in the kitchen and poured a tall glass from the water pitcher. He pulled an empty Coke bottle from the trash and rinsed it out to refill with water for David. Once downstairs, he realized he'd left without the golf club and balls, and had to go back upstairs to get them.

The outside world was pitch black by now, with only a few street lamps to light his way back to the parking lot. Each lamp was surrounded by a halo of circling moths and beetles, orbiting in rapid, tight circles, and occasionally flying off en masse like the seeds from a dandelion. He crawled back through the opening in the fence and saw David standing beside the stairs to the nearest entrance with his back to him. He was laughing.

"What are you doing?" Royce asked, dropping the golf club and box of balls onto the grass.

"Peein'."

"And what's so funny?"

"Peein'."

"Was I gone a long time? I still have zero concept of time passing, and I get distracted really easily."

David zipped up his shorts and turned around. "Nah, not long. Fifteen minutes, maybe. What did you bring?"

Royce fished the Coke bottle from his pocket and handed it over.

"*Gomawo.*"

Royce hoped that David-on-acid wouldn't break out too many more Korean words, as he had only learned a few polite phrases from Sun.

"I meant those, though,' David added, pointing to the sand wedge and balls.

"Oh, I felt like losing some golf balls. On purpose. I figured we could hit from the grass and try to knock them over or through the fence beside the tracks."

David nodded and picked up the wedge. Royce opened the box and dumped out the balls. David took a healthy swing, but he skulled the shot so badly that it skidded along the pavement at a 45-degree angle, ricocheted loudly off of a dumpster, and rolled right back to his feet. Royce doubled over, laughing so hard that he lost his breath. "I bet you can't do it again! Here," he said, leaning forward and pinching a handful of grass together. He placed the errant ball gently on the raised area. "It's easier with a tee."

David's second shot was much better, though it was very short, bouncing a few times on the pavement before rolling to a stop short of the fence. Royce noticed that every bounce disturbed the pollen covering the lot, throwing yellow dust in the air that glittered in the blue light from the street lamps. "That should make them easier to find," he mumbled.

"What?"

"I don't know."

They took turns, each hitting six balls from the box of a dozen. Royce's second and fourth were towering shots that easily cleared the fence and bounced over the tracks and into the woods, and David's third followed the same path. Royce dropped the wedge after his final shot and took off across the parking lot in a dead sprint, picking up golf balls with the joy of a child finding Easter eggs, and shoving them into his pockets. David took a different path, along the fence, but ran just as fast and found three more before turning and running back to the grass.

After two more rounds of thwack-and-chase were completed, and only four balls remained in play, a thick mist settled on the lot. Royce froze in place, studying the prisms that formed around the street lamps, casting rainbows that overlapped one another and created a canopy of vibrant color over the entire area. He placed his hand on his heaving chest and wandered toward the center of the lot, smiling as the colors shifted and re-formed like a kaleidoscope with every step he took. David called from the grass, trying to break Royce's concentration. "What's the definition of a bigamist?"

Royce turned toward his friend with a grin. "Italian fog. You told me that one already."

He wandered back to the grass and took the wedge. While his passion for chasing and returning with the golf balls had not faded, his arms and back were growing weak. It took three more rounds for them to blast the last ball over the fence, and by then a light rain had begun to fall.

"I don't want to go in yet," David said. "Do you?"

"No." Royce pointed the wedge toward the playground behind the Baptist church on the opposite corner. "We could go over there."

David nodded and led the way, shaking water droplets from his long wiry hair like a collie. They climbed the fence into the playground and took seats on the swings. The rain seemed to intensify with each kick of their legs to push themselves higher.

As Royce brushed the wet hair from his eyes, David quoted *Caddyshack*. "I don't think the heavy stuff's gonna come down for quite a while." They made two passes through the monkey bars, somehow managing to keep their grip on the wet steel without slipping, and took turns pushing each other as fast as they could on the merry-go-round. Within the hour, as they climbed to the top of the geodesic dome, the rain was coming down in sheets.

"Okay, I'm callin' it," Royce said, reluctantly. In the spirit of the trip, he was still a carefree eight-year-old, but his clothes were stuck to his skin, and he was cold. "I need to dry off."

They retrieved Royce's wedge from its place against the fence and trudged back to the apartment. Leaving their muddy shoes outside the front door, they changed out of their wet clothes. Royce joined David in the living room as he studied his collection of VHS tapes, attempting to put together an appropriate screening. Satisfied with his choices, he handed Royce three films. "A triple feature," he said, confidently.

The first in line was *The Adventures of Baron Munchausen*. "Terry Gilliam," Royce said with a grin. "I'm glad you didn't pick *Brazil*." He settled onto one of the floor pillows and rested his back against the sofa, barely moving as he took in the elaborate visuals, perfectly-flowing scores, and transcendent performances of the actors. He felt like he was watching a live show, rather than images on a screen.

After *Munchausen*, they watched *2001: A Space Odyssey*, a movie Royce had seen a dozen times, but now watched with brand new eyes. He nodded off a couple of times during the final film in David's trilogy, *Labyrinth*, but made it to the closing credits before he went off to bed.

"Thank you, David," Royce said, as he rounded the corner to the bathroom. "I had fun."

David flashed him a peace sign and a heartfelt smile from the recliner. "I'm glad you did."

Royce knew that David was horrible at goodbyes. He'd seen David artfully side-step any attempts at sentimentality as their mutual friends graduated and left town. He had so many more things he wanted to say, but swallowed the words and crawled into bed. His clock read 3:37 a.m.

✧   ✧   ✧

HE WOKE UP on his back, naked, sore, and parched. He blinked against the daylight, struggling to guess what time it might be. Chloe was next to him, sitting up against the headboard with one of her textbooks open and upside-down on her lap. She spoke softly. "Good afternoon. How are you feeling?"

"Like I got run over," he croaked. "And my mouth is so dry."

She handed him her glass of water from the nightstand. He sat up a little and drained the entire contents in a few gulps. His bedsheet was pulled up to his waist, but failed to hide a raging case of morning wood. He tugged it up higher, to cover himself.

"I know," she said, grinning. "I had thoughts about… doing something with that. But you're a little too smelly."

"How long have you been here? And what time is it?"

"A couple of hours. It's a little after two. David was up when I called, or at least he pretended I didn't wake him. He invited me over, but left for Sun's a while ago."

He pulled his right leg out from under the sheet, and found he had a large adhesive bandage on his knee. He reached down and felt another one on his left knee. "You took care of me, didn't you?"

She kissed his forehead. "They were pretty scraped up. You don't recall hurting yourself?"

He shook his head. Looking at the raw skin on his palms, he said, "I remember running. I *don't* remember falling."

She leaned to her left and placed her textbook on the floor, then back to her right to curl up against him with her head on his shoulder. "I hate to ask, but do you still want to try to do some shopping today? You don't have a TV and VCR yet."

He pulled her closer. "I still want to go shopping today, yes. But I want to shop for *you*."

She propped herself up on her right elbow and raised her eyebrows. "Explain."

"I've been thinking. I don't want you to have to plan ahead, anytime you want to spend the night with me in the new place. If there's a random Tuesday where we have dinner and watch a movie and you want to stay over, then you should. I want you to. Let's get all of your morning cosmetics and evening toiletries, and a couple of sets of clothes, a toothbrush, and whatever you'd like to wear to bed, and keep them at my place."

She patted his chest. "You have the best ideas, and I love you for them. Go shower, and I'll fix you something to eat."

CHAPTER 27

COMMENCEMENT

Ten days later, the spring tour ended in Covington. No one from Daughtry Village accepted Royce's offer to attend the show, which was as disappointing as the sales numbers from the phone campaign. But, surprisingly, the walk-up ticket sales for the show were outstanding, and he made a note to himself to investigate why.

Joey Vegas arrived in Dublin the next day, with a bank bag stuffed so full of cash that Royce felt sorry for its zipper. Joey and Bobby joined Royce and Chloe in the office, and Royce counted the money twice to verify Joey's total. He scribbled the numbers in his ledger book, then tossed the bag to Bobby, seated at the ugly mirrored desk, who pulled out Royce's $7,000 spring tour settlement. Royce recorded the balance and placed the cash in the safe.

When the older men walked upstairs to the kitchen, Chloe pushed back from her desk in her rolling chair and turned a 180 before extending her Keds toward his desk to stop herself. "Five thousand to your savings account for taxes, and two thousand to spend, right? Like your mother said?"

"Yes, thank you. That's the plan."

A couple of hours later, Mae returned from her errands. She asked Royce and Chloe to come upstairs to the kitchen. She directed Royce to a chair at the bar, pointing her stubby fingers, and he took a seat. She presented him with an oversized greeting card in a dark blue envelope, and a large gift wrapped in plain brown paper.

"This was supposed to be your graduation present back in December," she said. "But there were delays. So now it's kind of a combined graduation and house-warming gift."

Joey stood and adjusted his bolo tie. "I must confess that the delay was entirely my fault. When I learned what they were planning, I insisted they hold the presentation until I had an opportunity to sign the card. My apologies." He bowed dramatically.

Royce stood and shook the ringmaster's hand. He looked at Bobby, and then at Chloe, both of whom were smiling knowingly. He opened the card and read the kind words and well-wishes of everyone present, along with notes from every sales rep team except the Marshalls. He pulled at the brown wrapper and unveiled a framed print of a 1930s-era painting from an artist named Pasquale, featuring a red and white striped circus tent, with jugglers and acrobats practicing their acts in the side margins. The distressed wooden frame was a perfect complement to the print.

He beamed and brushed a tear from his right eye. "This is beautiful, y'all. Thank you so much." He hugged

Mae warmly and nodded a silent thank you to Bobby and Joey before collecting his things and returning to the office with Chloe in tow.

Looking at the print, he said with a sideways grin, "I'm both flattered and concerned that you were able to keep this a secret from me for so long."

She brushed her hair behind her left ear. "It wasn't easy. I was really excited about it! Especially since you have so few wall-hangings."

"What, so my Fahrvergnügen poster doesn't count?"

She wrinkled her nose and shook her head.

✿　✿　✿

At 8:00 a.m. on the last Saturday in April, Luke bounded up Kingston's steps and burst through the apartment door. "Second time in a calendar year that I'm helping you move!" He gave Royce a bear hug.

"And the last time I'll ever ask, I promise."

With the help of David and Chloe, Royce and Luke were able to load the pickup in half the time of the move from Leah's to Kingston, even with the new clothes and kitchen supplies that had been added. They formed a four-vehicle convoy to the duplex.

They made short work of unloading the truck, and the boxes and bags in their own trunks, and the guys worked on assembling the guest bedroom while Chloe set up the stereo in the living room. A few minutes later, she called out, "Murph? You have your first guests. You wanna get the door?"

Sun and Heather had walked over, carrying a basket of home-made muffins and pitchers of water and sweet tea. "Y'all are awesome," he said, kissing each of them on the cheek. "I'd offer you a tour, but you already know the floor plan."

A cool spring wind was blowing and, since the apartment lacked anywhere to sit, Royce directed everyone to the back porch to enjoy a break and the refreshments his new neighbors had brought. Soon, the low rumble of the delivery truck's diesel engine echoed through the cul-de-sac. Chloe grabbed Sun and Heather by the hands and asked, "Help me tell them how we want to arrange things?" They hustled to the front door.

"I don't envy those guys a single bit," David chuckled.

After the movers were gone and most of the protective plastic had been removed from the furniture, Royce called for Chinese takeout to thank his helpers. Heather and Luke were the first to leave after the late lunch. "Let me know when you get all these boxes unpacked. I'll swing by and throw them in the bed of the truck for David."

"Will do. Thanks, man. I appreciate your help."

David and Sun bid farewell a little while later. Royce suspected that she would be spending as much of the next three weeks at Kingston as she could, before David left. As Royce closed the door behind them, Chloe dashed to the bedroom closet and began unpacking her new clothes and toiletries. She arranged every item with special care, in drawers and on countertops.

He watched her with a lump in his throat. "You saved this until we were alone. Why?"

She cocked her head to the side. "Because it's nobody's damned business where I sleep, or what our private arrangements are."

He laughed. "You're right, I know."

She took his hand and led him on a slow tour through each room, moving several pieces of furniture a few inches back and forth until she was satisfied. "We only have two weeks before graduation to whip this place into shape. If you still want to play host and hostess with me, that is."

"I do. But you have finals next week. Are you ready?"

"I'm ready. Take me to your big new bed, love."

✿　✿　✿

Lancaster's graduates were each allotted four tickets to the commencement. Many of his classmates had difficult decisions to make, but Royce was lucky: his parents, Jennifer, and Chloe would all be sitting together in the gym to watch him walk. He had received his diploma in December, so this was only a formality. But it was important to his parents, and it gave him great satisfaction to share the ceremony with David, Carlos, and Nico.

He had another difficult question to ask Chloe, but he'd waited until after finals week was over. To celebrate the A's in both of her first classes, he took her back to the same Italian place where they'd eaten after their first golf match. "So," he began, tentatively, "I was thinking of asking Leah and her fiancé to come by the duplex after the ceremony. But I won't if you don't want me to."

She smiled a knowing smile, and reached across the table to brush a few stray hairs from his ponytail behind his ear. "Thank you for asking me. I know you fucked her, but *fucked* is a past tense verb, right?"

He nodded.

"You two are friends, and I want to meet your friends. Please invite her."

He phoned her later that evening as he sat on his new sofa with Chloe's bare feet in his lap.

"I'm so glad you called me, Royce! I wanted to ask if the dirt lot beside Kingston would be a good place to park for graduation. I'll have to be there early, like you, and I guess Matthew can walk around campus some, before he goes in."

He was pretty sure the lot would be available, and told her so, though he hoped to find a place on the street in front of Kingston. It was only a couple of blocks from the gym, but not easy to find if you didn't already know it was there. The primary lots on campus would be packed early in the morning with the cars of families and friends.

"I was hoping you two might come by my new place afterward. We're gonna have a little reception, and I'd like to see you."

"Ooooo, I'd like that," she said, with a weight to her words that suggested several reasons why.

"Okay, good. We'll be here all afternoon, after the

ceremony is over, so no set time."

"Thank you! We'll see you then."

His next call was to Nico and Carlos. He had already heard from David that both had passed their beastly courses and would graduate as planned, but he wanted to give them each the chance to brag to him personally, and to invite them to come by his new place with their families after the commencement.

✦　✦　✦

Royce and Chloe drove separately on Saturday morning, parallel-parking their respective Mazdas opposite Kingston and greeting Sun and David at the apartment. Chloe wore a pale green strapless sundress and white sandals, and Royce could barely take his eyes off of the narrow bikini tan lines that crossed her collarbones.

Sun was frustrated and tense, studying David's hair in the bathroom mirror and trying to find a way to stuff his unruly mane into his graduation cap. "Can I help?" Chloe offered. "I had to pull Royce's ponytail holder a few inches down the back of his neck, so it would rest underneath the cap. He looks like he's ready to begin his carpentry apprenticeship at the Plymouth colony."

Sun laughed. "I'm trying to fashion a bun on top, but that would make the cap sit higher than everyone else's. I think it's the best way to go, though."

"No, you're right." They worked together and eventually found the least ridiculous looking arrangement.

"Don't touch it," Sun warned, as David walked sullenly to his bedroom to get dressed.

Suddenly self-conscious of his own hair, Royce fiddled in the bathroom mirror while listening to Sun and Chloe talk in the living room. "Are you nervous about meeting the Carsons?" Chloe asked.

"A lot less than I would have been a year ago," Sun replied with a forced laugh. "We missed a lot of opportunities. I should have thrown myself at him, instead of waiting for him to ask me out."

Royce and David walked in the stifling heat to Centennial Arena. Lancaster had joined the Cumberland Athletic Conference five years earlier, just short of its one hundredth year of operation, and the college made a desperate plea to its benefactors for donations to build a venue for the Cardinals' basketball teams that would be comparable to the other schools in its league. In practical application for future graduating classes, however, it meant that commencement ceremonies would take place in a climate-controlled auditorium, rather than exposed to the summer swelter on the quad.

Royce was suddenly struck with the realization that this would be the last walk to the campus proper for him and David, a sidewalk they had taken together a thousand times before. He wanted to put his arm around his friend and thank him for all of the memories they'd shared, and for how profoundly he had influenced Royce's perspectives, but David was oddly quiet. Royce could only imagine how much he had on his mind, and absently fondled the tassels of his gold honors cord.

As they turned the corner, they fell in with dozens of other graduates, most wearing unzipped gowns that trailed behind them like capes. They entered the side door to check in as present with the commencement volunteers, then met with a team of lineup coordinators, who showed them to their seating sections. Royce found a few former classmates whom he hadn't seen since fall semester, and made small talk with them about their plans.

A pair of cold hands clasped against his eyes from behind him, and a familiar voice said, "Guess who?"

He smiled. "There could be only one Leah Renee Carlisle." He turned to face her and she wrapped her arms around his neck. Her blue eyes were as bright as ever, and he guessed that she had dropped twenty pounds or so since he had last seen her. He assumed it was due to spending so much time on her feet.

"So, have you and the good doctor set a date yet?"

"Next spring. April, I think. Write down your new address for me. I want you to come."

"I will."

They talked more about her job and her family, before her voice trailed off and the smile left her face. "You look happy. Does she make you happy, Royce?"

He nodded. "Euphorically."

They were interrupted by an announcement over the public address system, requesting that they take their seats. Royce found his in a small section where the honors graduates would be seated.

He looked over his shoulder to find David's section, and laughed out loud when he realized the only people separating him from Leah were a Carmichael, a Carmona, and the Carpenter twins. An administrator from the Dean's office took the stage and urged the graduates to memorize the faces of the people to their left and right, so they would know how to line up, and advised them to move into the tunnels beneath the grandstands and assemble along the hallways that led to the locker rooms. Royce's group would be the last to leave the gym floor, as they would be the first in line in the processional, so he was able to watch the opening flood of guests as they were allowed into the auditorium to scurry to the seats they considered to be the best.

✧ ✧ ✧

No FEWER THAN five university officials offered welcoming addresses prior to the keynote speaker, a low-level federal government official who had graduated from Lancaster in the Sixties. Her speech was boilerplate and generic. "Celebrate the past but look toward the future," and all that. He was happy to be among the first graduates to traverse the stage, and spent the remaining diploma distribution searching the audience for his group. He smiled broadly when he found Chloe, seated with Jennifer and his parents, about twenty rows up from the floor along the opposite side of the arena.

Sun was sitting beside her, so apparently she hadn't been able to find or identify the Carsons prior to the ceremony. Chloe had Royce's camera trained on him, and he offered *tatanka* horns to her against his cap.

He corralled Nico, Carlos, and David at the conclusion of the ceremony, and ushered them to the section where his parents were seated. He desperately wanted a couple of photos of the four of them together, in their caps and gowns, and he was grateful for their cooperation. He had told both Jennifer and Chloe to stay put, instead of filing out into the courtyard after the commencement, so he could more easily find them. The sea of humanity outside the arena was no place to arrange a photo opportunity. Chloe snapped a half-dozen shots of the boys.

Assuring him that they would see him later, his friends dispersed to find their own families. Royce hugged his sister and parents and thanked them for coming. Jennifer and Chloe were eager to leave to go set up the refreshments, and they dragged Royce's parents up the steps and toward the exit, waving over their shoulders to Royce.

He had one more appearance he needed to make, and departed through the side door en route to the southeast corner plaza. The English department professors gathered there every spring to greet their graduates around a fountain dedicated to the college's founder. He spoke briefly with Dr. Roberts and Dr. Gurski, and tried to dodge Dr. Dalton. Her black robe was unzipped to her waist and, naturally, she was wearing the pale blue sundress with embroidered daisies. He had no choice but to speak with her, though, once they'd made eye contact, so he accepted her congratulations and begged off as quickly as he could.

At the apartment, he kicked off his shoes and socks and removed his tie. Chloe and Jennifer had donned aprons and were busily cutting fruit and cheese in the kitchen, so he took a few minutes to poll his parents about his new place and his furniture choices. If they were anything less than proud and happy for him, they did not show it.

The doorbell rang, and Royce greeted David, Sun, and the Carsons. He had met David's parents only twice, when David had occasion to make a weekend trip to their place in Macon and invited him along, but had not seen them since he had moved into Kingston. He introduced them to his parents as Sun brushed past him on her way to the kitchen. Her hurried pace suggested the day had become a bit much for her to handle, and that she needed Chloe's company.

David shook his head as he watched her disappear down the hallway. "She's not having a great day. But here, I wanted to give you this." He handed Royce an index card with his Brooklyn address and phone number. "Get a magnet and stick it on your fridge. I don't have my work digits yet, but I'll give them to you when I can."

"Thanks! I need to give you my new information, too."

The doorbell rang again, and Nico bounded through the door with his parents and sister, Gina. The Contis were almost exactly as Royce had pictured them. Large and loud, like their son, and aggressively friendly. Royce had thought about the incongruity of meeting Nico and Carlos' parents for the first time on the day before they would leave Dublin for good, but relished the opportunity to put faces with the names and stories he had heard for the past few years. Mr. Conti was something of a legendary salesman in Ellijay, and his wife had started culinary school when their children had left for college.

Carlos and his mother arrived next, apologizing that his father, a journalist, had been called away a few days before the ceremony to cover the ongoing slow collapse of apartheid in South Africa. Mrs. Lopez was small and slight, but Royce could picture her in her youth as one of Mexico's best collegiate tennis players. She had groomed Carlos in the sport from the time he was big enough to hold a racquet. She was shy, and kept to herself, speaking hushed Spanish with Carlos. Royce picked up enough to understand that she wanted Carlos to stay as long as he liked.

He checked in with Chloe, Sun, and Jennifer in the kitchen. The refreshments had been a big hit, and several items were either empty or rapidly diminishing. He wrapped Chloe in a tight hug and whispered in her ear. "Do you need to leave soon?"

"No, I'm packed, so I have lots of time." She had planned to drive to Savannah after the reception to visit Mary for Mother's Day.

Their guests began filing out in the order they had

arrived. The Carsons were attending an ASPCA fund-raiser in Macon that evening, and needed to get home to prepare for it. David assumed Sun would be going back to Kingston with him, but she declined and returned to helping Jennifer and Chloe clear the kitchen.

The Contis and Mrs. Lopez needed to check into their hotel rooms, since they were staying in Dublin overnight to help with Carlos' and Nico's move back home the next day, and said their goodbyes shortly afterward. Just as Royce's parents and Jennifer were preparing to leave, the doorbell rang again. Leah burst through the door, pulling a short and slender young man behind her. "I hope we're not too late!"

"Not at all," Royce said, smiling.

Leah briefly introduced herself to the Murphys before making a beeline to the kitchen. Royce and his family attempted to engage the abandoned Dr. Cohen. "Matthew, please," he said. "Thank you for having us. I know Leah was excited to meet you all."

Royce left Matthew in the care of his family and peeled backward toward the kitchen to mediate anything that might come up between Leah and Chloe. He missed their initial pleasantries, but arrived just in time to catch Leah gushing. "I just *love* his new place! Are you living here with him?"

Chloe made eye contact with him over Leah's shoulder and tapped her chin. Looking back into Leah's eyes, she replied, "Not yet."

Sun sensed the tension, as well, and moved to diffuse

it. From the sink, she called out, "Chloe? Do you want me to keep these leftovers or not?"

"Let me look," she replied. "Leah, it was a pleasure to meet you. Royce has told me a lot about you." Leah snorted in reply.

Royce took her on a brief tour of the apartment, since she had scarcely had a chance to see it before pronouncing her affection for it, and then they joined his family and Dr. Cohen in the living room. After about five minutes of animated conversation, Leah announced, "We should go. We got here so late, and we don't want to hold y'all up. You were on your way out." Royce gave her a goodbye hug and shook Matthew's hand.

Chloe hustled to the front of the house to say her own goodbyes to his family, and whispered something to Jennifer that made her laugh. She and Royce walked them to the street, as he slipped a Mother's Day card into Kate's purse, and waved as they drove away.

Returning to the living room, they found Sun seated in the recliner. "Are you going to see your mother this weekend?" Chloe asked.

"No. They assumed I'd want to be here, so my dad surprised my mom with a trip to San Antonio to visit her sister."

"Okay, good! Then you're coming with me to Savannah. Like, right now."

Sun shook her head. "No, I couldn't. I don't want to impose on your parents."

"They run an inn! All they do is host people and cook

for them. I won't take no for an answer. You need to get away, and I'm taking you."

"Please don't argue with her," Royce said. "You won't win. Trust me on this."

Sun smiled. "You're right. A little spontaneity would do me good."

Chloe raised her hands in victory. "Yes! My shit's already in the trunk of the car, so let's get you to your place to pack a bag."

Royce hugged them both. "Y'all have fun. Be careful driving."

"Always," Chloe winked, with a big smile, and led Sun out to her car.

☉ ☉ ☉

HE ARRIVED AT Carlos and Nico's apartment just after nine the next morning, a few minutes before David and Luke pulled up. The Contis and Mrs. Lopez were running behind, so David had time to skewer his friends over a framed photo of Pope John Paul II and a ceramic sculpture of praying hands with a quotation from the book of John, which were additions to their coffee table he had never seen before.

"Sucking up to your Catholic parents, eh?" David laughed. "You need the graduation presents that much?"

Nico opened his mouth to reply, but thought better of it, and retreated to his room to finish packing. His father honked the horn of a U-Haul truck from the parking lot, and the crew set about loading it as quickly as possible.

The praying hands and Pope photo were the last two items to find their way into a box.

Royce had Nico and Carlos write down their parents' addresses and phone numbers in his address book, and gave them each a long embrace. "I love you guys. This wouldn't have been nearly as much fun without you. Please keep in touch. Anytime you want to come back and visit the ass of nowhere, you can stay at my place."

They agreed, and all three found themselves wiping away tears. Luckily, it was easy to make it look as if they were rubbing sweat from their foreheads.

☼ ☼ ☼

By the following Friday, David was confident enough with the progress of his packing that he called Royce at the office with an idea. "You and Chloe come to the Hound with us tonight. I've been cooped up here all week and I need to get out. Luke's coming, too."

"We'll be there."

The five of them toasted glasses of Smithwick's, shared laughter and retold stories, some of which Sun and Chloe had heard or witnessed, and many that they hadn't. David was more than happy to recall memories, and to talk about the future, but he redirected even the smallest hints of sadness or loss. Royce knew better than to try, but Luke made several overtures toward grand pronouncements. David shut them all down before they could find a voice.

On Saturday morning they met to help David load

his things. Dr. Carson had arrived at dawn with a rent-ed Penske truck, but leaned back and took a nap until the others arrived. Sun and Chloe started shuttling the dozens of packing boxes downstairs to the truck, as Luke, David, and Royce worked on the furniture. While struggling with his heavy dresser, the pain in Royce's fingers forced him to call for a break on the second floor landing. "How are you getting this upstairs in Brooklyn?"

"With difficulty," David joked. "I'm on the top floor of a three-story walk-up, just like here, but the stairwell is about half as wide."

"Shit," Luke said. "I'm not at all sorry I won't be able to help you up there."

The entire moving party was soaked through with sweat, by the time the truck was loaded. David wiped his face with a towel, then looked at Royce. "Help me do one last walk-through?"

They walked upstairs together and opened every drawer, cabinet, and closet. Satisfied that the apartment was completely empty, Royce grabbed David in a tight embrace. "I love you, man. Thank you for… literally everything. I'll miss you awful."

After a pause, David returned the hug. "Give me a couple of months to settle in, and come see me. I'll show you around."

Back on the street, Chloe gave David a goodbye hug. She joined Royce on the sidewalk and slid her arm around his waist. They both watched Sun, as she approached David and melted against him. He stroked her hair and whispered in her ear. Chloe had to turn her back to keep from sobbing. Sun took a few steps backward as he climbed into the cab of the truck. The diesel engine roared to life and, with a wave through the open window, he was gone.

"And that's how she tells him goodbye," she whispered, wiping her nose with the back of her hand.

"And she'll probably never see him again," Royce added.

But I will, he thought. *I'll make god-damned sure of it.*

By the beginning of August, Chloe had become so excited about the upcoming Lollapalooza music festival the she didn't let a day pass without mentioning it. The Atlanta performance would be held on Sunday the 18th, five days after her birthday, with a formidable lineup that included Living Colour, Nine Inch Nails, Fishbone, Siouxsie and the Banshees, and the headliner, Jane's Addiction. Her enthusiasm gave Royce the opportunity to employ some misdirection, allowing her to believe that tickets to the concert were his birthday gift to her, though in truth he had a much more elaborate plan in mind.

Jennifer and three of her friends were also planning to go to the show, and Royce asked her to buy his and Chloe's tickets when she got hers. He made it a point to have this telephone conversation while Chloe was in the office with him, so he could casually mention that the 13th was her birthday and revel in his ingenuity. They would all be sitting together on the lawn at Lakewood Amphitheater, and talked about packing blankets and other supplies. Royce also mentioned that he had recently learned a breath mint tin was the perfect hiding place to smuggle joints into a venue, and said he would bring a few for everyone to share.

In the weeks following the departure of David, Nico,

and Carlos, Royce's new friend group became Chloe, Sun, and Heather. It made perfect sense to him, especially given the fact that Sun and Heather were now his neighbors, and Luke reached out only seldomly. He and Chloe were invited there for her birthday dinner, and were not allowed to help. Sun put together a Korean seafood dish that was delicious, though Royce thought better of asking too many questions about what was in it.

After dinner, Chloe blew out the candle on a small cake, and they moved to the living room for dessert and gift-giving. She sat on the floor and dug into the wrapping of a box from Sun and Heather that contained a designer purse and wallet. "Oh, wow, y'all! I love it!"

Heather beamed. "We saw it a couple of weeks ago and agreed that it just *screamed* Chloe!"

Royce leaned forward and handed her a gold envelope. She smiled at him, self-assuredly, and opened a card she was certain would contain tickets. She was partially right.

She found two round-trip boarding passes to New York for the end of September, along with two tickets to *The Will Rogers Follies* at the Palace Theatre on Broadway. She sat, dumbfounded, looking back and forth between the two sets of documents.

"What is it?" Sun asked. Chloe rose and handed her the card.

"I thought we could play hooky on that Friday and fly up, and then visit David on Saturday," Royce said.

Chloe climbed into his lap, straddling him, and

delivered a rapid-fire series of kisses to his forehead and cheeks.

He laughed and took her waist in his hands. "Chloe? Baby? We are not alone." She took a deep breath and looked at Sun.

"Please tell David I said hello, and tell me honestly how he's doing." There were no tears in her eyes.

☼　☼　☼

ON LOLLAPALOOZA SUNDAY, they dropped the top on the Miata and sped north to meet Jennifer and her friends at their mother's house. Chloe covered her bikini top with a Henley, and wore short cut-offs and sandals. Her tan was as dark as Royce had ever seen it, and it was perfectly even. He knew a few shortcuts to the venue, so Jennifer and her friends followed him. Chloe bonded quickly with the girls, and spent the better part of the afternoon dancing barefoot in the grass with them. In between acts, they would gather together on the blankets and pass a joint, looking around for security personnel, who never made an effort to intervene. As the afternoon wore on and other attendees became emboldened, skunky gray smoke rose from dozens of groups on the lawn.

At sunset, a brief rain shower passed overhead, sending down cool droplets onto the exposed skin of hundreds of people who hadn't had the sense to apply sunscreen during the heat of the day. Lawn-dwellers formed tight groups and huddled shivering together in the growing darkness as they waited for Jane's Addiction's set. Chloe pulled on her Henley and leaned backward against him. "Do you think they'll do 'Three Days'?"

He wrapped his arms around her tightly and chuckled. "They'd better."

They would have to wait until the encore before the band played the song that kicked off the mix tape she'd made for him in December, but it was worth the wait. Jane's Addiction's crew brought out three more drum kits prior to the encore, and set them up beside Stephen Perkins'. Royce recognized Will Calhoun from Living Colour and Jeff Ward from Nine Inch Nails, and pointed them out to the others on his blanket. The band stretched the ten-minute song closer to twenty, allowing Dave Navarro to pile his epic guitar solos even higher, and extending the tribal drum breaks to take advantage of the extra talent on stage. Chloe became overwhelmed, as the pounding bass drums caused the ground beneath them to shake, and curled up into Royce's lap, facing him. She kissed him urgently, her tongue wild, as memories of their first night together possessed her. He ignored the prying eyes that witnessed the public display, and surrendered both to her bliss and to the music. There were maybe 18,000 people at the concert, but in that moment, they only saw each other.

The lawn lights burned brightly after the band left the stage, and the group gathered their belongings and folded the blankets. Royce and Chloe walked Jennifer and her friends to their car, and he gently scolded his sister for not coming down to Dublin yet to take advantage of his new guest room. He wasn't thrilled with the long drive home, nor with working the next morning, but he was already looking forward to the next milestone on his calendar.

✧   ✧   ✧

Six weeks later, they left the duplex early and drove to the Atlanta airport. Their flight was delayed, but they arrived at JFK in New York with plenty of time to spare. Royce had spoken on the phone with David several times, in planning the trip, and he had been given invaluable advice to help the first-time visitors navigate the city. He'd booked a room in a small hotel near the intersection of 55th and 7th, and hailed a cab at the airport to take them there.

"How long a drive is it?" Chloe asked.

"I'm not sure." Royce stared out the window, and channeled his inner Miyagi. "First time you, first time me."

Their room was tiny but well-appointed, and they curled up on the bed together to relax a bit before dressing for the show. David had recommended a deli on 46th Street, not far from the theatre, which was perfect, since their excitement had quelled their appetites. Chloe held his hand tightly and clutched her playbill to her chest as they found their seats at the Palace Theatre. Within the first ten minutes of the performance, she had fallen madly in love with Keith Carradine, and Royce spent as much time watching her as he did the show. She scanned the stage, left and right, and tapped her fingers to her chin as she took in every detail. By the finale, a reprise of "Never Met a Man I Didn't Like," she was on the edge of her seat, waiting for the proper time to stand and applaud.

After the curtain fell, they filed out with the other patrons, and made their way through Times Square. Walking unhurriedly, they stopped in various shops and studied every flashy piece of tourist bait that the area had to offer. In a small souvenir shop, Chloe walked toward him with purpose in her eyes and an *I Love New York* T-shirt in her hands, and requested that he take her back to the hotel and fuck her "New York style." He had no idea how to make love in a way that was expensive, crowded, and thoroughly exhilarating, but he gave her his best effort, as always. Twice.

✿ ✿ ✿

DAVID INSISTED HIS friends experience a true New York weekend, so he gave Royce explicit instructions on how to reach his place in the Park Slope area of Brooklyn by taking the subway from Times Square. Royce pulled his camera strap over his shoulder and called David from the hotel to let him know they were on their way.

Royce knew David had gotten an extreme haircut after his move, but chose to keep it from Chloe. His decision earned him a sharp elbow to his ribcage, as she saw David sitting on the steps of his building, waiting for them with a book in his hands. "Why didn't you tell me?" she called over her shoulder, as she ran up the sidewalk and leapt into David's arms.

David led them up the stairs to his apartment, the most compact two bedroom space that Royce had ever seen.

"Where's Dev today?" Chloe asked.

"Oh, he's probably at the movies. He's been seeing a girl from work, but he doesn't think I know."

David produced his green plastic bong and took a long rip before handing it off to Royce. "I'm glad you wore walking shoes. I take the subway to work and back, but I walk everywhere else. The Civic is gathering dust in Macon."

After the bowl was cashed, they strolled down to 9th Street and followed it southeast, entering Prospect Park at the Lafayette Memorial. David stopped at an elevated place on the sidewalk and motioned to his left. "That's Dog Beach, the happiest place in Brooklyn."

Royce took a few steps down the hill and adjusted the zoom on his lens. He snickered as he snapped a few photos of dogs splashing in the shallow pond. David led them north, through The Ravine, and then due east past the carousel. As they left the park, he raised his arms as if to make a presentation. "This is Crown Heights. Are you hungry? There's someone I'd like you both to meet."

They followed him a few blocks east, where he opened the door to a Greek restaurant. It was spacious, bright, and looked expensive. Royce silently wondered how much cash he had in his wallet, as he studied the dark wood, white linens, and wall art that incorporated every hue of blue and green. The hostess greeted David by name and escorted them to a table near the kitchen.

"This place belongs to Alexis' uncle," David began. "She's the head chef for the lunch hours, and he handles the dinner rush." The dining room was still half-full, even as the hour approached three in the afternoon, but Royce wrote it off as New Yorkers keeping later hours on weekends. Chloe reached under the table and squeezed Royce's hand. She recognized that David had been living in the city for more than four months, but it would still sting to see him with someone other than Sun.

Alexis pulled the bandana off of her head as she approached the table and shook her long dark hair. The threesome stood to greet her, and she enthusiastically shook hands with Chloe and Royce. Her Brooklyn accent was as thick as her ringlets and eyelashes. "I wish I could sit with you for a while, but we are two guys short in the kitchen today. Please, order whatever you'd like, and I'll cook it myself. On the house, of course."

Royce and Chloe thanked her, and studied the menu as she said goodbye to David and kissed his cheek. "Their moussaka and souvlaki are the best I've ever had, if you need a suggestion," David said with sincere pride.

"I was wondering," Royce said with a crooked smile. "What did you ask Dev to hide from you before you gathered the nerve to ask her out?"

David laughed. "I asked her out the same day I met her, as a matter of fact. I've *grown*, dude!"

After lunch, they took a circuitous route back to David's apartment, which allowed him to point out a few more of his favorite places, and to apologize twice for not being able to spend more time with them that evening. He and Alexis had plans to celebrate his birthday a few days early, because of their busy work schedules. At the steps to his building, he pulled two maps from his backpack. One was for the area around Times Square. "There are a ton of landmarks within walking distance of you, if you don't feel like going straight back to your hotel. And this one is for Central Park, if you're still planning to go there tomorrow morning. I circled some things you'll probably want to take pictures of."

Royce and Chloe fought back tears as they hugged him goodbye, again, and walked back to the subway. They took his advice and sought out the Museum of Modern Art, Radio City Music Hall, and Rockefeller Center, before turning back north to the hotel.

✧   ✧   ✧

HE POKED HER AWAKE early on Sunday morning and whispered in her ear. "Let's go to the park for a while, before we have to catch our flight." She grumbled, but did as he asked. They left their bags with the hotel concierge and walked north on Broadway. After grabbing a couple of coffees from a street vendor in Columbus

Circle, they followed David's map toward the Bethesda Terrace and fountain. She yawned as he shot photos of the landmarks, but took particular interest in the view of the Loeb Boathouse and the early-rising tourists that were beginning to launch their rowboats into the lake.

They passed a couple of joggers coming toward them at the entrance of the Bow Bridge, along with a photographer pointing his camera toward the west. David had suggested that they find the Lake Viewing Area on the north side of the bridge, but Royce stopped at the midpoint. "Hold my coffee, please? I need to tie my shoe."

She sat both of their cups on the bannister and smiled at her view of Central Park West and the buildings that were bathed in the orange morning light. After a minute or so, she shivered against the wind and grew frustrated. "Jesus, how long does it take to tie a…" She looked down to find him on one knee, holding open a black velvet box with a radiant cut diamond solitaire ring inside. She slapped her hands to her cheeks and stared at the ring with her mouth wide open.

"You don't have to marry me next week, or next month, or even next year," he said, "But please, Chloe, tell me you will, one day."

She nodded, wiping tears from her cheeks. She took his hand and pulled him to his feet. "I will. I will. I love you."

He slid the ring onto her finger and wrapped his arms around her. They held one another, lost in their own world, until a man standing nearby cleared his throat.

"*Excusez-moi.* My name is Lucien, and I could not help but notice your occasion." They recognized him as the photographer they had passed when they began their walk across the bridge.

"I see you have a camera," he continued, in a thick French accent, "and I thought you might like a photo."

Royce gratefully handed over his camera, and they posed for him. Lucien said, "When I saw what was happening, I shot a few photos of you myself. I would be happy to send them to you, when they are ready. Would you trust me with your mailing instruction?"

Chloe scribbled the Rosewood address on the back of one of Royce's business cards. They thanked him profusely, and began a brisk walk back to the hotel to collect their bags. She spent the entire two-hour flight focused on her left hand and squeezing his thigh with her right.

✧ ✧ ✧

Two WEEKS LATER, he returned from the mailbox to find her staring at the 8x10 photo they'd enlarged from the image Lucien had shot with Royce's camera. In the picture, the fingers of her left hand were splayed, displaying the ring, and she mugged with her eyes and mouth open wide. Royce's left hand was visible on her left shoulder, as he kissed her right cheek.

"I have a letter from Lucien," he said, ripping into the envelope. He'd sent two 4x6 prints, taken from his perspective on the bridge. In the first, Royce was on his knee, and she had her hands on her cheeks at the exact moment she realized what was happening. In the second, he was standing and they were locked in a passionate embrace. Lucien had taped the negatives to the backs of the photos.

She squealed and reached for her purse. "We have to go buy some more frames!"

THE END

"Brandy" — Looking Glass
© 1972 Sony Music Entertainment

"Cradle of Love" — Billy Idol
© 1990 Capitol Records

"Joey" — Concrete Blonde
© 1990 Capitol Records, LLC

"Stone Cold Crazy" — Queen
© 1974 EMI / Elektra

"Ways to be Wicked" / "Sweet, Sweet Baby" —
Lone Justice © 1985 UMG Recordings, Inc

"Let the Day Begin" — The Call
© 1989 Geffen Records

"She's a Beauty" — The Tubes
© 1983 Capitol Records

"The One I Love" — R.E.M.
© 1987 I.R.S. Records

"Driver 8" — R.E.M.
© 1984 I.R.S. Records

"Rio" — Duran Duran
© 1982 EMI

"A Girl Like You" — The Smithereens
© 1989 Enigma

"Let's Go" — The Cars
© 1979 Elektra Records

"You Make Loving Fun" — Fleetwood Mac
© 1977 Warner Bros. Records

"Enjoy the Silence" / "Personal Jesus" —
Depeche Mode © 1990 Mute Records

"Nothing Compares 2 U" — Sinead O'Connor
© 1990 Ensign - Chrysalis

"Overkill" — Men at Work
© 1983 Columbia Records

"Running on Empty" — Jackson Browne
© 1977 Asylum Records

"Sharp Dressed Man" — ZZ Top
© 1983 Warner Bros. Records

"Three Days" — Jane's Addiction
© 1990 Warner Bros.

"I Wanna Be Adored" — The Stone Roses
© 1989 Silvertone

"Under the Milky Way" — The Church
© 1988 Mushroom - Arista

"Sign Your Name" — Terence Trent D'Arby
© 1987 Columbia Records

"Cuts You Up" — Peter Murphy
© 1989 Beggars Banquet - RCA, Atlantic

"Lovesong" — The Cure
© 1989 Fiction Records

"How Soon Is Now?" — The Smiths
© 1984 Rough Trade - Sire

"Breathe" — Maria McKee
© 1989 Geffen Records

"Into Temptation" — Crowded House
© 1988 Capitol Records

"Who Wants To Live Forever"— Queen
© 1986 EMI - Capitol

"Need You Tonight" — INXS
© 1987 WEA - Atlantic - Mercury

"Give a Little Bit" — Supertramp
© 1977 A&M Records

"Carefree Highway" — Gordon Lightfoot
© 1974 Reprise Records

"Eternal Flame" — The Bangles
© 1988 Columbia Records

Mars Needs Guitars — Hoodoo Gurus
© 1985 Big Time - Chrysalis - Elektra

Boingo Alive — Oingo Boingo
© 1988 MCA Records

"Can't Find My Way Home" — Blind Faith
© 1969 Polydor Records

"Roam" — B-52's
© 1989 Reprise Records

"Guantanamera" — Jose Fernandez Dias
© 1929 Copyright holder unknown

Nomads Indians Saints — Indigo Girls
© 1990 Epic Records

"Black Velvet" — Alannah Myles
© 1989 Atlantic Records

The Real Thing — Faith No More
© 1989 Slash - Reprise

All Shook Down — The Replacements
© 1990 Sire Records